I0692811

Redemption
Twelve Readings from the Monks of Estillyen

A Scriptural Companion to
The Point: The Redemption of Oban Ironbout

WILLIAM E. JEFFERSON

Port Estillyen
PRODUCTIONS

Copyright © 2013 Port Estillyen Productions, Inc. All rights reserved. No part of this book may be reproduced in any form or by any electronic means, including information storage and retrieval systems, without permission in writing from the publisher, except by a reviewer who may quote brief passages in a review.

Pubished by Port Estillyen Productions
www.estillyen.com
https://facebook.com/estillyen

Cover Photo: Matt Gibson/shutterstock.com. All rights reserved.
Cover Design: Miriam Green
Interior design and typesetting: Creative Editorial Solutions

ISBN: 978-0-9856621-4-1 (soft cover)
ISBN: 978-0-9856621-5-8 (e-book)

Printed in the United States of America

5 4 3 2 1

ACKNOWLEDGMENTS

A very special note of thanks is extended to Claudia Volkman and Lynn Wehner, editors of *Redemption*. Without their encouragement, discernment, and artful way with words, the story now told would surely want for what it now possesses.

Dedicated to George Earl Jefferson,

whom I knew, and knew not

TABLE OF CONTENTS

INTRODUCTION

A JOURNEY TO the Isle of Estillyen is never in vain, if words of worth you seek to find. On this ancient isle, beyond the Storied Sea, knockers knock on doors that open wide, welcoming pilgrims inside.

On Estillyen's isle, words from ancient paths are purposely present. They mingle fresh, with messages milling about, filling up the atmosphere. In *Redemption,* some of the choicest words ever written you'll explore. They emerge from Scripture's store, in which thoughts of God are expressed.

Through mysteries you'll move with certainty. You'll come to see, "The further you go, the less you'll have, and the more you'll find."

There is much to be gained by lingering long amidst past prose. The haste of life through headlines blazed is paused, hushing present's rushing ways.

A letter penned long ago by St. Paul the Apostle speaks of hidden treasure waiting to be found. Words new they are not, yet wondrous words they are. St. Paul claimed that "all the treasures of wisdom and knowledge lie hidden in Jesus Christ."

The pages gathered in *Redemption* reflect but a flicker on this treasured figure of light. The crown jewel of treasures all is Christ. He is the Redeemer. He is the author of the script. He is the noun and subject of redemption.

"Blessed are those who have not seen and yet believed." Christ spoke these very words to his disciples. Many willingly wish not to believe. Why? All manner of notions knot themselves into reasons for casting Christ aside.

There is held, by some, the idea that to be contexted within redemption's story means abandoning wisdom and knowledge. The ancient and the mysterious are shunned, for want of brighter perception. From distant days of ancient ways the skeptics flee, in search of a different kind of light. Much they see, but truth is held at bay.

The perfect prism for peering at matters great is not a prop or props. Instead, the story of redemption centers on the person of Christ—the Word Made Flesh. Divinely choreographed through culture, space, and time, the story lives. Life it gives. Redemption it offers.

Journey now to the Isle of Estillyen....

THE ORIGIN

Redemption: Twelve Readings from the Monks of Estillyen is a companion work to the novel, *The Point: The Redemption of Oban Ironbout*.

In *The Point*, the readings are in synopsis form. Here, the readings are offered at length, as they originally would have been given by the monks of Estillyen.

The Scripture narratives offered as Estillyen readings are not simply passages pasted on a page. They are presented in dramatic fashion, by monks who gather audiences in quaint Estillyen structures. Their audiences travel from afar to explore the words so uniquely woven into message form.

Estillyen monks—with literary names like Saga, Narrative, Plot, and Writer—bring to light ancient texts of Scripture. Audiences are offered much to ponder, concerning words and how they bring meaning to life.

The work that flows from the Isle of Estillyen frames truth with fiction. That's the way of Estillyen. The story of redemption and human worth, which unfolds through the vivid cast of characters on the Isle of Estillyen, is...what?

That's for you to decide!

THE MESSAGE-MAKING MONKS
OF ESTILLYEN

TO FULLY APPRECIATE *Redemption: Twelve Readings from the Monks of Estillyen*, a degree of context is essential. The Isle of Estillyen is a most intriguing land, a pilgrimage destination. It's an ancient harbor known for gifting words of worth to the present.

The surest information to be derived about the Isle of Estillyen is found in the novel *The Point: The Redemption of Oban Ironbout*, the companion work to *Redemption*. The story of *The Point* is brought alive by a rich cast of colorful characters.

There is the reclusive Oban Ironbout, who lives on Estillyen's Point. His tale of pain and redemption runs through the heart of the novel. Equally compelling are the characters of Hollie and Goodwin Macbreeze, who travel to Estillyen on a pilgrimage—and find much more, as their lives become inseparably intertwined with Mr. Ironbout and his mysterious past.

Hollie and Goodwin join fellow travelers. All have journeyed to Estillyen to hear the readings of a group of monks, who craft their messages around compelling Scripture narratives. While on Estillyen, Hollie and Goodwin take in twelve monk readings—the *Redemption* series.

The Point opens with Hollie and Goodwin in the town of Century, as they are looking for signs to the Estillyen Ferry. They hold a weather-beaten map, but are uncertain about which route to take. Eventually, they meet Mr. Kind.

The three strike up a friendly conversation—and, in due course, decide to have a sack lunch in Grims Park. The following excerpt is from chapter one of *The Point*, which is simply titled "Lunch at Grims Park."

The dialogue, and Mr. Kind's comments in particular, provide important background and context before we move along in this volume to the twelve readings of *Redemption*. During their enjoyable lunch and conversation, Hollie asks Mr. Kind about the Isle of Estillyen....

"Do you know much about Estillyen, Mr. Kind?" Hollie asked, as she turned her head in his direction.

"Oh, yeah, well, actually a fair bit. You do know Estillyen is an ancient word for *still*?"

"Yes, I read that. Goodwin's grandfather had a couple of old books on Estillyen. In fact, I have a booklet in my backpack."

"So you know there's a fishing village, Port Estillyen, with a few hundred people, a monastery, and an abbey. The monastery is run by the ancient Order of Message Makers, which dates back centuries."

"I just hope we don't end up bored," Goodwin said. "Although I'll hike, hit the trails, maybe fish, while Hollie does some painting."

"I'm sure you'll love it," Mr. Kind said with an affirming smile. "The gray granite they use in the village sparkles like diamonds in the winter sun. Fine people, those Estillyens. Hardy. Must be. The wind can howl across the isle so fierce it can freeze a lightning bolt. Yes, for sure. Good time of year to be heading over to Estillyen. This is actually the best, I'd say.

"There's a small infirmary on Estillyen, run by the sisters. They're called the Sisters of Good, or Good Sisters—either way."The infirmary is best known as the Good Shepherd Infirmary. If your body decides to be sick for a while, you couldn't be in a better place. Spotless and as quiet as a bath towel stowed away in a wooden cupboard.

"There are three little lakes up on the far side of Estillyen known as Lakes Three. They're quite near each other, but you can't see one from the other. Tale has it, cranes swoop down periodically, picking up fish from one lake and dropping them into one of the other two. That way, the three lakes stay in touch—fish messengers, they call 'em, couriered by cranes."

Mr. Kind suddenly stuck his cane straight out in front of him and started making little jabs at the air, like he was jousting with an invisible butterfly.

"Brilliant. So the lakes really exist?" Hollie asked.

"Sure enough, you'll see. Estillyen has a way of not being like other places. It has an Estillyen-sphere, its own sort of atmosphere. The message makers, the monks, they're a wonderful, dedicated lot. No doubt a little nuts, I suppose, but passionately so. They'll make you think, mind you, but not all overly intellectual-like. No, that's not their thing, though they're plenty smart.

"They have a knack for sticking words together in ways they don't normally run, to help you see things you don't normally see. They make their words jump into lines like little frogs, yet they're not overly wordy.

They call words *thought wrappers*. Yeah, I believe that's how they say it. Thoughts are invisible. They need visibility to be transferred. They need apparel. They have to be wrapped in words.

"On Estillyen, the whole idea is about stilling, contemplation, reflection. Those message makers are very much a mind of mission, they are. They see words from ancient paths as pillars for the present....

"What most folks don't know is that those message makers come onto the mainland every six months and spend an entire week just listening and observing. They discover what messages are floating around, filling the atmosphere.

"Strange in one way, but not in another. Lots of people are strange, I suppose. I'm strange, I suppose. The monks spend an entire week on a kind of message retreat, exchanging what they see and hear.

"Now, get this. They move their months and weeks forward with each visit— know what I mean?"

"I'm not quite sure I do. Do you, Win?" Hollie asked.

"No, don't believe I do either," Goodwin said.

"Well, it's like this: Say this year they would come to the mainland during the second week of September, and six months later they'd return the first week of March. That's twice a year. So next year it'd be the third week of October and the second week of April. The months advance and the weeks with 'em.

"The way they see it, in twenty-six years, they'll have experienced a full year— all fifty-two weeks—on the mainland, a week at a time, simply by advancing and rotating their dates. That allows them to experience all the changes a year can bring, even though it takes 'em twenty-six years to get through a year."

"Fascinating," said Hollie. She and Goodwin stared out across the park, with their heads cocked slightly upward. They watched the clouds drifting by, just above the roofline of the two-story library at the far end of Grims Park. Hollie rested her chin in her hand. Goodwin sat motionless, with his fingers interlocked on his lap.

"Messages are sensitive to seasons, you know," Mr. Kind said, while he reached behind his head to tug on a patch of white hair sticking out of his straw hat. Hollie noticed his hair and its texture, thinking it reminded her of a horse's forelock.

"Smart bunch, those monks are. Focused on tales from Scripture, you know? They've got a series of readings called *Redemption*. They'll lead you all over those ancient tales 'til your eyes begin to cross and your mind begins to smart from expansion.

"The monks don't just read lines, as if they were reading a speech or a story. They like to get the audience involved, volunteering. You'll see.

"No, the monks, they have a way of losing themselves, probably like young Hollie here and artists down through the ages. Good to lose yourself. The further you go, the less you'll have, and the more you'll find," Mr. Kind said. Spontaneously, he began to hum and mutter in a chirpy rhyme, "That's what you find. The more you lose, the more you'll find. The more you lose, the further you go. That's what you find...."

"That's the ticket, by Job—'In this life look for peace, not paradise.' Now, that's Estillyen. Peaceful, but not paradise," Mr. Kind said, scratching his smooth chin, as if calming an itch.

"Have you spent a lot of time on Estillyen?" Hollie asked.

"Aye, a fair bit, I'd say, a fair bit. Good to see younger people like you making the trek. You know, words really do matter," he said, his eyes staring straight ahead. The conversation paused for a moment, as all three just sat staring out from the long wooden bench in the corner of Grims Park.

"The monks on Estillyen all go by pseudo-names: Saga, Narrative, Plot, Story, and the like. All the names are related to storytelling, message making, readings. Scripture is their craft. They have a way of becoming the message. That's kind of how they speak of Christ. Let's see, how do they put it? He's a, a medium of..." Mr. Kind mused. He removed his hat and placed it on his knee and momentarily shut his eyes. "Old Narrative, he used to...yeah...no...oh yes...he was fond of saying that Christ was the medium and message of God...something near to that, sure enough."

Mr. Kind sat back on the bench, rubbing his palms on the legs of his tweed trousers. A smile swelled his cheeks; they flushed bright pink.

"Sounds most intriguing," Hollie said.

"You've heard of Alpha and Omega, haven't you—the beginning and the end?" Mr. Kind asked.

"Yes," Goodwin said.

"Well, it's something like that. Those monks view Christ as being a composition of message and medium. You know, his words were so powerful, they told truth what to do."

"Never thought about it like that," Goodwin said.

"No, don't expect you have...."

The three sat there calmly, watching sparrows flap their wings in a small, nearby puddle.

"The birds remind me of children running through sprinklers in the summer heat," Hollie said.

"They do know how to make a splash," Mr. Kind said.

"Well, Sir, it's been a privilege visiting with you, but I suppose we better get moving along," Goodwin said....

"Fascinating," Hollie said. "Not sure what to say to thank you, Mr. Kind."

"No thanks needed," Mr. Kind replied. "I'm obliged for your company, very much so."

"Hollie's right, we've greatly enjoyed talking with you, Sir," Goodwin said extending his hand to Mr. Kind. Hollie followed suit.

"Maybe we'll reconnect when you return," Mr. Kind said.

"We'll be back in a month and a day," Hollie said.

"I'll mark that down. I'll stop by Blyer's on that date and see if I can spot you. You'll want a cup of coffee or a snack, I suppose."

"That's the plan, on the morning ferry," Hollie said. "We'll definitely look for you."

"We'd better move along, Hollie. See you, Sir, and thanks again."

"Oh, here, take this with you." Mr. Kind said. He reached into his pouch and pulled out a small, folded slip of paper and handed it to Hollie.

"Thanks," Hollie said, wondering what it could be. She put the slip in her pocket, as she reached out to give Mr. Kind a snip of a hug and a pat on his shoulder.

Hollie and Goodwin cut across Grims Park towards Estillyen Way. At the edge of the park, Hollie turned and looked back at Mr. Kind. He smiled and gave a wave with his cane. A stream of passersby entered the park and passed in front of Mr. Kind. Hollie continued to watch, but when they cleared, Mr. Kind was gone.

Goodwin turned to Hollie and asked, "So, what about the note—what does it say?"

Hollie pulled the paper out of the pocket of her bright-green jeans. She placed her hand inside Goodwin's arm, just above the elbow. Softly she read, "'My words are not my own' (Jesus Christ, circa AD 32)."

They just looked at each other and didn't say a word. Excited but silent, they began to walk in the direction of the Estillyen Ferry....

The redemptive messages that Hollie and Goodwin took in on their Estillyen pilgrimage now fill the pages of this literary work. It's time to read and, no doubt, ponder. Interesting monks await your presence. The audience you are.

READING ONE

⊰•◦•⊱

SETTING THE SCENE

To the Isle of Estillyen we journey for the first reading in the *Redemption* series. Our location is Quill House on the Bend[i], where the story to be told stretches back to the dawn of days, when Eden had a garden lush.

Therein, words flowed without disquiet to merry hearts. That is, until the day a distorted message made its move on Eve. Words set aloft, making meaning new, changing hearts and minds. Satan's Scriptural début it was — the ancient actor of witty words, with a knack for hacking truth to bits. History had no hedge against its first distorted message. The medium slithered in, wanton of sin.

At Quill House, midmorning has arrived; an eager audience sits in a welcome circle of wooden chairs. Glances they trade, smiles too. Anticipation is marked on every face. They wonder what words they'll hear — and, from them, what images might appear.

The Reader's name is Epic. He belongs to Estillyen's ancient Order of Message Makers. Epic is one of the most delightful and gregarious monks on the Isle of Estillyen. Not a measure of eccentric appeal does he lack.

The Reader, though, reads not alone. He is aided by the Voice. For each Estillyen reading, volunteers are chosen from among the audience. The number is most often three, yet one Voice they become. Lines they are given. The Voice speaks in unison, casting an air of wonderment and questioning into the setting. The Voice helps prop and prompt the themes and topics, as drama builds.

Indeed, the Isle of Estillyen is a place long associated with the spirit of contemplation, as robust readings stimulate reflection. To the land of Eden, via Estillyen, we go. The stage is set beyond the garden gate.

To the reading...

Did God Really Say?

*Now the serpent was more crafty than any of the wild animals the
Lord God had made. He said to the woman, "Did God really say,
'You must not eat from any tree in the garden'?"*

*The woman said to the serpent, "We may eat fruit from the trees in the
garden, but God did say, 'You must not eat fruit from the tree that is in
the middle of the garden, and you must not touch it or you will die.'"*

*"You will not surely die," the serpent said to the woman. "For God
knows that when you eat of it your eyes will be opened, and you will
be like God, knowing good and evil."*

GENESIS 3:1-5

READER: Adam and Eve lay netted in nightmares on Eden's soil: Reproach
of conscience seized and squeezed their tortured souls. Long was the night that
lingered to consume the light. Hours of eerie, thick darkness crept, gifting its
chilly blankets of doubt and despair. Reeling nightmares rendered perplexing,
macabre images, which elbowed hearts deeply troubled.

Creation's leading man and woman tossed and tussled in painful estrange-
ment. Darkened dreams drifted into their subconscious state, bringing no flight
of fancy. In their dreamy world they ran; they fled; they grasped, yet there was nowhere to go. Stark separation from joy laid them low. Sorrow stole their slumber.

So it was. Then morning broke. Joltingly, Adam and Eve awoke. At break
of day, the nightmare did not flee. Morning did not dawn and chirp away their
sorrow. As heavy as mud were their hearts. It was their first morning outside the
Garden of Eden. Welcome to reality new. Sullenness has come to call!

As sinners new, they must begin anew. They must cope, no matter what!
On behalf of the human race they were paired. They had awakened to a new,
conditional state. Mutually impaired they were, a state not to be rubbed away
from frenzied, bloodshot eyes. Creation's travail had begun. Adam and Eve were
now inhabitants of the wilderness—refugees of Paradise.

The couple's intimacy with God on the Garden grounds must have been
as close as a petal to its rose. Now plucked, they were out. Cool wilderness soil
pressed against their bare soles. Upward it spoke with a sullen, dulling effect.

VOICE: What did the soil say? Did it really speak?

READER: Not audibly, of course, but speak it did. It spoke like this: "Though upright you walk, you were made from the soil beneath your feet. Privilege has passed. Do you feel the dirt pressing, telling? It speaks of who you really are."

VOICE: It's so sobering. Is there a single word that describes how Adam and Eve might have felt?

READER: You mean, can a tiny word find a descriptive spot in such a magnanimous plot? Yes, Voice, I believe it can. Try the word *loss* on for size. Loss—that's the linking, lingering word coursing through the lines of this tragic tale. The crafty one did them in, bringing a losers' loss.

So upright they were! Suddenly they cowered low, forfeiting dreams not seen. Their chested jewels of privilege were barely touched. All was swapped for skins stitched, wilderness wear.

The story of Adam and Even began on humanity's high ground. Consider it, Voice: They were the first to hear God's thoughts coming forth in words. Morsels of meaning, divinely dispatched, filtered into their hearts and minds. Verses between the Trinity and the pair flowed as naturally as love to the heart.

Words from God to man passed, and from man to God returned. There was no in-between. No need of mediation or clever devices. Meaning was transferred without distortion. God's words settled directly on their hearts and minds, something like manna floating down from heaven. It could have been rather different, though. God might have crafted mankind in a limited form, simply parroting words.

VOICE: How is that? I mean, can God do the unimagined?

READER: Why not? God is God! He chooses his choice. Are you suggesting God needs to consult someone before making his moves?

VOICE: No, not at all. It's just that God is always supposed to be the same, unchanging, or so I'm told. You know, the same tomorrow as today?

READER: If it makes you feel better, Voice, I'll use the word *suppose.* Suppose God did make such a parroting person—a voice without choice. He would not truly speak, converse, and share from the heart. God would say, "Good man, parrot person." Parrot person would reply, "Parrot, good man." God would say

"God good." Parrot person would say "Good God." Consider for a moment how meaningful that scenario would be to God and man. Voice, parroting is not a Godlike attribute.

Let's continue our story. In the Garden of Eden, aspirations filled the air like butterflies at summer's peak.

VOICE: Reader, that sounds like a fairy tale!

READER: Does it now? It was so, Voice, this Garden of Paradise. It was so very real. No dread, no dark side. Despair was not present, not even known in Eden's land. Nor did want or worry have a place. No tempers flared. Adam and Eve shared a depth of communion with God no one else has ever experienced.

Paradise lost, it has been described—this paradise so briefly occupied. Oh, the sheer brevity of it! The brevity speaks hauntingly to the gravity of the tale, turning sad to sadder still.

Adam and Eve had hardly arrived when beginning found its end. Their exile came about so rapidly that Garden dust was yet to settle. Transitioned through, they were. It was God himself who gave them a little shove into wilderness weather.

Everything had been going swimmingly well in Paradise. There was no need of reprieve. That was, until the fateful day Eve spoke with the serpent.

VOICE: The serpent—you're referring to Satan, right?

READER: That would be the one—the master of evil. The serpent appeared in the Garden, parceling and parsing words. This inauspicious character is introduced as being very crafty…more so "than any of the wild animals the Lord had made."

Voice, Satan has an uncanny knack for spinning words. Ever so clever is this evil one. He offers conversational lines that are most sublime. Never does Satan say what he means or mean what he says. He is consistent, though, and most persistent.

VOICE: He is?

READER: Trust me, Voice. He isn't what he seems to be because he always is as he is. Satan mediates messages with disfigured verse. Each and all are dispatched with malicious intent.

Crafted in God's image, Adam and Eve were creatures unique, the object of God's delight. Listen to the ancient text, Voice: "Let us make man in our own image, in our likeness, and let them rule over the fish of the sea and the birds of the air, over the livestock, over all the earth, and over all the creatures that move along the ground."

That is what God said to God, when God decided it was time to get on with making man.

VOICE: What do you mean "God said to God"? That sounds peculiar to me.

READER: Voice, haven't you ever thought of the Trinity conversing?

VOICE: No, not talking…more like sailing together in heaven—that's how I see God—floating in and out, merging 'round about.

READER: I see. Sailing but not saying—interesting image of the Holy Trinity. Hold it there, suspended in your mind, as we consider what it is God said.

Special is this directive of God, to God, with God, about man to be. It bears a unique collaboration, not present in other acts of creation. No verse exists which says, "Let us make a zebra," or "Let us make a manatee." References to "us" and "our" indicate that the image God etched in man was requisitioned by the Holy Trinity. Sanctity of life resides, does it not, in these words of God designating man to be?

VOICE: How is that? Sanctity of life—that's an issue of great import!

READER: Right you are. Think of this: God spoke up for life long before man was formed. Discourse preceded dirt. The origin of humanity was conversation within the Holy Trinity. In the purity of the divine mind, humanity was pictured, envisioned, spiritually encrypted.

VOICE: Never thought about it like that. It's like forming the form before it's formed.

READER: Indeed, that's the idea, Voice. Were it not for that original divine discourse, forever in no-man's land is where man-not would be. Man-not would be amidst the ether of nonexistence. There, in vast nothingness, in emptiness, touching nothing and never being touched is where man-not would be.

VOICE: That's a scary thought, Reader.

READER: Yes, but if you were there, as nothing, as man-not amidst the ether, you would not be scared.

VOICE: That's what scares me. I don't want to be nonexistent.

READER: You make me smile, Voice. You are not nonexistent and will never be. But you might have been.

VOICE: I'm not sure I can think like you, or should think like you. You know what I mean?

READER: Let's think about it. Consider, though, how emptiness waits to be scooped into the something God decrees. Like the starting shot on the field of play, God's creative call sets elements streaming into form and place. Until that point, nothingness knows nothing of what it might be. At God's command, the heavens aligned, constellations filled the skies, and the first ocean wave splashed its force and foam onto virgin sand and beach.

The creation of the man, though, was not simply a command. The narrative describes the act. God "formed the man from the dust of the ground and breathed into his nostrils the breath of life, and the man became a living being." *Yatzar* is the Hebrew word for formed. It conveys the idea of God acting as a potter, shaping and sculpting Adam from the dirt.

God breathed into his mold, allowing life to flow. Breath of God's Spirit rushed in, filling heart and soul. The breath of God carried a string of divine-like attributes, meant to root and lodge.

VOICE: How you word it—it makes the human race sound so much more than human, somehow.

READER: It was so. But so was the reality of Satan. Satan's entrance into the Garden scene is curious, dispelling the picturesque tranquility. The appearance of Satan in the plot is rather like seeing one's sails rip apart, far at sea. One minute the vessel is lunging forward, racing through the waves with sails unfurled. Heartily they are swelled with gust.

Then, suddenly, rips appear. The rips begin to chase each other up and down the sails. The vessel stalls. It stops. It begins to bob.

VOICE: Satan in the Garden? How can it be?

READER: Ah, your question is cast in an ocean great! Satan has a way of appearing. He was on a mission. What else can one say? Certainly, Satan was not just wandering through; he didn't become disoriented on a devil's jog.

Satan's début in Scripture is in the Garden, conversing with Eve. Suddenly there he is. A demonic force has entered to oppose and counter the divine. He was there to rip Eden's sails apart—disfigure creation's canvas!

His cameo role in the Garden is even more perplexing than his part in Job. This is the beginning of time, yet there he is. Is he a fantasy, like many believe? Or should we say, disbelieve?

God chooses to reveal what he reveals. The drama is his. Beyond knowing are God's reasons for the mysterious moves he makes. This, however, is exceedingly good, not bad.

VOICE: What do you mean by saying exceedingly good?

READER: If you knew all God knows, Voice, God would be rather limited, would he not? Or you would be like God, which is the very point that undid Eve.

God being God, without reason to man, is God being God, as God should be. The characters of Scripture come and go. God alone knows the story complete. Satan appearing in the Garden, no matter how bizarre it might seem, was no surprise to God. The reason why extends deep into the divine realm. Let it rest there. It's not your worry.

What's evident from the scene is that Satan is there to tempt and test the will of God's newly created beings. He makes his move. Silently Satan slinks. He is there to prey and pounce on human will, showing it can bend and yield.

Satan enters the scene. His opening line is not a greeting, which one might expect. No "Hello, Eve, let me introduce myself. I'm Lucifer, the adversary of God." His first words, instead, form a question: "Did God really say you must not eat from any tree in the garden?" This line tossed to Eve is the first question recorded in Scripture. Satan was indigenous.

VOICE: Indigenous, that can't be. We're talking about Paradise, not hell.

READER: Yes, I know. Remember what we said about God being God?

VOICE: Sure, but…

READER: Then we must trust beyond our knowing. Indigenous he was. The crafty one knew his way around. He possessed an inside track. Was not Satan aware of the words God had spoken to Adam and Eve?

Perhaps, like a chameleon, he hid perched on branches, eavesdropping, watching. With wily eyes, he might have watched as God welcomed his original pair, giving them an instructive stroll around the Garden. The serpent's weapon—what was it, Voice?

VOICE: I suppose his words—what he said?

READER: Precisely. He struck at Eve, not with fang and venom, but with words. How close the serpent must have been to speak as easily as he did. There was no calling out to Eve, no shouting from afar.

In an instant, it seems, the crafty one could have easily lunged and had an eye-for-an-eye. Imagine Eve running through the trees with one eye snatched away. What a horrific sight! Or perhaps, on the throat his wily eyes he might have fixed. His aim sharp, he might have pressed deep his fangs, injecting a venomous flow through Eve's tender skin. Into the blood his poison would pass. Death would chase life away. Satan would have his prey.

Physical harm, though, was not the method of Satan's destructive blow. That was too limiting. The attack came via little morsels, the careful placement of chosen words.

The prize for Satan was much greater than the breath of Eve. Satan's goal was to scar and disfigure the spirit. His aim was to twist the spirit to such an extent that it would cost God dearly to affect a remedy. This was Satan's mission. With the right sinful twist of words, all would be warped, sullen, and sad, including God.

This is what Satan knew. This was his devilish desire. Satan wanted God to bear wounds from this infamous strike. Out of immense nothingness God had spoken the universe into being. At the center of it all was Eden's Paradise with Adam and Eve. Oh, how Satan must have abhorred this newfound life God had rendered. It all came to be without the slightest nod to Satan. He was not called or consulted. This, too, Satan knew.

In Eve, Satan saw his opportunity not simply to destroy a single woman or man. Satan's ill effect could cast the whole of creation into a monstrous death roll. This was his mode of operation, his prowling perversion. No pithy, piddly prize for Satan. Big game was his aim.

Expelled from heaven's realm, the wandering devourer would show God a thing or two. Give God a blow. The crafty one may be a castaway, but he could still hack away at Paradise. Satan seethed. To seek destruction was his code. God's fleshy uprights would taste sin and rejection—he, Satan, would see to it.

VOICE: Can Satan really think like that? It seems so incredible, so devious, so scary.

READER: Surely Satan thinks. What of his modus operandi? Have you thought of that?

VOICE: Yes, to an extent. I can't figure it out, though—such a manic rage against God.

READER: Impossible it is to know what rolls through Satan's wretched, wicked world of thought, although one can imagine what he might have considered as he peered across the beauty of Eden's Garden.

He may well have imagined, "I AM, why not I with Eve—there in the center of your paradise so green and lush? Who better than I to make good your wondrous scheme? I AM, we could have done a deal, you and I. After all, I was once a celestial being, a great bearer of light. You could have cut me in, set the past aside. Think about it, it was eons ago, our spat. We could have started anew, you and I.

"Sure, I would have dropped my wings, no big deal. There I would have been, your chosen one, reassigned, ready to father it all. Reborn, if you wish, but a celestial man. Instead, you ended up with little imps of dust with nostrils puffed. I AM, you needn't have stooped so low, to make creatures from the dirt. I could have done you proud, and your planet, too. Come on, can't you see what you missed in not calling me? Surely your wisdom must have waned, not realizing all this could have been meant for me and you.

VOICE: Are you serious? You are, aren't you, Reader?"

READER: Yes, Voice, it's far more than a silly thought in this magnanimous plot. In Paradise, Eve was unaware that she had been drawn onto Satan's turf. Morsels from the crafty one danced in her ears; words flowed to the core of her understanding. The most critical question Eve had ever heard was posed as a proposition of doubt. Satan questioned what God had said. Satan's words sliced at God's. Consider the sails, Voice. Can you see them?

VOICE: I can. They are white and puffed—but slit.

READER: So right, Voice. In Eve's heart and mind, words dueled and echoed. "Did God really say, 'You must not eat from any tree in the garden'?" Eve entertained these words bearing hidden hooks. The question Satan asked was not for want of information. Cleverly his line was cast. He was simply conversing. This was the first temptation of Eve. Slice!

Adam and Eve were novice conversationalists, mere babes up against the master of lying lips. The question to Eve could have gone unanswered, been referred to Adam, or been taken to God. It was not to be. When the first question to humanity was carefully lobbed by Satan, Adam was silent. There was no rebuke or rebuttal on his part. By injecting a line or two, Adam could have quickly shooed the crafty one away. He could have told Satan where to go.

VOICE: Where? Where would Adam have told Satan to go?

READER: Well, where else? To God, of course. God was the sure source for information about what God really said. If not that solution, Adam might simply have said to Eve, "It is time to go." Instead, the conversation continued. Adam's silent presence spoke not against but in consort. Adam allowed Eve to converse, to entertain Satan's salacious words.

Satan's misinformation to Eve was a trick. She felt obliged to correct him. Eve knew that she and Adam were not restricted in the way Satan implied. God was not banning their access from all the trees. It was just the one. Eve felt compelled to answer. She wanted to explain, to speak, to clarify the facts.

She told Satan what he already knew. "We may eat from the trees in the garden, but God did say, 'You must not eat fruit from the tree that is in the middle of the garden, and you must not touch it, or you will die.'" With each word of engagement, Eve slid deeper into Satan's pit.

Satan didn't pause to thank Eve for her helpful clarification rendered by feminine intonation. Rather, he crept closer still, to the strategic intent of his distorted message. "You will not surely die," the serpent said to the woman. "For God knows that when you eat of it, your eyes will be opened, and you will be like God, knowing good and evil." This line was Eve's second temptation. Slice!

Words dispensed with Satan's hooks. The word *when* is a hook, is it not? Satan did not say *if* you eat, but *when*. Then, two more hooks: Your eyes will be opened. You'll be like God. Not just God-likeness, but like God. That's what you'll be, Eve, like God. The hook of implication was also embedded in the serpent's message.

VOICE: Implication…what's implied?

READER: Plenty. In particular, the notion that God had not been forthcoming with Adam and Eve. He'd been holding out on them. Was God, for reasons of his own, manipulating Adam and Eve? Why was he restricting access? Why didn't God want them to gain the knowledge he possessed?

With a few little lines, the serpent cast a swelling cloud of suspicion over God. Masterfully he crafted his message. Slice, slice, slice. Blending truth with lie, the serpent's message became ravenously tempting and taunting to Eve. Consider the blend. The lie straight from the liar's lips: "You will not surely die." The truth: You will see life differently, knowing good and evil, like God. The lie: You will be like God. The truth: You will be very unlike God.

The ultimate promise: You will be like God. You will be God, not an approximation of God-likeness. No longer will you troupe around in human skin, bearing godly attributes. God you will be, and as God, you will set the Garden rules, make the arrangements. You'll do as you please on Garden grounds.

Then, as swiftly as it had begun, the conversation between Satan and Eve ceased. Three characters are center stage in the Garden drama. Only two exchange lines, on which the destiny of the created order was balanced. Drama, deep drama, filled the air. Heaven peered down. Angels of light, busied by creation's launch, looked to God for affirmation. Can you see them, Voice?

VOICE: I can! They look disturbed, curiously worried. Think of it, worried angels. I see them. They have no smiles.

READER: All the while, angels of darkness, the fallen, hid in Satan's shadow, clinging to his twisted tail. They gnawed at the dirt and inadvertently paused to peer up at their master. They watched their adored matador, Satan, as he inched ever closer to crippling creation.

Suddenly, softly, they began to chant the bitty lines their master strung. Did God really say? You will not surely…Did God really say? You will not surely… Did God really say? You will not surely…That was their mumbled mantra. Faster and faster they chanted, as the volume began to grow into a riotous rumble.

VOICE: Did Satan's demons really chant like that?

READER: Did they not? With every beat of her heart, the wayward will of Eve rose. Without a hint of disapproval from Adam, the crafty serpent waited for Eve's response. Satan's forged smile concealed his fangs. Behind his sealed lips, bitter venom dripped. Feverishly hot it was.

Heaven waited! Destiny waited. With bated breath, all of creation waited for Eve, for Eve to choose, for Eve to make her move.

"When the woman saw that the fruit of the tree was good for food and pleasing to the eye, and also desirable for gaining wisdom, she took some and ate it. She also gave some to her husband, who was with her, and he ate it." Eve reached for that which was pleasing to the eye and desirable for gaining wisdom. This pleasing desire was the third temptation of Eve. Rip, slice, rip.

Do you see the sails now, Voice?

VOICE: I do! They're falling, flapping, failing.

READER: The grasping motion was perpetuated by the message. The message, not the fruit, was the great embrace. Eve reached for words—the promise to be like God, not merely to be image-bound.

The serpent's distorted message achieved its aim with maddening effect. Sin had slithered through the garden grounds, finding its wily way to the human heart. There it deposited itself and swiftly rooted. Sin's fertility would wait for posterity. Adam and Eve were delivered into darkness. Just as God had said, they would surely die.

Adam and Eve cast caution to the wind—and with it, life. They embraced the message, swallowing swiftly its scripted words. Aspiration rose, and will moved. Human will is such that it can swell with the force of the ocean tide. Whatever qualms Eve may have possessed were rolled away by her wanton proclivity.

VOICE: Reader, sorry, but that word *proclivity*—I like the sound of it, but I'm not sure what it means.

READER: It has to do with penchant—one's desire or weakness—the way you are prone to be if left to your own devices. This is the great sin, when temptation rises and the will lunges with proclivity. To embrace a distorted message meant that the message of God had to be let go. No need of God. The new beings somehow thought they could maneuver around their Maker. This is the core of rottenness, for which Eve reached.

There would have been a huge problem of being on par with God. What was to become of God—creation's keeper? Consider it, Voice. A garden, like a kingdom, cannot stand divided. Tiny feet of human beings cannot fill divine shoes. God can fill human footwear, and, indeed, this happened, but that is a reading for another day.

The story of the Garden centers on messages in a competitive mode: one true let go; one distorted embraced, hacking the other away. Some things cannot be replaced. God cannot be replaced. Those original sails cannot be replaced.

Inventive creatures, human beings are. They create all manner of gods and messages. The great attraction of many, though, is to reside in a world that is God-exempt. This is but the same deception of Eve. God's exemptness aids in this feeling of being God, of representing the highest order. With God exempt, there is no deferring to the divine.

Voice, presumption is humanity's middle name, resident in every heart. From ancient parents, presumption is handed down. It was deposited that fateful day that Eve, with twitching ears and wanton eyes, grasped the object of her undoing. Proclivity of will brought on sin's plague.

Listen to more ancient words, Voice. "Then the eyes of both of them were opened, and they realized they were naked, so they sewed fig leaves together and made coverings for themselves." Adam and Eve heard God "as he was walking in the garden in the cool of the day, and they hid from the Lord God among the trees of the garden."

With fig leaves adorned, among the trees, humanity's first couple hid from God, their Maker. "I was afraid," said Adam. "The serpent deceived me," said Eve. Little chirps of confession appear not to detect the magnitude of sin's curse, which would roll out from the Garden and into the world beyond.

"The Lord God made garments of skin for Adam and his wife and clothed them." At creation's dawn, the sacrificial age began. Having placed Adam and

Eve at the center of the universal stage, the curtain would have to fall. Adam and Eve, the world's first Godlike creatures, now bore the mark of sin. Created in the image of God, though, they were not disposable.

Human beings had been grafted into God's existence. They were there for a reason. God wanted them. God would not give up on humanity and go away. God would respond. A long and circuitous route of redemption would be deployed.

True it is. Guilt seeped into shame for Adam and Eve, while fear and anxiety crept over the state of their new condition. The intimate environment into which they had been placed soon fell silent.

The gate of Paradise was closed. The world, and its Garden within, would never be the same. Cursed was the ground, and to cursed ground Adam and Eve would return. To death's embrace they would go; surely they would die!

The ceiling of Rome's Sistine Chapel is adorned with scenes painted by Michelangelo. Among these magnificent frescoes is one from Genesis entitled Original Sin and the Banishment from the Garden of Eden. Michelangelo depicts Satan luring Eve into his deceptive ploy.

Perched in a tree, the serpent reaches out to Eve with the offer of fruit. The crafty creature sports a feminine torso but one with masculine qualities, broad shoulders and muscular arms. An equal blend of genders is seen in the face, while the thighs segue down to large, reptile-like extrusions. They coil around the tree, disproportionate in size to the main body of the figure.

Eve is below the tree, lying nude on her right side, her left arm extended upward. Her fingers appear to be touching the serpent's left hand as she reaches for the fruit. A blonde-haired Adam stands upright, examining the tree with intense curiosity.

The scene blends seamlessly into an adjoining fresco of Adam and Eve being expelled from the Garden. A red-robed angel hovers in the air, pressing the tip of his sword to the back of Adam's neck. Shocked, confused, and frightened, the couple is reluctantly forced to step into the wilderness unknown.

Voice, the pace of modern advancement has a way of distancing ancient sagas from the present with exponential force. The story of the Garden of Eden carries with it a mythical undertow tugging at all that follows in Scripture. It's a story both passionately believed and readily dismissed. As brilliance appears to mount, numerous skeptics and cynics gnaw at the umbilical cords of faith and belief. They want to tether free of ancient times, when human beings lacked the accoutrements of modernity.

Just the same, my dear companion of rhyme, faucets gushing so freely today with messages of disbelief will tomorrow only drip. Morphing like chameleons, from one generation to the next, messages of distortion and disbelief have their momentary appeal. As time moves on, they will all drip dry.

This is not the way of messages, with words that are God-inscribed. To such words, fate bows, knowing full well their origin. Voice, numerous are the Garden's lessons, not least the meaning of words and messages sent.

Words matter...some far more than most.

"Did God really say, 'You must not eat from any tree in the garden'?"
THE SERPENT, GARDEN OF EDEN, CIRCA THE BEGINNING OF TIME

READING TWO

◆━━◆━━◆

SETTING THE SCENE

Reading Two it is, and what words might you expect to find in a story told in Estillyen's Silo on the Mound²? Words in the *Redemption* series are known for linking up in peculiar patterns.

The words one and all like to move about with meaning sure. Their disposition vis-à-vis the audience, though, is more akin to coasting through than carting, but they're never laissez-faire. As one of the monks, Saga—in fact, our Reader for today—tells us, "Ah, mystery mixed so sweetly with surety and reality."

Saga is a simple, humble monk who lives in the tradition of St. Francis of Assisi. For Reading Two, Saga is joined by Brother Herald, a more senior monk.

Readers two they are. That's the way the drama works whenever the character of Lucifer makes an entrance, which shortly he will do. This pugnacious role of Lucifer is always assigned to a senior monk. The Estillyen monks are rather fixed on certain notions, this being one. They insist on setting apart the Readers of Scripture narratives from the Readers who act out the counter cause of Lucifer.

Further, Lucifer travels not alone. He has chosen devotees—twelve, in fact.

In Reading Two, Eden is so very distant now, as the daunting shadow of Mt. Sinai looms. Yes, you are there, at the mountain's base. Tablets of stone Moses possesses. Commandments Ten will soon lie in multiple bits and pieces.

They're ready. Reader and Voice trade nods; throats are cleared. A mantle of silence descends on the room. The reading is set to begin at precisely 12:00 p.m., which now it is.

To the reading...

Picking Up the Pieces

Moses turned and went down the mountain with the two tablets
of the Testimony in his hands. They were inscribed on both sides,
front and back. The tablets were the work of God; the writing was
the writing of God, engraved on the tablets.

When Joshua heard the noise of the people shouting, he said to Moses,
"There is the sound of war in the camp."

Moses replied: "It is not the sound of victory, it is not the sound of
defeat; it is the sound of singing that I hear."

When Moses approached the camp and saw the calf and the dancing,
his anger burned and he threw the tablets out of his hands, breaking
them to pieces at the foot of the mountain.

EXODUS 32:15-19

READER: From God to Moses the tablets of stone were passed. With a single fling of indignation, they lay on the ground in pieces. The Law of God lay broken to bits. Never read. Never adored. No chance to be abhorred. The magnanimous message, in medium of stone, had swiftly become a heap of litter.

Jumbled were the words and letters God had inscribed. With his own finger, God had etched them in the Commandments Ten. Not six, or eleven, or some other number, but ten. This was a message of divine intent. This was a brief compilation, a succinct summation of God's thoughts, inscribed in words.

VOICE: Why stone as choice of medium?

READER: Inscribed in stone, letters do not scatter or move about. They are fixed, set, no blotting out this for that. No dropping a word or two to free up space.

But there is more. The medium speaks, does it not? A medium is a message, but what message does it bear?

VOICE: Reader, pardon me. I know you've only begun, but I just want to be clear. A medium is a medium, and a message is a message, right?

READER: Go on, Voice, I sense more in your query.

VOICE: The former, being the medium, does not usurp the message, surely?

READER: Good question, Voice. To which I offer this reply: A message is not a message, apart from the medium that makes the message known. Show me a message without a medium. Oh, I could cruelly send you on a search of such a specimen. Though that I will not do, because you would go and try. Forever I would wait for your return!

Therefore, regarding this matter of message and medium, the former, being the message, is never what it is indivisible from the latter. Into every message, the medium contributes elements of its essence to the message. It's not unlike letters conveying words. Words need letters to make them known, but the letters shape words to appear and sound the way they do. Indivisible are the two.

Look at me, Voice. Am I not a medium with a message? So it is with you.

VOICE: I think I'm still with you, mostly.

READER: Lest we trail away, let's go back to the tablets of stone—and our story of words and letters on the ground. We were considering the medium—stone it was. Stone does not smile or hug. It's not warm and friendly. It's not human. Stone is cold if not warmed by the sun or something else. It possesses no blood. It has no pulse. It's made of granules, grains, once popular for telling time.

Stones are not new. They are old. Inscribed stones are not rare. As cornerstones they often speak, dating dreams. At entrances they frequently appear, speaking words of conviction. Embedded in memorials, they speak of honor and sacrifice. Their most common use, by far, is to name and date the dead.

Markers they are called, headstones over those at rest below. Once those resting walked upward, talking, jostling. Now they rest—inscribed, dead, and dated. Inscribed markers speak of permanence, though their etchings fade. They are bastions of permanence in a world of impermanence.

This they are, rather like the tablets handed down. Imagine the tablets, the work of God, the never-changing One. God who speaks words never fading. His work of permanence reduced to rubble. The tablets were heavy enough to be inscribed—yet brittle and thin enough to break.

Ever so carefully, no doubt, Moses must have carried them down from the majestic summit. The weighty stones held fast against his chest. That is, until Moses saw what he saw. That's when he flung the burdensome weight.

VOICE: What did he see?

READER: Wait, Voice—don't rush the reading.

The medium, with its message intact, hit the ground, smashing into pieces. One can imagine the pieces there—random bits of stone with broken words scattered from context and meaning.

"You shall," the most frequent of words God inscribed, lay there in a triangular scrap. "Idol" is visible in one stone's small square. Next to the idol scrap rests a stone strip bearing the phrase, "but showing love to a thousand...."

Is it hard for you to see them, Voice?

VOICE: No, I see them as you say. Several are bunched together. Others lay round-about.

READER: Words broken, loosed from medium and message, lay on the ground, speaking still. Curiously, they became a message new. With diffused meaning, words and letters called out from the heap.

The collective shatter formed a new kind of meaning. The message was more like an eagle's nest fallen from its cliff. In the eagle's nest, babies chirped. Chirping want, chirping fear. The shattered stony bits lay chirping, too. One by one, stones chirped of shame and confusion.

God's words etched in stone signified not only surety of source but also the new reality of God communicating with man. The coziness of the Garden was gone, long gone. Laws etched in stone formed the new communicative mode. Do you see, Voice, how it is the message cannot break away from the medium?

VOICE: It's just that this is not a simple matter: messages making meaning, molded in medium. I guess I need to consider this more fully.

READER: There is a great deal to consider relative to those disjointed pieces broken on the ground. The stone tablets were given by God to guide and mold the Israelites into a new way of being. Words inscribed in stone were to be inscribed on their hearts and minds, not departing. They were to divert devious words from wandering hearts, like the words that deceived dear Eve. "Did God really say?" was Satan's slithering plea.

The silt of Noah's epic flood, teamed with the sands of time, ultimately smothered Eden's paradise. Together they heaped history high, layered thick, covering the once sacred ground buried deep. Where the tree of life went, Scripture does not say. It's safe to surmise that those mysterious leaves were not fossilized in an abandoned plot, no matter how deep and indistinct.

Ah, mystery mixed so sweetly with surety and reality. That's the way of God, Voice, gracing the known with that which is so otherly divine.

VOICE: Reader, wait, Sir, if you will. I'm with you, but these stories are all about ironclad matters, surely. Yet you speak of mystery with such…how might I say it…with such zeal.

READER: Mystery is good, Voice. It places present reality in the place it should be.

VOICE: Where's that?

READER: Present days of fast-paced ticking are prudently placed, tethered to the past and facing eternity. God's words fuel and foster imagination no one can shatter. Letting God be God, planting the tree of life and knowledge, too. This notion is grain-ripping for those who demand proof for everything. Seeking proof at every turn can blind you, Voice. Beware.

The generations extending from Adam and Eve were quick to reap quite appalling press. Among those early generations of posterity, there was little prodigy. Rather, the move was a rapid descent into a kind of deranged debauchery.

The divine image borne in man grew increasingly faint. The image acted much like a heart symbol carved in the bark of a tree. In time it spreads apart. Its form is obscured. The twist of character swiftly manifested itself in Gomorrah-like passion.

It seemed God became so grieved that, for a while, he wanted to get down on his knees and pray, but to whom? Ancient words testify to it! They do not deny it. Listen to words from Genesis: "The Lord was grieved that he had made man on earth, and his heart was filled with pain."

VOICE: God grieved…his heart filled with pain…how can that be?

READER: I know, Voice. It sounds bizarre in a way, but so it was. Surely, all the heavenly hosts mourned pitifully upon hearing that God was not well. A sight not seen in all eternity this was: God in pain. The hosts watching must have hovered behind stars and constellations to help lessen God's consternation. Who is it that speaks to God when the foreordained exhibits disdain? Does God need comfort?

Oh, it's true, Voice. God was in serious pain regarding creatures vain. This, too, is a mystery great, is it not? The picture of God in pain. That's not at all how God is so often depicted. Insufficiently real and without depth, God rides upon the canvas of so many tawdry paintings. God is real. Pain is real. God in pain is doubly real. The beings God had created had faltered. Who was to blame? Was it the mold, the maker, or what was made?

The day God spoke to Noah, the fate of flesh was sealed. To Noah, God said, "The end of all flesh is come before me; for the earth is filled with violence through them; and, behold, I will destroy them with the earth."

The end of all flesh. How such news must have sounded to Satan! What a welcome epitaph for Lucifer to read, inscribed over humanity's grave. The human race, diseased by sin, destroyed by Satan, drowned by God! What could be more appealing for Satan? God and Satan, once again, named in united action. No victory for humanity, only loss. Forever Satan's smirk at God would be his delight. To God he could always say, "I could have told you, but you never asked."

Noah's ark was it, a single clan aboard, with captive critters bobbing up and down. Waters rose, humanity sank. Crying, clawing, clinging, choking, they slipped into the watery waves of death. Silently they floated, as rain pelted down on cold, dead flesh.

Consider it, Voice. It was so. Can you see the scene?

VOICE: Yes, I can.

READER: Yet a rainbow of hope appeared in the sky. God would begin anew. Seasons chased one another through the years, and God's grief eventually ebbed. God got well. In time, characters of a different sort emerged.

Abraham appeared. In him God found a different kind of man. One night, God took him out under a starlit sky. "Look up at the heavens and count the stars," God said. Abraham received a great promise. His descendants would be numerous, not unlike the vast array of shining stars on which he gazed.

Abraham was looking for an architect and a city whose builder and maker was God. God was looking for a people to carry out his plan of redemption. God needed a peculiar people, a stalwart lot, with priests and prophets willing to meticulously record their exploits and plots. Their prophetic words would ensure God's redemptive message. That is to say that, once God spoke through the prophets about what was to be, it had to be.

VOICE: God setting in motion what must be—it's such a mesmerizing thought to consider. What will be is by his decree, it seems. No matter what, I guess.

READER: That's the way it works with God and inspired verse. Once inscribed, the words of prophetic promise are placed along future's trail. Then, when history catches up with the future and becomes present, that which was to be *is*.

VOICE: Spellbinding! This line of thinking is so encompassing—almost beyond reason.

READER: Does that trouble you, Voice?

VOICE: No, it's not troubling…well, maybe somewhat.

READER: It is an amazing story, Voice. God needed a people sensitive to his Spirit, people who would fill and swell scrolls with words rendering the thoughts of God to men. The scribing work would begin with the Law, which would set the stage for the message of grace. One day grace would appear, bearing a most unusual face.

This scribing work on behalf of God required a people especially prepared to weather centuries of persecution and retribution. It's no easy work, scribing for God. Thoughts of God scribed as words have a way of stoking great complaint and fierce opposition.

Abraham's starry promise would take time. A severe famine swept across the land where Abraham's ancestors were to live out their thriving existence. This forced Abraham's lineage to leave and migrate to Egypt. In Egypt, the Israelites were enslaved for 400 years. Think of it, Voice, a decade times ten, times four little years—layer upon layer.

Four hundred years is a hardly a tick or two of time. Nations—and kingdoms, too—can dissolve and disappear in the space of so many years. During those long centuries, the Israelites did not busy themselves with conquests and nation building. Instead, their hands were plying mud and straw. They were brick makers.

With every single brick made and stacked, God was forging a stalwart people of priests, prophets, kings. Denial was their culture—their fate, daily drudgery. Confinement was their playground. Luxury and advancement were seen only from afar. People free walked with a different gait than slaves casting bent silhouettes under the Egyptian sun.

As centuries passed, the Israelites became more convinced of who they weren't than who they were. With each passing year, they moved farther from their nomadic ways. They were people of bondage. The Israelites lived and died, but always with a sense of dying without truly living. Prospects seemed nil, bricking the dreams others possessed. Yet patient is God, working in ways that cannot be seen by eyes other than his.

VOICE: Reader, pardon me. About your lines—will they lead back to the tablets lying on the ground?

READER: Most assuredly! We're there! The enslaved Israelites finally fled Egypt by way of the Red Sea, following Moses in an amazing saga that we'll not touch on here today. For three months they journeyed in the desert before making camp at Mt. Sinai.

The ominous site was selected by God. This was the place God chose to pay a visit, to lay down the Law, along with a host of conditions. Worlds apart from Eden's Paradise, Mt. Sinai showcased a side of God man had not seen.

Days before God would appear to the Israelites en masse, he summoned Moses up to the top of the mountain and instructed him on how to prepare for this unprecedented occasion. He gave Moses a worrying message to spread among the camp. This is part of what God said: "Be careful that you do not go up the mountain or touch the foot of it. Whoever touches the mountain shall surely be put to death. He shall surely be stoned or shot with arrows; not a hand is to be laid on him. Whether man or animal, he shall not be permitted to live. Only when the ram's horn sounds a long blast may they go up to the mountain."

In this great throng of freed brick makers, God saw temple builders in waiting, prophets and priests who would foretell of the coming of the Messiah. Their role was preordained. Their deliverance from Egypt was already deeply embedded in God's story.

Through Scripture God would work, effecting his mission. Stories with real-life characters would reveal the will and ways of God. God thoughts would be incarnated in human story. The good and the bad, the evil and the saintly, all had a part in the stories that would unfold. The exploits of men and mates seal their fate. In scrolls they would come to rest, encased in God's story.

What man curses, God may bless. What is cherished, God may loathe. It was all to be revealed in story, showing God to be the source of indisputable virtues. God knew he, too, would play a part in his own drama. Now and then he'd slip in a little handwriting on the wall, or drench a poor king with dew. Can you imagine it? King Nebuchadnezzar, in a field covered with dew, eating grass among the beasts!

VOICE: Is that story true—King Nebuchadnezzar drenched with dew, eating grass in a field? Surely that's a fairy tale just slotted in.

READER: Voice, my friend dear and near, be wary of those who speak of airy and fairy. What's been scribed and come to be was done with great sanctity. Let that point in you rest. Consider the message in the making and the meaning made. Don't run along outside the story—that's where you'll get lost, stuck among the thorns. I ask you, how did poor old King Nebuchadnezzar contract such a disease?

VOICE: Don't know—I guess God gave it to him.

READER: Now you're thinking within the story, not apart from it. Through messages and mediums, God creates, reveals, reckons, and restores. From the medium of self, God's communication flows, not unlike a divine pulse emanating throughout the cosmos and down to man.

Mt. Sinai was the great exception in revelation's roll, the time when God came down as he is, not incarnate in the flesh. He came down to stay awhile and speak his mind about the trajectory of man with God. Mt. Sinai showcased the seemingly insurmountable gulf between God and the human race. How different things had become since those early Garden days, days of walking near and talking dear.

Make no mistake about it: The medium was the message at Mt. Sinai. The mountain, the acts of God, the appearance of God—everything mediated a message with meaning. The image of God was impossible to ignore. The image, yes, is that of a majestic creator draped in wonder. At the same time, though, the image is frightening. God demands distance. He's ready to rain down terror and retribution.

Voice, this is what the Israelites heard and saw standing there at the base:

*"On the morning of the third day, there was thunder and lightning, with
a thick cloud over the mountain and a very loud trumpet blast. Everyone
in the camp trembled. Then Moses led the people out of the camp to meet
with God, and they stood at the foot of the mountain. Mount Sinai was
covered with smoke, because the Lord descended on it in fire. The smoke
billowed up from it like smoke from a furnace, the whole mountain
trembled violently, and the sound of the trumpet grew louder and louder.
Then Moses spoke, and the voice of God answered him."*

The Israelites were meeting their maker, the mysterious God who rescued
them from Egypt. Movement around the mountain was allowed only when
the ram's horn blared its haunting sound. Merely touching the mountain at
the inappropriate time meant certain death. Execution was inevitable, stones
thudding against the body, arrows piercing flesh. Dead, the victims would fall.
Their defiled bodies were not to be touched. Dead, they would bloat and rot in
the Sinai sun.

A few months earlier, the Israelites were bent over, working mud and straw.
Now they were to ascend Mt. Sinai and meet the God who created the universe.
"When the people saw the thunder and lightning and heard the trumpet and
saw the mountain in smoke, they trembled with fear. They stayed at a distance
and said to Moses, 'Speak to us yourself and we will listen. But do not have God
speak to us or we will die.'"

Precipitous beyond compare was humanity's fall from Eden's garden to
Sinai's mountain. Everything had changed. A child running to his parents with
outstretched arms is not the picture of Mt. Sinai. Yet Moses said, "Do not be
afraid. God has come to test you, so that the fear of God will be with you to
keep you from sinning."

The people watched from a distance as Moses dutifully climbed and disappeared
into the thick darkness of divine presence. Mt. Sinai is a comprehensive drama, directed by God. The juxtaposition of God and man is most telling. God is up there.
The Israelites are down below, cautiously moving about as the drama builds.

Smoke billowed not of its own accord, nor did the trumpet blast. The
mountain didn't suddenly decide it was time to tremble. The mountain was a
medium, Voice, as well as a message. Indivisible they were in transferring meaning. Together they spoke of God, for God. It was God's communicative act.

The smoke billowed; the mountain shook. The madding trumpet blast grew louder and louder. Then, out of the dense smoke, the voice of God was heard. Medium and message were fused by God with dramatic effect. The skies rumbled with energy; thunder exploded; lightning charged through the sky.

Unquestionably, the most pivotal event was God giving the Ten Commandments to Moses. "Come up to me on the mountain," God said, "and stay here and I will give you the tablets of stone, with the law and commands I have written for their instruction." The Israelites watched once again as Moses ardently ascended and disappeared into the mysterious cloud. As he did, "the glory of the Lord looked like a consuming fire on the mountain."

During the Mt. Sinai experience, twice Moses fasted for forty days and nights. Without food or water, he would lay prostrate before God. It was during Moses' first fast that the people in the camp lost their mooring.

"They gathered around Aaron and said, 'Come, make us gods who will go before us. As for this fellow, Moses, who brought us up out of Egypt, we don't know what has happened to him.'

"Aaron said, 'Take off the gold earrings that your wives, your sons, and your daughters are wearing, and bring them to me.' Rapidly, the people stripped off their jewelry and offered it to Aaron. He took the jewelry, melted it down, and fashioned an idol cast in the shape of a calf. The people were elated and said, 'These are your gods, O Israel, who brought you up out of Egypt.'"

When Aaron saw the reaction of the people, he made an altar and placed it in front of the golden calf and announced, 'Tomorrow, there will be a festival to the Lord.'" The brick makers of Egypt had gone mad, casting off all restraint to indulge in revelry.

The events in the camp did not catch God unaware. God saw the people bowing down and worshiping, bestowing praise on the golden calf for its power to deliver them from Egypt. God told Moses that the people had "become corrupt" and "quick to turn away." Moses quickly retreated down the mountain with the inscribed tablets in his hands.

As Moses started down the mountain, God said, "Now leave me alone so that my anger may burn against them and that I may destroy them." Moses begged God to reconsider, reminding him of the Egyptians and what they would think upon hearing God slaughtered his chosen people in the desert.

Moses pleaded, "Remember your servants, Abraham, Isaac, and Israel, to whom you swore by your own self, 'I will make your descendants as numerous as the stars.'" Moses prevailed.

What about the great adversary of God during all of this? Did you ever think of that, Voice? One can imagine Satan scouting out Mt. Sinai, drawing near enough to see what was up with God coming down. He's always on the prowl, and with such a dramatic occurrence unfolding, it's hard to conceive Satan would be clueless concerning God's whereabouts. It is not every day that I AM decides to come down to occupy a mountain and inscribe words in stone.

At this point in the reading, Saga looked behind him and nodded to Brother Herald. Slowly Brother Herald stood, taking not a single forward step. From the corner of the room, he voiced his lines, which spoke to the heart of Satan's intent, depicted through the character of Lucifer.

LUCIFER: Silence, imbeciles; Lucifer demands quiet! Can't you see I'm peering and hearing, perceiving and parsing? That's I AM communicating, you stupid lympheads! I need the full extent of my faculties to peer with pure perception.

More than much I've seen and heard in my existence. Never, though, have I seen I AM congregating with fleshies on a mountain. This is big, my devotees. Get your wits twitched. You gotta be at the bottom of your game, low, I mean really low. No telling what's gonna happen here today. Be ready to respond to my every twitch, to every point on the compass. Dial your eyes in. Fix them sure on our cause. No hyperventilating—keep all of your inductors open.

No sir, not small at all is this I AM extravaganza. I can detect the future talking with the past. They're streaming into the present. They know nothing of time. They're like liquid mercury flowing in to hug each other. There's heavy spiritchitis going on here—heavy, I tell you! It's putting red rings in my eyes. It's making me cough. I AM is billowing that smoke. Stay clear of it, I tell you—one strong whiff and you'll be obliterated.

I've got news. I AM is on the move! He's scripting something new. He's on some revelatory roll. That's not good. I AM spins a good line, but his ways have become untoward. Fraternizing with fleshies was the last straw—that's the move that snapped the angel's wing. Just look, I AM congregating on a mountain, out here in the desert with imps. Why, oh why? What, oh what does I AM see in these mud molds?

I'd rather congregate with mice. The instant I laid eyes on fleshies, didn't I tell you I despised 'em? Have I wavered one iota? Lucifer never wavers. Puffed up mud with little spirits, that's all they are. Big deal, mud breath. They have no idea what's on the far side of the stratosphere.

I AM might have called on me to look after a few constellations, to give him a hand now and then. Not now; there's not a chance. He's lost it, becoming enthralled with fleshies, putting on this show for fleshies out here in the wilderness. You can't be God and go prancing around with fleshies. That's as bad as angels riding pigs. Did you devotees ever see angels riding pigs? That's not a question!

Of course you haven't. Angels don't ride pigs to and fro in heaven. Would you expect to see Elijah's chariot drawn by flying baboons? Don't you reckless delinquents go getting any ideas. No pig-riding for my devotees. I'd smash you, pigs and all.

It's not right, I tell you, seeing I AM getting all mushy with fleshies. I AM's become so unlike his former self. He says in the fleshy good book he never changes—'Same he'll be, as he used to be.' Fleshies have no way of knowing what was, scooped out of the mud like they were. I was around in the days of what was, and I wasn't scooped out of miserable, mucky old mud.

In those days we were alliterated—word-spun, in a manner of speaking. Suddenly in the heavens we soared. Naturally, I soared higher than the rest of the flock. No wing-flapping for me—very little, anyway. Soar I did, and all the angels of light used to gather just to watch me soar. My maneuvers were extraordinary, providing updrafts for the lower ranks.

Hey, you're getting me all dreamy with your owl-like watching. My chosen band of twelve, Lucifer is speaking to you straight, in a manner thereabouts. One day we'll have to take over, set things right. Get your minds wrapped around the mission. This Sinai day is pivotal. You hear me—pivotal. I AM's showing his hand.

I AM's confused, all defused, drowning all the fleshies except for that nuthead Noah and his kin. Bobbing up and down in a big boat—it's all become some kind of joke, a divine game. Packing a vessel full of baboons and ostriches, what a sight! There're constellations to rule, hemispheres to hover through. There are much bigger fish to fry than fooling around with fleshies and ostriches. Who's looking after the abyss anyway?

I'm just saying, I AM's work is serious business, with lots of elements and eyes looking in your direction. Pause a moment. Look at me—your leader, Lucifer—what do you see? Quiet. I'll tell you what you see. You see no quiver, no wither, no dilly dance of dither. You see Lucifer, through and through. Now suppose, perhaps, let's discuss it, old chaps. Do I look like a question looking for a mark, or a note without a line? On the contrary, I'm thought sublime, the centrifuge of subterfuge.

I'm expeditious, always malicious, saying this and meaning that. Practicing pure quackery is any fool who thinks he's discovered a way of knowing what Lucifer knows. I am today what I wasn't yesterday and will not be tomorrow. Look, see my shadow? Now you don't. Oh, what force I feel.

You can count on me! Just watch the tally. Lucifer is the medium; Lucifer is the message. One and the same, I am. Yesterday, today, and some days, I forever creep, carting off, laying low, exacting my blows. Constantly inconsistent I am, never dealing straight, always tempting the fate of fools—that's the way of Lucifer.

Imagine, my devotees, you're chosen—you are my corpus dozen. Be proud. Look proud. See how near to my presence you are. Just let your minds fill with me, Lucifer. Simply the sound of my name is beautiful, is it not? Enunciating my name should be a ritual, a rite. Hearing my name is like hearing the sound of war. It makes me want to run on scorpions, or dance on the beach atop broken shells.

You know what? Since this Mt. Sinai outing is shaping up to be some kind of memorable day, I think I'll let you speak my name. Yes, you heard me right. Close your dropped jaws, close 'em! You'll speak it in unison. I know it's most unusual, but just the same, when I say "Speak," you will say "Lucifer" three times. Say nothing more, and say it softly with passion. Keep your heads slightly tilted back, and one eye closed. Now, in unison, speak.

LUCIFER'S DEVOTEES: Lucifer, Lucifer, Lucifer.

LUCIFER: How perfect! You're making my centrifuge spin. It's so tonal and harmonial, so full and complete. I'll tell you what I'll do—just once more in unison. This time add a fourth "Lucifer," and before it add the word "oh." Ready, one eye open, now speak.

LUCIFER'S DEVOTEES: Lucifer, Lucifer, Lucifer, oh Lucifer.

LUCIFER: Delightful, simply delicious, but I'm concerned that I'm letting you become too loquacious. Be as you should, my devotees, and who knows? One day, I might let you speak. You know, say a sentence each. I might even ask you a question and listen as you speak. What a privilege you would be afforded! We'll save that for some great honor, a special rite of passage.

Quit wiggling. I see your wanton desire to smile, that look in your eyes.

Have you forgotten the cardinal rule? Only at the sight of war and disaster do you smile. It's pain that gives us thrill, perks our pot, boils our brew. Now shut it, and be forever grateful that you have been acknowledged by Lucifer.

Listen to me, let's slink around this hillside, get on that ridge. Maybe I AM will regain some of his senses and torch the fleshies. He likes fire and brimstone, you know.

Demon Backrider,[3] are you ready? As you sit backward, keep your eyes peeled. Not even for an instant are you allowed to turn around and look forward. To the rear, your eyes must always scan. Cover my back. Do you know how fast I AM's angels can move? That's not a question!

Now get ready to slink when I give the word. Two seconds max, we'll be there. I want a single line of slinkers, my devotees. Slinker one, hold on to my belt. The rest of you follow suit. Now, slink!

See, we're here. Whoa, I AM is all stoked up. We've arrived in the middle of the action. I can't believe it. Down, you imbeciles. Quit trying to see too much. I can peer and hear for all of us.

The fleshies are having a party! I'm stunned. No, I'm not; I'm never stunned.

What am I then? That's not a question! I'm elated! Fleshies whooping it up, worshiping a golden calf. I AM is probably reeling. What a day for us to show up. I AM can't hide this, can't avoid seeing what he's made. Fleshy, muddies, they've gone wild—brilliant!

I really should break into the present sphere, but this is not the day. We'll do our peering from the spirit world, not seen, not heard.

Whoa, there's Moses! Hey, skinny Moses, why don't you show us some magic tricks? Where's your stick for frog making, cattle killing? Look at your buddy Aaron, golden calf making. Is that his new profession?

What's that Moses tossed? I can feel spiritual tremors. Give me room, you imbeciles! Let me zoom.

Whoa, I know that script; that calligraphy is unmistakable. Moses has just shattered I AM's instructions. That's what it is. It can be nothing else. I know all about that divine constriction—Shall This, Not That, Look Unto Me, No Other...

Lucifer speaks, and it is done. No need for calligraphy and engraving stones. That's what you get, fooling around making fleshies. They're a bad species. They're full of spiritual rabies, thanks to me. Just trying to prove a point— my access was not denied.

This mountaintop deal must be to corral those brick-making fleshies into something special. Typical, that's the way I AM thinks. Working with slaves, underdogs. I AM's so enmeshed. Why didn't I AM just empower Pharaoh? Here's what I say about the brick-maker muddies. Ashes to ashes, mud to mud, they'll never shake off their crud.

Ah, chaos, I never dreamed a single day could be so delightful—golden calf, I AM's words in a pile. Oh, skinny Moses is furious!

We've watched, and we're out of here. I AM is busy, but he might still detect my presence. He's got a mess to clean up, pieces everywhere. Start slinking now, backwards, single file. Devotee twelve, start towing. You take the first backward step, and pull on devotee eleven. I'll keep watching and tell you all the news.

We're gonna have to fix our eyes on this chosen tribe. Now slink. What I command, I demand. Slink, you imbeciles, slink.

Brother Herald finished, saying, "And so it was, as Lucifer and his devotees slinked away." *He closed his eyes for a few seconds, and, without a trace of a smile, he took his seat.*

READER: Of the stone pieces lying on the ground, nothing more is said. Perhaps they were left to lie distorted, like a memorial bearing a somber message in their jumbled state.

God words they are. Words, words, words—saying let light be, moving mountains, raising the dead, and striking down those who disregard what I AM has said.

The ancient story of Mt. Sinai has a way of forcefully colliding with the present. This is expected. The stories of Scripture are diverse, layered with messages and meaning.

They can, indeed, be most provocative to modern sensibilities. Scripture's compilation, though, is what provides the meaning for all its bits.

The psalmist writes, "God looks down from heaven on the children of man to see if there are any who understand, who seek after God." Man, in contrast, looks up to heaven, and not without a sense of challenge.

Turning to Mt. Sinai, a rather ominous image arises—arrows piercing, stones smashing. Are they not there, Voice?

VOICE: They are.

READER: As the chosen ones move on into the Promised Land, there, too, much amazement is recorded in the stories told. These are often the parts so many readers like to skip, but that only gives detractors ease. It prompts disquiet, rumblings of naiveté.

Questioning the nature of God is a subject enormously valid. What if, just what if, Voice, you enter heaven. Then, as you begin to poke around, you find what looks like a park. It's a model of Mt. Sinai with all its billowing and blast. But it's not a park, you discover. It's the side of heaven where God goes to let off steam, which sometimes turns out not so keen.

Be honest, Voice, along such lines have you ever mused?

VOICE: Well, I…

READER: Rubbish is your rebuke, and rightly so. It will not happen.

Though does that diminish the validity of query? The point is worth a pause. Those who have experienced the harsh reality of what life can dish out often look to heaven with eyes exceedingly leery. The young man who has experienced the wrath and beating of an angry father looks to God. What image does he hold? A young woman who carries the stigma of incest as a life sentence—what does she see when she gets down on her knees to pray?

The world knows no shortage of abuse. Incidents live on, embedded in wounded hearts. Some wounds act as a kind of invisible leprosy, eating at the soul. Violence, beatings, abuse—the sheer craziness of it all. That's life for those with fathers bent on evil, not on good.

Bring on counselors in waves. They're needed everywhere, platoon after platoon; bring them in. People need solutions for broken hearts, troubled souls. If the compulsively disturbed see God as impulsively charged, what is their view of heaven? Is heaven a destination where timid souls are to walk as if on eggshells for eternity? Such perceptions, Voice, have a way of pulling passengers from the train.

Real help, real hope is to be found along ancient paths. Words do matter. The image of God, emerging through Scripture, is a lifelong study. Few subjects are more important. What a person imagines God to be will have great bearing on the world they see.

Honesty is not the enemy. Parts of Scripture can evoke so much cognitive dissonance it can make a person want to read the tales therein with a one-eyed patch. The story of Mt. Sinai is no exception. Retribution with stones and arrows for touching the mountain is hardly a passive image of God. At one point, God's anger burns to within an angel's feather of annihilating the Israelites.

What if Moses had thrown in the towel rather than throwing down the tablets of stone? Who would have intervened with God? What's more, when the Israelites finally got ready to break camp, God informed Moses he would not be going. "But I will not go with you, because you are a stiff-necked people and I might destroy you on the way." Moses again pleaded with God. God eventually had a change of heart and told him, "My Presence will go with you, and I will give you rest."

VOICE: Reader, that line you just quoted: "My Presence will go with you, and I will give you rest"—does that promise still abide?

READER: Consider it sure. There is reason measured full and overflowing for the story of Mt. Sinai, but it is not understood if clipped and hung in isolation. Scripture has amazing symmetry when viewed through the lens of God on a mission with medium and message.

Mt. Sinai was the entry point of the Law and the message it bears. It's a message most strategic, not easy or free of burden. By design, the Law was heavy-laden and inseparable from a God of purity and justice. To tweak it, water it down, would be to tweak and water down God.

Without Mt. Sinai, there would have been no transfiguration on a mountain high, and no appearance of the One who transfigures "you and me."

The psalmist writes, "The law of the Lord is perfect, reviving the soul. The statutes of the Lord are trustworthy, making wise the simple. The precepts of the Lord are right, giving joy to the heart. The commands of the Lord are radiant, giving light to the eyes. The fear of the Lord is pure, enduring forever."

The brick makers of Egypt had no recourse but to become the people God had destined them to be. They were the chosen ones and ever so deeply entrenched in God's plan.

The Mt. Sinai appearance was long booked in God's diary, and his audience was where it was destined to be. The Israelites were chosen not because they were more special than other people. They were made special because they were chosen. They were the chosen ones to march into history representing the Lord their God, laying down ancient paths that would one day open to all.

Before ominous Mt. Sinai was left behind, God instructed Moses, "Chisel out two stone tablets like the first ones and come up to me on the mountain. Also make a wooden chest. I will write on the tablets the words that were on the first tablets, which you broke. Then you are to put them in the chest."

The words were once again carved in their medium of stone. They were now protected. God had picked up the pieces. It was time for the message to move along.

Words matter…ancient words matter especially.

The tablets were the work of God; the writing was the writing of God, engraved on the tablets.

MOSES, SINAI DESERT, CIRCA 740 BC

READING THREE

—◆—

SETTING THE SCENE

Centuries. Are they not like massive gobblers gulping down disappearing dates? Days, weeks, months, years—how swiftly they slide from present's sphere. Here now, then not.

Alive once each day was, with plethora of words, images, and sounds. Speaking, calling, congealing, wheeling and dealing. It is not true; under the sun is nothing new? Present tense is always spent. Seed for centuries' feed, till each is full and potted in the past.

Along the path of ancient days we step. A story we find, not dead but alive, speaking words not to be whittled down. A king, a fiery pot, and a scroll, all central to the plot. A story placed along redemption's path. Who put it there? Slit by slit, bit by bit, now it's yours, a gift to receive.

Readers Narrative and Brother Extol[4] will lead the way. All readied they are to read. Perhaps, the zealous word *zeal* is the most apropos for Brother Narrative, though the punchy little noun can just as easily be applied to Brother Extol.

Narrative is welcoming the guests to Three Pond Cottage,[5] one of Estillyen's most quaint structures. Brother Extol is seated on a high, dark-blue stool on the far side of the room. Silently he sits, watches, and listens. Volunteers for the Voice are quickly chosen. Narrative explains that his reading, among other things, will touch on the theme of self. He encourages his audience to listen carefully.

The final point Narrative raises is one of pain. He speaks of it now. A question he lobs, and an answer he serves. "Who believes in a God who knows no pain or chooses to ignore it? Such a God would be crueler than pain itself, dropping his painless message on the pitiful creatures below."

To the reading...

Scroll in the Fiery Pot

Whenever Jehudi had read three or four columns of the scroll, the
king cut them off with a scribe's knife and threw them into the firepot
until the entire scroll was burned in the fire.

JEREMIAH 36:23

READER: The Israelites departed Mt. Sinai with the Ark of the Covenant in tow. Forty years through desert sands they wandered. Sheltered in the gold-clad Ark were two stone tablets, bearing the Ten Commandments. The tablets were the second pair God had inscribed. Moses shattered the first set and chiseled stones for the second.

Forty years of moving here and there but going nowhere was the Israelites' course. That's the way of wander. It knows not destination or stilling position. It moves by scent and intuition, with fortuitous ambition.

VOICE: Who were these wanderers anyway? I'm not quite sure.

READER: The same generation that passed through walls of salty mist and then witnessed the divine dikes burst, drowning all of Pharaoh's charioteers. That's who they were.

They wandered through decades of drift. Death stalked them, snatching them away. One by one, two by two, they fell, until the entire generation was wandered through. Their soles never touched the mystical land of promise, where captives freed would build a nation new, of priests and kings. They found no desert exit, crossed no Jordan to cool their heels.

They were laid to rest in no man's land, the desert of wander. No nation, no home, just wander land. Even Moses and Aaron were buried there. Only valiant Joshua and Caleb had breath to make it through and lead the chosen people to their appointed destination.

Across the Jordan the Israelites moved in mass migration. And so it was, the past was washed away as through the halted river flow they stepped. In those intervening years of desert time, the brick makers of Egypt had wandered themselves into a living force, set upon seizing history. Joshua led the charge into the land long occupied with peoples warring, bearing, and caring. These peoples, though, were not yet revealed as heirs, in God's great redemptive plan.

The Israelites marched where milk and honey flowed, and with the promised fare came suffering. Wailing cries filled the night air. Blood oozed from place to place, as the reapers came to call. They came to claim space for the divine drama to unfold.

VOICE: Is it so, Reader?

READER: It is, Voice.

VOICE: Is it right?

READER: It must be, Voice. God has a way of purifying Providence with the way he holds his scales and weighs his weights. Enormity of price and mounting toll were exacted by this history new, as the past was tilled and plowed for the present's sake. In the distance far, a sacrificial lamb would appear, providing reason for history's shove. Yet in these early acts, only God knew the reason of reason's sake.

Scripture, such as it is, hides not in shame what its tales reveal.

VOICE: For sake of divine image, Reader, it seems God might have extracted a bit of this or that from a story or two. I've read a little bit about the carnage that went on.

READER: Voice, the story of choosiness entering the land of promise is history raw. It's the story of history incarnating itself, making ready for the epic casting call.

As the Israelites marched and moved, with the Ark in their midst, there was sorrow sure. Cries of mothers with babies clutched resounded, as did those of sons, daughters, fathers, animals. The lot, by sword and spear, fell into pools of blood their bodies bought.

This is the arena into which atheists and skeptics quickly leap and howl. They heap blame and shame on this God, which the supposed nutties avow. It's the troubling lines on which the skeptics walk, drawing crowds by rebuffing divine nets. They argue that if such history is true, God should simply be removed, forgotten. Cast aside your delusion; balance yourself with proper press and proof.

Why is it, though, such ardent disdain is not stamped across the stories skeptics call fairy tales? You know what I mean, Voice, stories like Noah's flood and Jonah's whale. Those are the ones they like—and the bits they use to aid their cause.

Atheism is a way of seeing God as *not*. Believing in God's nonexistence is still a form of God-centered thought. God-not belief is a religion of ignoring God, disputing God, replacing God. It's a belief-of-God-in-question.

For some people, atheism is a moral decision—a way of reconciling the realities of suffering and pain with the notion of a loving God.

VOICE: Yes, but, Reader, doesn't Scripture say, "The Lord is righteous in all his ways and loving toward all he has made?"

READER: It does, Voice.

VOICE: Is it so?

READER: It is!

VOICE: Then how can this picture of genocide be erased, reconciled?

READER: One day all will be erased, Voice. Heaven and earth will pass away. For now, Voice, know this. There is reason beyond knowing. Knowing is limited. Knowing knows little of what is known in vast expanse. Only the Creator of knowing knows all of what is known.

The stories in Scripture's store, with all their provocation and detail, are there at the will of the One who brought the text to be. There is not the slightest hint of covering the trail that leads to suffering's source.

This thought is worth many a pause. Do you like pausing, Voice? Or would you rather walk that indignant line of resentful angst? Craft your balancing beam? Draw a crowd?

VOICE: A Voice I am, but I'm a Voice who listens. I'll pause; I'm pausing.

READER: Voice, God is not squeamish about reality—and the cost of suffering matters greatly. Belief is purified by pain. The world knows pain aplenty, and numerous are those who suffer, many wretchedly so. A message of truth, void of pain and price, would be most suspicious and remiss if offered to a world of suffering souls. God's message is not that sort.

Who believes in a God who knows no pain or chooses to ignore it? Such a God would be crueler than pain itself, dropping his painless message on the pitiful creatures below. Most disturbing would this image be, to beings born, one and all, into an existence where pain comes to call.

Voice, tell me, who were the Israelites to argue with God?

VOICE: I don't suppose they could, really. Not after the misty sea parted and they were on their way.

READER: So correct you are. The Israelites were chosen to be the leading troupe in the epic drama they neither dreamed nor conjured. The Israelites were plucked and planted. A tulip bulb doesn't argue its fate or curse its petals. The tulip emerges as intended—yellow, red, or another delightful shade.

Do you see them, Voice?

VOICE: I do! I like tulips.

READER: God's method of molding message is inclusive of rut and gut, not limited to stories of angel dust. It's among the sinners that God finds his saints.

Rather revealing is this process of divine revelation. A secretive process divorced from reality it's not meant to be. The messianic message the Israelites brought had to be storied in culture, space, and time. This required distance from other religions. A single generation removed from the Egyptian brickyards, the Israelites were a people far too impetuous to mix and mingle with cultures and gods unknown.

They proved themselves to be a people prone to absorb every whiff of promise that wafted their way. Without distance, in a historical wink, they would have absorbed the spiritual climate surrounding them. Their messianic message would never have been written. No foretelling, no appearing! Pause, Voice. Consider those last few words—and the vast expanse of divine messaging.

No foretelling, no appearing!

For now, enough of this dialogue, Voice. Let's direct our thoughts to the scroll in the fiery pot, shall we?

VOICE: Yes, sure. I'm not departing.

READER: The sixth century BC was in full swing. The threat of Babylonian conquest had become the source of constant chatter in Jerusalem's streets. These were the days of the prophet Jeremiah. Some 700 years of Israelite history had been scrolled away by the time Jeremiah came on the scene to make his mark.

Jeremiah's ancient record is long. It's a tale of woe and promise—and not at all a typical narrative, with a beginning, middle, and end. More like a war correspondent, Jeremiah sketched reports of mayhem and devastation. In the middle of his reporting, he had a way of abruptly sprinkling in a mix of prophecies, revelations, and poetry, as well as the details of a prophet's life.

Jeremiah's words King Jehoiakim of Judah didn't want to hear. Some of the prophet's most descriptive prose comes via recorded prayers. Listen Voice. "See how the siege ramps are built up to take the city. Because of the sword, famine, and plague, the city will be handed over to the Babylonians who are attacking it. What you said has happened as you now see." To God thus he prayed.

With the force of a stoked furnace, God's charging word is brought through the prophet. "But look, you are trusting in deceptive words that are worthless. Will you steal and murder, commit adultery and perjury, burn incense to Baal and follow other gods you have not known, and then come and stand before me in this house, which bears my name, and say, 'We are safe,' safe to do all these detestable things?"

At this point in history, God's chosen people were no longer looking to the God of Abraham, Isaac, and Jacob, as had their ancestors. The popularity of God had ebbed. Visions and dreams had faded.

Jeremiah's message was more than a trivial scroll of words. The chosen people God called out of Egypt were to walk with such words, pinned and placed on door and heart. These chosen ones, of all the earth's inhabitants, were to move in the flow of words. They were to be seen weighing, obeying, talking, musing, always considering the words God had placed in their midst.

The prophet Jeremiah created no small stir. As prophets do, he continually pointed to God as the only true source of help. This God-dependant tone was set way back in Moses' day, just before he died in the Sinai desert at the age of 120.

Moses spoke of the future and the prospects for a chosen people in a promised land: "This day I call the heavens and the earth as witnesses against you that I have set before you life and death, blessings and curses. Now choose life, so that you and your children may live and that you may love the Lord your God, listen to his voice, and hold fast to him. For the Lord is your life, and he will give you many years in the land he swore to give to your fathers, Abraham, Isaac, and Jacob."

This was the plan. A modeling nation set apart to become the children bearing the chalice for the coming king. Such an extraordinary plan, Voice.

Plans, though, do not always go as planned. There were long stretches in Israel's history when only a small minority carried pins and clasps bearing ancient words from the prophets. During the reign of king Jehoiakim, this was especially true. Whirling winds and worry had carried away such acts of dutiful devotion.

Instead of "Listen to his voice, and hold fast to him," by the sixth century BC, the prevailing mood was to "ignore, let go, look elsewhere." This, of course, was the eventual unraveling of Israel and Judah. Time and time again, Israel's leaders would grasp, with swift embrace, *not* the words of the prophets, but alternative and attractive messages from foreign lands. The words they possessed, they dispossessed.

Passion for religion, though, had not departed. It was merely diverted. Heaven's divine eyes watched, as the Israelites plunged into idol worship.

Jeremiah penned God's righteous indignation: a divine complaint with horrific consequences. Through the prophet God spoke: "They have turned to me their back and not their face. And though I have taught them persistently, they have not listened to receive instruction. They set up their abominations in the house that is called by my name, to defile it."

VOICE: "Abominations"—not a word I'm accustomed to hear, Reader. A strong word, it seems to be.

READER: Yes, Voice, listen to what the record attests. "They built the high places of Baalin the Valley of the Son of Hinnom, to offer up their sons and daughters to Moloch, though I did not command them, nor did it enter into my mind, that they should do this abomination, to cause Judah to sin."

To Moloch the Israelites turned. The tender flesh of their children they sacrificed. With sobbing, heaving tears, to Moloch they gave the dearest gift that could be brought.

How does one make such a leap, Voice?

VOICE: Not sure? But certainly not casually.

READER: Consider the raw reality of it, Voice. Phantom voices speak. "Goodbye, child so dear, the blameless one we barely knew. Precious child so pure and perfect, pass now to Moloch, with the praise of his protectors roundabout.

"In sweet serenity, rest there in Moloch's arms. Limp, for long, you will not be. In the surety of Moloch's strength you'll rise. Forever safe you'll be, to play and roam so free. A gift given, a choice chosen, your life for aid of the living.

"Awaken now, our love, to the sound of praise and your protectors singing roundabout."

Imagine it, Voice. How could it be that to Moloch, "the detestable god of the Ammonites," they would turn?

Listen, Voice, to Milton's poetic prose speaking of Moloch in *Paradise Lost*:

> *"Moloch, horrid King, besmeared with blood*
> *Of human sacrifice, and parents' tears;*
> *Though, for the noise of drums and timbrels loud,*
> *Their children's cries unheard that passed through fire*
> *To his grim idol. Him the Ammonite*
> *Worshiped in Rabba and her watery plain,*
> *In Argob and in Basan, to the stream*
> *Of utmost Arnon. Nor content with such*
> *Audacious neighbourhood, the wisest heart*
> *Of Solomon he led by fraud to build*
> *His temple right against the temple of God*
> *On that opprobrious hill, and made his grove*
> *The pleasant valley of Hinnom..."*

JOHN MILTON, PARADISE LOST, I. 392–405

Parents fainting, falling. Who can console such sorrow with embrace or words? Those ghastly, ghostly lines yet linger in the air. Do you hear them, Voice?

VOICE: I do.

READER: What tragedy at work in the sin, sick of soul corruption. Faint and final lines I hear.

"Oh love, I know, I know, I equally want to die. I truly do. But we mustn't let our sacrifice, so great, be in vain. Feel not shame, there is no blame.

"We have given. There is nothing more to give. You will not forever grieve. Let it be. Let us cleave as one in Moloch's open arms."

VOICE: Was it really so?

READER: It was, Voice. It was.

Sacrifice to Moloch: sacrificing to satisfy a deity dead, a mask without a face. Through Moloch's hollow mask demons run like rats from side to side, popping up through holes of mouth, ears, and eyes. That's sacrifice to Moloch. The rattling of tambourines dampened the cries of children, while a strange sacrificial scent lingered in the Promised Land air.

It was into this very chilling, killing air of madness, the words of the prophets were dispersed.

God told Jeremiah, "Take a scroll and write on it all the words I have spoken to you concerning Israel, Judah, and all the other nations from the time I began speaking to you in the reign of Josiah till now. Perhaps when the people of Judah hear about every disaster I plan to inflict on them, each of them will turn from his wicked way; then I will forgive their wickedness and their sin."

That was the directive, pure and simple. Scroll it in. Speak it out. Words scribed would speak for God. Words scribed take their place, stroke by stroke.

Into the well of ink the quill is dipped, drawing up a bit of blackened ink. Out of the little pool the quill rises high, pretending to be a beak. With the precision of an eagle's eye, it carefully applies the cross of a "t" or dot of an "i." The motion is as gentle as that of an eagle smoothing the feathers of its eaglets.

As Jeremiah received his oracle from God, he dictated it to his scribe Baruch, who formed and fashioned the words onto the scroll. Months of dipping, dashing, and dotting ensued. When the scroll was finally ready, Jeremiah instructed Baruch to take it to the temple and read it out loud. He did as he was told. Word after word, Baruch read from the scroll in the temple courtyard.

His reading was soon overheard by the king's officials, who became greatly alarmed by what the prophetic words had to say. They summoned Baruch to appear before a select group of officials for a private reading behind closed doors. When those gathered heard what had been scribed, "They looked at each other in fear and said to Baruch, 'We must report all these words to the king.'"

They questioned Baruch about the origin of the message, and he readily explained that Jeremiah had dictated all the words he had dutifully scribed. The officials told Baruch to go into hiding, and to find Jeremiah and tell him to do the same.

King Jehoiakim of Judah was a force to be feared when it came to prophets and words. The prophet Uriah, Jeremiah's contemporary, had earlier escaped to Egypt, fearing the king's wrath. King Jehoiakim, though, had Uriah tracked down and captured.

This is the record, Voice. "They brought Uriah out of Egypt and took him to King Jehoiakim, who had him struck down with a sword and his body thrown into the burial place of the common people."

King Jehoiakim liked turning prophets into object lessons. King Jehoiakim stiffened his spine against their prophetic messages. Instead of listening to their advice, he aligned himself with Egypt and Assyria. This, too, was part of Jeremiah's accusation. "And now what do you gain by going to Egypt to drink the waters of the Nile? Or what do you gain by going to Assyria to drink the waters of the Euphrates?"

The origin of Jeremiah's message was God, who spoke of turning so that Judah's disaster might be averted. There was a choice to make—words to believe, words to reject. At the core of all cultural quests are diverse messages offering alternative ways of seeing, being, and knowing what is known. Messages always compete. In open societies, messages having at it is a very lively sport.

Even in societies where words are often strictly controlled, messages diverse never die. Resembling seeds scattered here and there, they find all manner of cracks and crevices to root. Like wild mushrooms, people go to pick them. Savory are some; poisonous are others.

Jeremiah was both the medium and message of what God conveyed. Baruch transferred the message to the medium of scroll, extending the message into the public sphere. This is how all messages move along. From its origin, message links with medium to make its meaning known. At that point, replication depends a great deal on persistence and popularity. The popularity of Jeremiah's message was not what King Jehoiakim had in mind.

Jeremiah's scroll, with its steely words of warning, was the focus of immense concern for King Jehoiakim. Upon receiving the report from his officials, the king dispatched his aide, Jehudi, to seize the scroll. Jehudi was instructed to bring the scroll to the king's winter apartment, where the king waited, seated in front of a fire.

In short order, Jehudi appeared with scroll in hand and entered the room. King Jehoiakim had his officials present to witness the occasion. The king ordered Jehudi to read aloud Jeremiah's words.

King Jehoiakim of Judah, however, had little regard for God and his prophet Jeremiah. He had the prophet's scroll brought to his winter palace, where it was read by the king's aide. Seated cozily by a fire, the king listened, but not as one would expect.

For in defiance King Jehoiakim sat. "Whenever Jehudi had read three or four columns of the scroll, the king cut them off with a scribe's knife and threw them into the firepot until the entire scroll was burned in the fire."

The king and his officials showed no fear. There was no remorse, no ripping of robes and clothes. Bit by bit, slice by slice, God's words, Jeremiah's oracle, and Baruch's scroll were pitched into the fiery pot.

During this whole affair, what might have been King Jehoiakim's posture? Voice, what do you suppose?

VOICE: Good question. I don't know.

READER: Can you see him, Voice?

VOICE: Well, sort of in my mind's eye. He's very intentional. His profile is serious, though his posture is not. He sits with a kind of smirk or grin on his face.

READER: No posture can commend itself to what the will has bent. His feet up or down, on a stool or not—where were they placed?

VOICE: The king's chair blocks my view.

READER: I see.... Erect, was he? Forward-leaning perhaps, but somehow the setting of the scene does suggest a casual frame. I too envision his eccentric smile, the resting of the head on the chair's upper pad.

To the words of the psalmist he would have been wise to turn. For there he would have read what God can do. "He has struck down many nations and killed mighty kings."

King Jehoiakim was not concerned. He was now on the throne, determined to prevail where weakling kings had failed.

Consider it, Voice—what a powerful play on a winter's day!

VOICE: I'm with you. I'm still in the room. I haven't left.

READER: Let your mind continue to paint the picture. The aide assigned to this urgent task entered the room. He bore the scroll in question. No doubt, all eyes were trained on the medium of quilled words, God's message through the prophet.

This was not a quick copy purchased on the temple grounds. The scroll would have taken months of tedious work to produce. Every detail of the rare object had to subscribe to the strictest regulations. The papyrus could only be obtained from an official source. The black ink was made from a special mixture of carbon soot, tree sap, and water. Each letter inscribed was afforded its own space, never to touch or invade the assigned space on another letter.

Knife readied and blade sharp, the king sat before his audience in front of a warming fire. In comfort and repose, the defiant deed against God and prophet Jeremiah was performed.

The comfort speaks, does it not, Voice?

VOICE: It does; it must. What does the picture say to you, Reader?

READER: There was no trembling, fear, or dread in the chamber on that winter's day. This little war with God would be won in warmth, without nipping out into frosty air.

There was no need of discussion or time of prayerful angst. No pause. No wringing of hands. No calling on a higher order. King Jehoiakim himself would slit the scroll, section by section, piece by piece. He sliced through phrases, decapitated words, reducing prophetic prose to ashy bits.

Frame and fix the story in your mind, Voice. Won't you?

VOICE: Yes, it's there.

READER: Adorned lavishly in impunity, the defiant king displayed his honed skill of penknifemanship. Even while seated, he was the master of slit. Slit, slice.

Can you hear the slitting sound, Voice?

VOICE: I didn't at first. I was thinking in silent mode. But hear it I do! It dominates. The king slices. No one speaks. Slicing riotous sounds fill the room. It's like repeated severing.

READER: With an act of true bravado, Voice! The king released each scrolly bit from his fingertips. His eyes bulged with delight, as he watched the slit bits float down into the fiery pot. What an act of majestic malevolence!

Due to the king's unswerving resolve, recognition was bestowed. History has awarded King Jehoiakim a special place.

VOICE: It has? Are you sure?

READER: Indeed, Voice, it has. A standard-bearer he is, the consummate character of self. What a man, what self-determination—self defying God on that winter's day beside the warming fire. What a selfy self he was!

How can it be that so much stalwart determination could be exhibited by a single man? Have you considered it, Voice?

VOICE: No, I'm ever so curious, though.

READER: I'll tell you how the said king achieved the pinnacle of self. By letting self rule—self as king. That's how the king's demeanor was achieved. The irony, oh, the irony, Voice!

VOICE: What irony?

READER: Don't you see it, Voice? The very narrative King Jehoiakim sliced to shreds now holds him fast. He is captured there, preserved as if pickled in the words. He's dotted and dashed. He is strung up by the very lines he sliced away. He is sealed forever in the story, penknife in hand, never to escape.

Jehoiakim's jots and tittles have been witnessed on scrolls vast and pages more. In sundry languages, generations have come to learn of this defiant king, this patron of self, this character poor, dispensing words to ashes.

Envision how the great adversary of divine dots and dashes would have delighted to have been in that chamber watching the king's fiery exposé. One can only imagine where the great adversary of truth might have been on that chilly day.

Since God's moves are always a matter of disquiet to Satan, is it not plausible to consider him there? Surely he could find a way to slither 'round, peering from afar by aid of his miraculous farsightedness.

Perhaps he was even there but invisible, clinging to the ivied wall and staring through the chamber windowpanes.

Narrative paused, turned around, and nodded to Brother Extol. Narrative quietly stepped backwards out of the line of sight. Brother Extol stood in front of his blue stool and cleared his throat. He allowed a few seconds of silence to settle as he twitched his eyes. With riveting clarity and energy, he began to speak.

LUCIFER: Listen up, my devotees. Lucifer's got a job for you to do. Get over there in the gutter, all of you, quick. Don't utter a peep. I'm gonna climb this wall with Backrider. I'm gonna cling from that shutter. Straight up I'll go. Keep looking, Backrider. I'm getting ready to ascend, to peer inside that chamber window.

I saw Jehoiakim's fleshy aid, Jehudi, carrying Jeremiah's scroll. More than see it, I could smell it. Jeremiah's dumb scribe has been hovering over it for months, licking on the papyrus with soot and tree sap. What a smell—horrid! I've always hated the smell of scrolls, those old wordy wraps. Don't get it, not at all.

What do I want you to do, my devotees? Exasperate conditions—that's what I want you to do. Remember, placid is never good, never desirable. Your minds should always be fixed on menacing up messes that alter conditions. Think falter. Faltering the faith of fleshies is the core of your cause. Swell with conviction. While you abide with me, you know your mission. Falter, falter, falter. Fix that word in your spines. Let us so bequeath: We shall falter faith to fleshies everywhere.

This reality world was I AM's idea, filling up the planet with fleshies. Right from the get-go, that was his commanding notion. I was around. I heard it. "Go forth in yonder expanse and multiplyist thyself. This I have given unto you. Reproduce, never reduce. Subdue, inhabit, multiplyist. Migrating wildebeests have nothing on you. Show nature what you can do. Multiplyist. Fill, fill, fill the plains and move up the hills. Multiplyist."

Well, we're gonna fall, fall, fall their spurious faith. Look at 'em. Everywhere they move they carry out their subduing ways. Since they were made from mud, they think they own the turf. It's so disagreeable with my evil innards. I hate the sight of 'em. But how can you avoid 'em? What do they know? Have they ever soared through a hemisphere or floated in and out of heaven? I have! If they only knew what they don't know. They couldn't take it, discovering their utter insignificance. They'd all start running around like headless hens. They do anyway.

What good are they? No better than a bunch of rotten figs, that's what they are. Now, devotees, grab hold of your coarseness and fix your minds on menacing, exasperating. Did you hear me? That gutter is a huge trough, plenty of room to do all sorts of exasperating. You can all lie in it, all comfortable-like. When you're in there in sentinel-mode, and I'm up the side of this wall, here's what you do.

I want you to pull in a fleshy. Scare him spitless. Get hold of one of the priestly kinds, grab him by the beard, and pull him in. Tell him who you are.

Straight out, say you're Lucifer's devotees, demons from the netherworld. Tell him you have come to help him. Have some fun.

"I'm here to watch you, fleshy; don't want to see you falter, no, certainly not. Tell me about your faith, fleshy. Is it deep and indispensable, or undetectable? You're more than a fleshy reprobate, some recluse on the loose, aren't you?

"You look to me like you're seeking a roost full of richness. Have you seen that mark of genius on your face? You, my friend, are a long ways from mud. Have you taken a good look at yourself in the mirror lately? What do you see? Surely it's not falter?"

Then, when his eyes are all wild and dreamy-looking, pull out one of them fleshy mirrors. Say to him, "Have a look, see the face of stalwart indispensable faith. Here, peer in this little looking glass." Then while he's peering at himself, transfer your images into the mirror—not all at once, though. Rotate them slowly, one after the other. Then whisper in his ear, "Mr. Fleshy, now's the moment for your faith to falter."

While he's all gasping and trembling, tell him, "Fleshy, haven't you heard, there's war about, and it's just on the horizon." Then, breathe on him, and watch him pass out. When he does, kick him out of the gutter.

When he wakes, he'll think he's had a visionary dream, and he'll start running through the streets like a madman, screaming of war. Then grab another fleshy and do the same. Don't you see how to do it, you demented lot? That's how you exasperate conditions. Make it happen; I'm counting on you. You gotta have a mind for coalescing, for exasperating. Even from a gutter you can make fleshies flutter and fan out carrying your message. Now get to it!

Steady, Backrider, keep me covered. This ivy's full of bugs—creepy, crawling things. Even though we're invisible, we can't stay up here too long. The ivy will begin to wilt, and all these little butterflies and such will start dying, falling down and gathering attention. Then next thing you know, a crowd will be over here praying to the wall. We don't want to draw a praying crowd, no sir, a bunch of fleshies rocking back and forth, moaning. Nobody wants to be perched up above that commotion.

So we're going up to peer, and then we're outta here. See, six little pulls and we're here. Done, arrived. I like the height! Can you see if the imbeciles have got any fleshies in the trough? That's not a question!

Here, let me zoom my eyes. Okay, I'm peering. Hmmm…hmmm… hmmm…it's unbelievable. That pukie King Jehoiakim is slicing up old Jeremiah's scroll and pitching it into the fiery pot. This reminds me of the time Moses shattered I AM's tablets.

The more Lucifer saw, the more his eyes bulged. He watched as the king tenaciously sliced up the scroll and then dispensed it, section by section, into the leaping flames. Clinging to the ivy-covered wall, Lucifer continued to stare through the window. Backrider remained perched high, scanning out across the courtyard for anyone or anything that might be approaching.

The scene was so thrilling for Lucifer that he became lost in the moment. He felt venomously vitriolic. His long, scaly tongue pressed full against the frosty glass. His hot breath fogged the windowpanes.

LUCIFER: Give me the scarf 'round your neck, Backrider. My peering is fogged.

Satanic saliva dripped on the windowsill, as Lucifer's toes curled with delight. Frightened sparrows fluttered and flew, as Lucifer clung to the wall, making strange groaning and snorting sounds.

Lucifer watched as Jeremiah's words turned blackened burnt. The ivy began to wilt and wither. Ladybugs, caterpillars, and crawly things harboring in the ivy all fell dead. They dropped along the wall's stone base. It was, for Satan, a day of immense satisfaction, even though the words "satisfied" and "Satan" are immutably exclusive.

LUCIFER: Get ready, Backrider. I'm slinking down and then we're gonna pass through the gutter and pick up the devotees. I want to try a new dance routine tonight, make some smoke. Down. Down. Oh, I like that word. It's so direct and to the point.

Sliced papyrus, charred to ashy bits. When the serfs get round to shucking out the ashes, we'll drop back by and scoop 'em up. What a delightful souvenir. Let's get out of here.

Brother Extol paused and became as still as he was before he began to speak. Without acknowledging the audience, he settled back upon his stool. He looked straight ahead with a pleasant expression on his face, as if watching the setting sun. Narrative stepped back to the center of the room.

READER: Jehoiakim destroyed the medium but not the message. The burning of the scroll did not go unnoticed. God instructed Jeremiah, "Take another scroll and write on it all the former words that were in the first scroll, which Jehoiakim the king of Judah has burned."

God gave Jeremiah a special message for King Jehoiakim: "Thus says the Lord, you have burned this scroll.... Therefore, thus says the Lord concerning Jehoiakim king of Judah: He shall have no one to sit on the throne of David, and his dead body shall be cast out to the heat by day and the frost by night."

Some two decades later, Jerusalem fell. The year was 586 BC.

The message was not to blame for King Jehoiakim's rebuff. Will and matters of the heart set messages apart. What some ears perceive, others disbelieve. Some ears hear not beyond the hearing. Some eyes see not beyond the seeing. The reason has a great deal to do with the trajectory of heart.

Ancient words, Voice—that's what I implore you to consider. Ancient words infuse the present with wisdom sure.

Along ancient paths, through the corridors of time, words in stories rich have filtered into open hearts and minds. Into countless souls they've swirled, calling, convicting, and prodding the will, saying, "Move away from self and discover what Scripture has in store."

All messages come forth with strategic intent. If there is no intent, there is no message. Words that matter most capture the heart, drawing one into the realm of God's intent. This is the purpose for which they were sent.

Words matter...some exceedingly more than others.

The king cut them off with a scribe's knife and threw them into the firepot until the entire scroll was burned in the fire.

THE PROPHET JEREMIAH, JERUSALEM, JUDAH, CIRCA 605 BC

READING FOUR

———•-•———

SETTING THE SCENE

In Dairy House,[6] a pair of Estillyen monks dutifully move to take their seats. Contrast the Readers two. Consider the scene. Behold their positions. The curious are gathered; they fill the room with watching eyes. Watch with them.

In the center of the room, Plot quickly settles into his antique, ladder-back chair. Next to the chair is a round black piano stool, on which an amber glass of water is rested.

"Welcome, friend or foe, to this house where messages are made and flow. My name is Plot. Today we have a message to explore. It comes from the ancient paths of the prophets—Isaiah, to be exact."

In the middle of the doorway leading to the kitchen, the older Brother Say[7] calmly steps. He places a wooden chair in the doorway and takes his seat. His long legs extend into the reading room, while the upper part of his body remains centered in the doorframe. Brother Say offers a mild smile and a polite nod.

You see, but what? Who is the friend? Who is the foe? No doubt this you know. Still, consider the image now perched and pressed in your mind. In the doorway, neither in nor out. Not near, not far, the message bearer waits. What will he say? What spell of words shall he cast to undermine Scripture's truth?

Wait not. Moments are now ticking. Very soon you will hear Plot say, "Scripture sourced divine, through people, culture, and time, bears a reflective, iridescent image of God on every page."

What will Brother Say say?

To the reading....

Lips Unclean

In the year that King Uzziah died, I saw the Lord, high and exalted, seated on a throne; and the train of his robe filled the temple. Above him were seraphim, each with six wings: With two wings they covered their faces, with two they covered their feet, and with two they were flying. And they were calling to one another:

"Holy, holy, holy is the Lord Almighty;
the whole earth is full of his glory."

At the sound of their voices the doorposts and thresholds shook and the temple was filled with smoke.

"Woe to me!" I cried. "I am ruined! For I am a man of unclean lips, and I live among a people of unclean lips, and my eyes have seen the King, the Lord Almighty."

ISAIAH 6:1-5

READER: The year was 742 BC, way back in history's hold, when the prophet Isaiah received his most extraordinary vision of heaven. This was the year that Judah's King Uzziah died—a year of changing, rearranging. Isaiah was a prophet in the land.

The threat of war filled the air. People were keenly suspicious. They whispered; they muttered; they worried and wondered. National identity and fate were uncertain.

The king was dead. Now what? What was to become of the Israelites and their southern nation, Judah? They knew they were God's chosen people inhabiting the Promised Land. This they believed. But were they still? Where was God? Was he still in their midst, or had he moved along, preoccupied with intricacies of other ethnicities?

VOICE: The vision sounds so extraordinary.

READER: Oh, yes, an extraordinary scene it was, what the prophet saw. His vision brimmed full with meaning. Isaiah peered straight into heaven. There was God on his throne, with angels flying to and fro, calling back and forth, speaking words of praise in angelic voices. The prophet's words once scribed are fresh, moving the mind and perking the imagination.

An old movie reel spinning silent frames was certainly not what Isaiah saw. No, it was more like the curtain of heaven had suddenly been pulled back. God was center stage, seated high on his throne. The cast of heavenly beings were wired and miked. The vision was vivid, the sound sublime.

What the prophet witnessed, though, was no theatrical play. A stage set it wasn't. There were no fabricated walls, props, or hollow gadgets. This was heaven, where substance streams with meaning along hallowed halls, never ending. The prophet was given a glimpse, a snapshot into heaven's realm, where communication forever flows.

VOICE: Reader, pardon me, but why is the word *heaven* so often stitched to those two little words *will* and *be?* You know what I mean—like it isn't really there but will be one day.

READER: Right you are to ask, Voice. Those two words *will* and *be* follow heaven around, as if on a lead. Isaiah saw not what will be; he saw heaven.

Heaven is, was, and always will be, Voice. It's the eternal corpus from which God's communication moves out into the cosmic realms and down to earth.

Think, Voice, beyond harps see. There may well be harpy tunes in heaven's sphere. Likely so, they'll occupy some corridor, but just where I do not know. However, be certain of this: In heaven's realm, knowledge itself will chime and rhyme with heaven's rhythm. Knowledge vast will glide forth on wisdom's wings. Knowledge there knows no end.

Dig a million layers deep, and only the top layer of knowledge can be reached, under which a billion layers reside. All the while, from the bottom millions of layers continue to grow and grow.

VOICE: Are you saying that knowledge forever grows?

READER: Are you voicing a contrary notion? Voice, dear Voice, intricacies of the cosmos are never still. The uninvented is there invented. Wisdom and divine intent swim along, tethering everything together. The notion of heaven being a boring place arises from people with the naiveté of plants.

VOICE: Naiveté of plants?

READER: Yes, Voice. What do plants know of creation's great panoply, as they root and seed in soily spots? It's inconceivable to think that God, who created it all, would design heaven as boring. Heaven is far more than a mass snoring chamber, lit with lava-lamp luminosity.

Is that what you want, Voice, lava-lamp luminosity?

VOICE: I'm not sure what lava-lamp luminosity is, but if it is boring, I'd rather not have it.

READER: Good on you, Voice.

Certainly boring is not the vision Isaiah saw, when into heaven he peered and doorposts shook. The prophet was so awestruck by what he saw that he felt he would die. The contrast was so stark from his life in Judah that he felt ruined. That's the precise word he used: "ruined." Isaiah saw himself as still alive, but among a people as good as dead.

VOICE: Reader, why did the prophet feel so done in?

READER: Lips, that's why.

VOICE: Lips? What do you mean?

READER: Yes, lips, Voice. Isaiah dwelt in a land of unclean lips, idol worshipers, gossipers, and muttering spiritists. There were even lying prophets lying around. In contrast, the prophet peered into the very throne room of God. The disparity was startling. In the realm of God, there is no mutter, no crafty chatter, no prophets puffing puff.

The disparity Isaiah perceived was not a bit of falling short. It was an enormous distinction between the realms of heaven and earth.

Voice, look upon my lips, if you might. See them move. They're eager, always eager. Touch your lips, Voice. Are they eager, too? Sure they are. They long for motion.

Lips are such an exquisite part of the human anatomy, extending as they do from the face. They express sentiment beckoned by heart and mind. Their ability to pucker, press, and position convey what words alone cannot say. What a coveted position they possess! Tirelessly they move. Like eyelids, lips too can seal and close.

Lips project a pose. They shape the face, signifying quickly a sign to friend and foe. Powerful they are, exceedingly so, with a strength vastly disproportionate to their size. In the time it takes to bat an eye, a single pair of lips can sway battalions to charge and die.

Voice, lips are far more than pink seals for the teeth and gums. It's not so much a matter of munching and lunching that brings lips their renown. Nor is it their beauty cast. Rather, it's what they launch.

VOICE: What lips launch?

READER: Yes, precisely. Lips launch words. Lips need no coaches. They carry out what the heart has in store. They're ever so ready to ply and comply. Haven't you ever heard the little rhyme, "Lips Lips Upon the Face"? It goes like this:

> *Lips, lips, the pair, oh how we adore our place upon the face.*
> *Below the eyes and nose, above the chin we sit.*
> *To us words rise, as they receive their call.*
> *We clothe them with form, propel them to function.*
> *Through us they all must pass, whether it be to bless or bite,*
> *for wrong or for right.*

Isn't that nice, Voice?

VOICE: Yes, indeed.

READER: It's such an ancient rhyme, but ever true.

This fact is what brought the prophet Isaiah such consternation. Desperately distressed he was, knowing that God heard every word uttered in the land of promise. In Judah, words had gone awry, propelled by muttering lips, forming all manner of distorted messages. Isaiah knew how messages compete, spawning both good and evil.

Listen to an excerpt of what the prophet had to say to the lying prophets: "When men tell you to consult mediums and spiritists, who whisper and mutter, should not a people inquire of their God? Why consult the dead on behalf of the living?"

The Israelites were consulting the dead on behalf of the living. The lips of the spiritists were busy. So too the craftsmen making idols. Isaiah writes, "As for an idol, a craftsman casts it, and a goldsmith overlays it with gold and fashions silver chains for it. A man too poor to present such an offering selects wood that will not rot. He looks for a skilled craftsman to set up an idol that will not topple."

Isaiah spoke too of what God saw as he looked down from his throne on high, watching the idol worshiper with his idol. "Half of the wood he burns in the fire; over it he prepares his meal, he roasts his meat and eats his fill. He also warms himself and says, 'Ah! I am warm; I see the fire.' From the rest he makes a god, his idol; he bows down to it and worships. He prays to it and says, 'Save me; you are my god.'"

In this land of lying lips, one might think such acts were on society's fringe.

VOICE: I suppose you'll say it wasn't so.

READER: How did you know? Have you read my lines?

Right—spiritists and idol worshipers were in vogue. In those days of Promised-Land culture, messages were running about, telling, congealing, speaking for truth, but lying lies. Many were the words dispersed by lackeys lacking worth.

Projected from lip to ear, words bear messages that multiply and grow exponentially. Muttering picks up a head of steam. It mutters, mutters, puffs, puffs—until the muttering is out of control. Unstoppable, muttering mutters on.

When heaven opened before the prophet Isaiah, his eyes saw majesty, holiness. "Woe," he cried. "I'm ruined." We're all ruined, he thought. When Isaiah compared the flow of heaven's verse, with the mutter of land-locked lips, he felt cursed, doomed. Isaiah had peered into heaven and heard an amazing symphony of sound. In contrast, the sound in the Promised Land was something of a cacophony. It was at that very point a miracle occurred.

VOICE: It did?

READER: A true miracle it was. No magic tricks, wands a-waving. Rather, an angel appeared. A six-winged angel came to Isaiah, speaking words of comfort and absolution. Listen to the prophet's account: "Then one of the seraphs flew to me with a live coal in his hand, which he had taken with tongs from the altar. With it he touched my mouth and said, 'See, this has touched your lips; your guilt is taken away and your sin atoned for.'"

A six-winged angel flying with a burning coal, speaking, touching lips—is it not mysterious?

VOICE: Are they extinct, the flying seraphs?

READER: What a question, Voice! Are we to believe the supply of coal is also extinguished? Let God be God, majestically mysteriously, as he truly is. Does that trouble you somehow, Voice?

VOICE: No it's just that…well I'm not sure.

READER: Majesty—mystery in realms beyond realms of knowing—God is there.

The sear of burning coal from heaven's altar was the signet of Isaiah's commission. Listen once again to the prophet: "Then I heard the voice of the Lord saying, 'Whom shall I send? And who will go for us?' And I said, 'Here am I. Send me!'"

When the burning coal touched Isaiah's lips, his words changed. His entire disposition was instantly altered, transformed. He went from a ruinous state to one of readiness. Isaiah knew the worth of words. The prophet was eager to run with God's message. "Send me," he said. He was compelled. There was work to do, words to carry. Society was on edge. War was on the horizon.

And so God did. Isaiah scribed his words, spoke his lines, and challenged those who had turned from God. With King Uzziah dead and King Ahaz on Judah's throne, conditions were not at all good. Wars and rumors of wars abounded. Judah's fate was most uncertain. Judah had enemies.

In those days, Assyria was warring against Israel. Israel was desperate for Judah to join an alliance against Assyria, which included Syria. King Ahaz was obstinate.

Therefore, Israel and Syria mobilized their armies and marched on Judah. The diktat to King Ahaz was simple: Join the alliance or be conquered. When word was received that the combined armies were advancing from the north, Isaiah describes the mood in Judah this way: "The hearts of Ahaz and his people were shaken as the trees of the forest are shaken by the wind."

Shaking in the wind…. Lying prophets, spiritists, mutterers, all quaking with fear. It's seems no one had a solution to the crisis. That is, except for the prophet Isaiah. He had a word from the Lord for King Ahaz. This is what he said: "Be careful, keep calm, and don't be afraid. Do not lose heart because of these two smoldering stubs of firewood."

Isaiah then made King Ahaz an amazing offer to prove the validity of God's protection. He told the king, "Ask the Lord your God for a sign of confirmation,

Ahaz. Make it as difficult as you want—as high as heaven, or as deep as the place of the dead."

A sign as high as heaven or as deep as Hades. All the king had to do was ask.

VOICE: A sign?

READER: Yes, Voice, a sign. The kind of happening that has a way of happening when God gets involved. A little dew on the ground here but not there. The sun stands still, as it did for Elijah. A shadow moves backwards down a flight of stairs. "As difficult as you want," Isaiah told the king. That was the offer.

VOICE: What did he do?

READER: Nothing. He could have watched a flaming shadow leap around the room, the sun stand still, the moon eclipsed, but he did nothing. King Ahaz was not only defiant. He was dismissive.

Are you the dismissive sort, Voice?

VOICE: No, not me.

READER: King Ahaz had no regard for the prophet or his advice. He brushed him aside. He had a plan of his own. He would make a treaty with Assyria and ignore Israel. The consequences of doing so would prove grim.

Isaiah swiftly rebuked King Ahaz. This is what he said: "Therefore the Lord himself will give you a sign: The virgin will be with child and will give birth to a son, and will call him Immanuel."

VOICE: What? What was it King Ahaz heard? That sounds so unbelievable.

READER: Voice, surely you're correct. These were not words the king anticipated hearing. He probably expected the prophet to say something like, "Therefore, King Ahaz, your years will swiftly wither. When the sound of war begins to echo up the valley, be sure you..." or, "When you hear the sound of horses' hoofs and the myrtle tree begins to shed its leaves, know this..."

Isaiah was caught up in the drama of the hour. War was on the horizon. Injustice filled the streets. So what does the prophet do? He suddenly prophesies that a virgin will give birth to a son called Immanuel.

Ah, Voice, take it in, the mystery of it all!

VOICE: How can this be? Are you sure this precise turn of events is in the record?

READER: Voice, you have an endearing quality about you. You're earnest. These were not ordinary words from the prophet's lips. Isaiah spoke prophetic words jumping into lines, lines jumping into stories. The prophet Isaiah spoke of the distant future, some 700 years on the horizon. It was with the sensibility of spirit that the prophet Isaiah spoke. His heart and mind carried the words his lips dispersed, but it was the Spirit of God that prompted the prophet to speak of a virgin and Immanuel.

Tucked away in Isaiah's scroll are numerous words from this prophetic vein.

Words like "For unto us a child is born," and "Unto us a son is given, and the government shall be upon his shoulder; and his name shall be called Wonderful Counselor, The Mighty God, The Everlasting Father, The Prince of Peace."

Does that sound ordinary to you, Voice?

VOICE: No, not at all.

READER: Dispersed from the prophet's lips were also haunting words about this Prince-to-be. Words like "He was oppressed, and he was afflicted, yet he opened not his mouth; like a lamb that is led to the slaughter, and like a sheep that before its shearers is silent, so he opened not his mouth."

The role of a prophet can be explored from many angles, but the thrust of words in message form is always at the heart of the prophet's cause. Into a competitive marketplace of messages, man is born. Messages exist not simply to give words a place to hang out and play. They are there to call and beseech, to preach and teach.

Critical analysis and historical criticism offer their due in assessing Scripture's text, but the ancient words of Scripture offer something more than simply material to be inspected. These ancient texts have earned the right to be respected, to be cherished.

What is it that you cherish, Voice? Anything?

VOICE: Cherish? I'm not sure what you mean.

READER: Consider it, Voice. The sheer presence of all these words streaming in to corral around a manger and a cross. Does it not lead one to pause, to experience awe? The words of Scripture not only spell out this and that. They are spellbinding, full of prophetic wonder. It's all rather mystifying how these words came to be. They come forth with such diversity, but singularly sourced they are.

The sourcing of Scripture's words, one and all, is a matter great. The sourcing itself speaks of reaching, telling, wanting, and calling.

VOICE: Reader, I might be getting lost, that is unless you are. Which means we both are.

READER: I won't allow it, Voice. Listen sharp, with vigorous intent. The meaning of words extends far beyond their distinct descriptive definition. Meaning has much to do with how words are woven together and follow one another down the line. Context, too, is extraordinarily valuable to know. A letter signed from a loved one in a distant war holds greater worth for its recipient than a million words without the loved one's signature attached.

Every word in a line, and each line in a message, invariably leads back to where the line was formed.

VOICE: Where's that?

READER: At the intersection of who and why, that's where. It's there all words must pause and bow to the one who paid the price and put them in the line. Without who and why, the words know they never would have been sent. At the junction of who and why, they discover the reason they were gathered and then dispersed—some to heal, some to deal, others to kill.

Every word that finds itself in a message is there for a reason based on source. Massively important is this feature of all messages, but significance soars to the stratosphere when the source is thought to be God. This single element adds depth of meaning to every word in Scripture. The words are not just there to define bits. They are there as divine bits speaking forth a collective meaning.

Source transcends medium and message, signifying meaning. This principle is constant, whether the source is from the gutter or God. Scripture sourced divine, through people, culture, and time, bears a reflective, iridescent image of God on every page. This image, if seen, is as pleasing as moonlight's full face on a meadow's pond. The one who made the message known shimmers there, enhancing its meaning. Can you see the pond, Voice? How the moonlight's full face shimmers upon it?

VOICE: Surprisingly, I do. It's nice.

READER: The words of Scripture clothe God thoughts. Through a marathon of generations, God moved the drama along, stitching this with that, creating a collective feat of words to reveal the mystery hidden throughout the ages. Isaiah's promise of Immanuel was long in waiting, but then it came. There was a virgin giving birth. Mary was there with child, just as the prophet Isaiah said she would be.

Skeptics argue, "Where's the proof for Scripture's tales? Where is the proof—you know, what is there to show? Show me the Ark. Show me a chariot wheel at the bottom of the sea."

All the while, enigmatic proof rests not just in the aptitude of words woven in the lines, but also in the shadows between the lines. This is a most enlightening place to look.

Ponder, Voice, just how the vast body of prophetic prose came together. Consider the divine casting call that superintended it all. All the words, bit by bit, in they came, joining a single story.

In Isaiah's day there were many who turned their backs on God's prophets. The Israelites, like King Ahaz, were looking elsewhere for answers, not to scrolls. There were all manner of excuses and abuses. The passion of the day was for the words of spiritists and idols carved, not scrolls scribed.

The Israelites were the message makers of God, chosen to weave words in redemption's plan. They were to live out the Law, which emanated from the ancient paths of the patriarchs.

In those years now so distant, the Israelites were at a crossroads for survival. Isaiah's advice was: "To the law and to the testimony! If they do not speak according to this word, they have no light of dawn." This was the path to which Isaiah pointed. Isaiah saw no middle ground: Either speak to God or else speak to "the dead on behalf of the living."

This type of environment, of course, would be ideal for the master of deviant words.

VOICE: Who's that, Reader?

READER: I speak of Satan. One can imagine him on the move, peering about, sniffing war in the air, sensing despair. Would he ever wander far from God's chosen people?

Lucifer was hardly naïve concerning the strategic role the Israelites played in God's redemptive plan. Messages flowing forth from false prophets and lying lips—for Lucifer what could be better? Imagine him here.

Plot paused, turned his head, and nodded at Brother Say, who was still seated in the doorway. Brother Say calmly and deliberately rose. He coughed, cleared his throat, and began to speak.

LUCIFER: My devotees, listen here. Give me your ears. Lucifer is speaking. We need to get busy wreaking havoc. The environs are too calm, too complacent. We need some rumbling and rioting. Besides, you're becoming like lazy lizards, all lackadaisical. I'm not having it.

I have a plan, so gather 'round. I'll spring up on this high rock, have a seat, and give you a lecture. Listen to the morsels from my lips. They are choice. If a single word is borrowed, fret not, every syllable has been Lucified. That means they were reborn within me before breaching out. Each word has been graced by my sense of magnanimous wonder, my lips.

Come close, my band of devotees, I'm not in a whispering mood. I'll teach you a thing or two about communicating, about bouncing words around, about making people frown. I'll certainly not speak to you in parabolic fashion, roundabout. I'll speak it straight, spit it out. My words flow as directly as demon darts.

Did you ever look closely at my lips? That's not a question. Do so! You must admit, they are exquisite specimens. What shape they possess, full of form. See how I can make 'em pucker? I bet you didn't know I can switch 'em around. Watch—see how the bottom one is on the top, the top one's on the bottom? They move just as well as before. See?

However, this contortionist show has very little to do with the true power of my lips. That is preserved for what they project, not how they pucker. This brings me to the point of our important gathering.

Now, don't interrupt me, and don't fidget and get me distracted. When I'm done speaking, I'll look at you real close, study your eyes, to see if you understand. If you look more stupid and quizzical than normal, I'll know you got confused. You'll be in real trouble. Don't be. Listen up, listen good. This is communication of the highest importance.

Now, here's the scoop. As you know, I AM's got this deal going on about fleshies pinning on words, reciting, and remembering. He wants fleshies to pin 'em on, write 'em above their doorposts, put 'em in their sandals, and weave 'em in their hair. Sing 'em, shout 'em, and spout all about 'em. That's I AM.

Here a word, there a word. You know how adamant I AM is about words, inscribing stone tablets, making the fleshies cart 'em around in that ark all over the desert. Drag 'em across the Jordan. He is so connected to his words. I AM gets blistering bent out of shape when his words get messed about.

So what are we gonna do? I'll tell you what we're gonna do. We're gonna get I AM blistering bent out of shape by messing about with his words. Yeah, that's right. Go ahead—applaud. Cough three times. Let me know it's from your heart. Go ahead, in unison.

The devotees did as they were told; in unison they coughed.

LUCIFER: Good. Good. Very good!

Okay, this is the plan! I've been scheming it for a good spell. We're gonna sponsor a National Security Fair. Yes, you heard me, imbeciles, don't look like stunned sheep. You see, ever since King Uzziah died, the kings up north have been coming and going like vessels on the Nile. Oh, how I loved the sight of the Nile, all blood red—how enthralling it was!

Anyway, let me get back to my point. The fleshies are all in a dither about the prospect of war. They are looking everywhere for answers. Of course, what could be better than fleshies bowing down to idols, prophets telling lies? Fleshies are doing exactly what I AM hates. Superb time, it is! We need to be out there coalescing, exasperating, and winning our way with demonic cohesion.

I AM was so far afield when he came up with the idea of fleshies! Don't worry, I know, I know—I'm not gonna go off on a tangent about I AM making fleshies. I'll hold back. If I go down that trail, you'll be at the bottom of this massive rock for days, maybe months.

Hmmm, there's not too much mud down there, is there? I just don't want you to get mud in your eyes, or clog up your ears. You're my audience, the corpus for my corruptious, and the receptors of connectivity. My message comes to you without distortion.

As I was saying, the National Security Fair. We'll have it right here in the capitol. We'll spread the word that it's being sponsored by an anonymous patriot, one who is concerned about the welfare of the nation in troubled times. Now that Assyria is on the move, we need to make our move. We need to sow terror and sorrow, reap some havoc, get everyone running wild and scared. Doesn't that encourage you?

We can do it! We can do it! Oh, I know we can do it! Now, here's what you do, in order to do it. Go out there and round up all the spiritists and sorcerers you can find—you know, warlocks, wizards, and such. Tell them they will be at the fair. Tell them that if they refuse, I'll obliterate 'em. I'll send 'em so far into the abyss that they'll descend beyond the descendible.

Get this: Their job is to instruct the fleshies in the art of muttering. That's the main topic—actually the only topic—that will be presented at the National Security Fair. Listen to the slogan: "Learn to mutter, save your mother. Learn to mutter, save your brother." Isn't that great? I'm telling ya, devotees, this is gonna be exciting, inviting.

The spiritists and sorcerers will be our duly appointed representatives. They'll explain why everyone, in these days of heightened security, needs to be suspicious in order to be auspicious. The spiritists will say that all fleshies everywhere, for the sake of the nation, must learn how to mutter. They'll turn the notion into an appeal, a quest of necessity, of national security. I've thought of another good slogan: "Learn to mutter, not just utter. Twist your lips, so the king won't slip."

We will have lots of booths, which will be occupied by the spiritists, sorcerers, warlocks, and witches. I'm not sure which of that lot I like the best! At any rate, they'll all be real smiley, wearing uniforms and robes the way fleshies like it. You can each pick a sorcerer or warlock of your choosing. Then you'll stand behind 'em, invisible, watching over their shoulders. Your job is to make sure they do a good job of mutter-teaching.

Here's how you enforce your control. Make sure each one of 'em brings a small mirror to slip inside their witchy robes. You know, pocket-sized. Then when you come along, have 'em pull out their mirrors and act like they are adjusting their locks. Tell 'em to bring their mirrors up close to their faces, no further than a fleshy foot away.

Then, with your orchestrating means, call up my image. At first, the only thing to appear will be my right eye. It will fill the entire frame. They won't know what it is or who it is. It will be a live cast, but it won't really be me. It will be my simulated double. Tell 'em to slowly extend their mirrors forward to arm's length. As they move their mirrors outward, my eye will zoom down in size and my face will begin to emerge. By the time they reach arm's length, my entire face will fill the frame. I'll stare right at 'em, blink my eyes, and disappear. The ground will shake, they'll be so terrified.

Then, when they peer back into their mirrors again, they'll see you looking over their shoulders. Every now and then, press your claws into their backs. Also, be sure you breathe on their necks. Just make sure you circle back once in awhile to breathe. Not at regular intervals, though—keep 'em guessing. Add some eerie sounds to your breathing to let 'em know we mean business.

I'm not gonna go into all the intricate details right now, sitting on this rock. The basic idea, though, is to teach fleshies to shift words around in distorted form. That's the main goal. We want to get the fleshies looking to our instructors as authorities on security.

Let me give you a few examples. Take the word *Israel*. Now, at the fair, everyone will be all abuzz about security. The spiritists, sorcerers, and such will say, for security purposes, the word *Israel* must never be said on the streets. If anyone wants to say *Israel*, they are to mutter *surreal* instead.

You try it, mutter-like. Watch me first. I'll nip the side of my bottom lip with these two teeth, just barely nipping the lip on one side, and then I'll say *surreal*. Watch. "Surreal." Did you see how I distorted my lips? Slurred the word *surreal*? Try it. Nip and hold the side of your bottom lips, and say *surreal*.

See how easy that was? That's what we want happening all over the fair. Just imagine all the instructing, all the slurry enunciating. Now take the name I AM. Instead of fleshies saying *I AM,* teach 'em to mutter *ain't I.* Instead of saying *king,* tell 'em to mutter *sling.*

You just keep it rolling and rolling, muttering on and on for the sake of national security. And here's the best of all: Our witchy instructors will inform the fleshies never to use the word *security,* and implicate themselves as mutterers. Instead of saying *security,* they are to mutter *sorcery.*

The instructor core will also teach the fleshies how to doublespeak. When fleshies want to say *love,* they're to mutter *hate.* If they want to speak of *heaven,* they're to mutter *hell.* Before long the fleshies will be so confused they won't know what they're saying. In no time, we'll have all the fleshies speaking our language. Ah, what a plan!

Now, look up at me. Is there a glow around me? I'll allow you to answer with a nod. Oh, good, thought so.

Now, let me see, have you got it? I don't see you looking any more stupid than normal.

You want to practice muttering a bit? When you go to round up the spiritists and warlocks, you want to be able to demonstrate, ruminate, and pontificate on the subject of muttering. Show 'em you're experts. Show 'em *surreal* for *Israel.*

Tell 'em you learned it straight from the lips of Lucifer, who taught you from the rock.

We can do it! We can do it! Oh, I know we can do it!

Brother Say paused and slowly blinked his eyes a couple of times. He scratched the side of his nose and quietly sat down in the middle of the doorway.

Plot offered a gentle smile and began to speak.

READER: The images of God arising from Scripture's text are many: creator, judge, even an eagle flying high teaching its young to fly. There is the shepherd leading sheep to pastures green, and in the year King Uzziah died, the majestic king high and exalted upon his throne.

There is another image to consider in Scripture's making, though, which is rather astounding to grasp.

Behind the epic story of tales and tribulations is the message maker who wove it all together, not by happenstance, chance, or a quick divine glance now and then. No, it required remarkable constancy to achieve the prophetic consistency that Scripture displays from page to page.

Someone had to be the word watcher, the word inspirer, to ensure that all the words would fall in line in keeping with the story. Words do not say to one another, "Hey, would you like to trade places? No, the lines of Scripture are fixed, forever set. A story here breathes meaning into a story there, as all the words hold their lines together.

In their act of showcasing letters, not all words are created equal. They may look equal—that is that, and this is this—but source coupled with intent affixes their weight. The words of Scripture are not unlike bees placed on a divine trajectory to intercept the heart.

Curator of every prop, selecting each person in the play, God had a most significant job to do. God was there, assuring that Aaron's staff would bud on cue. Dry bones rose with skin and sinew when the prophet commanded, and God obliged. God was not slouching around, stealing long naps, letting his troop of message makers set out on their own.

Look not at the words alone, but beyond, to the weaver of words— and ask, "Who's there?" For those with eyes to see, in the shadows between Scripture's lines is God's face. Like a full-faced moon on a meadow's pond, it shimmers there. Through culture, space, and time, with prophets' pens and psalmists' prayers, words fell into lines. Why, you may ask. The answer is strewn throughout Isaiah's scroll, but in succinct summation there is a verse from the prophet that draws it in:

"Shower, O heavens, from above, And let the clouds rain down righteousness; let the earth open, that salvation and righteousness may bear fruit; let the earth cause them both to sprout, I the Lord have created it."

Salvation and righteousness—these two words tend to summarize why the vast supply of words have come showering down from God. That iridescent image of God, residing in Scripture's text, reflects back upon the Father's face. The Father willingly let go, sending the Son, yet brought forth, in perfect time, words arrayed to aid his redemptive mission.

Words matter…particularly those scrolled long ago.

See, this has touched your lips; your guilt is taken away and your sin atoned for.

ANGEL FROM HEAVEN, JUDAH, CIRCA 742 BC

READING FIVE

SETTING THE SCENE

At Quill House on the Bend we once again meet, this time to reckon with Reading Five. Epic, the Reader, offers a broad smile to the guests seated in a circle roundabout. Soon they will hear him say, "The pendulum of time swings and sweeps, brushing the present into the past's repose."

Not just yet. The Reader, as you know, does not read without a Voice for voicing. As usual, volunteers for the Voice are not wanting. Three are quickly chosen. Epic, though, so it seems, wants to be assured his Voice is up to the task. Now, to the Voice we hear him speak—"Let's have two lines of practice, just to help set your voices in unison. Try saying this: 'It's time for tea. It's nearly three.'"

"It's time for tea. It's nearly three," the voices three recite.

"Perfect!" Epic said. "Nice high pitch, slow and deliberate. Don't worry about how slowly you speak or ask a question. Actually, the slower the better. Unison is the key. Another one: 'I wonder what's happened to Clive. It's nearly five.'"

"I wonder what's happened to Clive. It's nearly five," they say in unison.

"Perfect," Epic affirms.

As everyone is getting set, a rather plump-looking monk wearing a black habit has just appeared in the narrow hall. Without looking directly at anyone in the room, he slowly walks behind Epic and sits in the lone chair stationed by the fireplace. Epic welcomes him and introduces him as his longtime friend and colleague, Brother Tell.[8\] Epic tells the audience they will begin with a verse from St. John, who speaks of what he saw in witnessing the person of Christ. No doubt, we'll also hear an illicit tale or two from Brother Tell.

To the reading…

The Word Became Flesh

*The Word became flesh and made his dwelling among us. We have
seen his glory, the glory of the One and Only, who came from the
Father, full of grace and truth.*

JOHN 1:14

READER: Words wither, many much swifter than others.
The pendulum of time swings and sweeps, brushing the present into the past's
repose. The present always goes; it never stays to become tomorrow. It can't
wait. Another present takes its place. Once swept into the past's vast repository
of days, the present becomes like all the rest: gone, parceled in the past.

Voice, Listen to a few ancient words from Solomon by way of Ecclesiastes:
"There is no remembrance of men of old, and even those who are yet to come
will not be remembered by those who follow."

Words of wisdom, these words remembered, not lost and forgotten. For
most words this is not the case. As time's pendulum swings, the words of most
men, and those of their kin, disappear without a whisper.

VOICE: Why? Why do the words disappear without a whisper?

READER: Do you not know, Voice? The mooring for words spoken is life. When
death comes around, the words attached to life depart with the departed. What
was spoken soon fades and falls away. Eventually the words are forgotten. They
enter the vast repository of *was*. Their echoes are no more.

The present is history's living patch, abiding between the future and the
past. The present has paths to both, but is owned by neither. The present daily
reaches, stretching for the future, yet with each passing hour it surrenders and
slips into the past. Today's yarn spins swift into the behemoth hemp of yesterday.

Second by second it secedes. It cannot hold. Each forward grasp is matched
by what must be released. The past, with a force unstoppable, gobbles at the
present, pulling in those words no longer to be heard.

There are, however, words of exception. Though swept into the past's
vast repository of *was*, they do not sink. Instead, they float like buoyant
buoys, calling, reminding, warning. Words of exception they are, ringing out
with meaning, beauty, and provocation. Such words have a knack, a way of
reemerging in the present sphere. Although into the past they're truly swept,

they can't be held or smothered away. They keep casting lines that draw them back into present time.

History records notable figures who've managed this remarkable feat of casting lines that speak out in time. There is one figure, however, whose words and lines are so incredible that the present daily plies them to chart its future course. Like ocean waves, his words wash upon the shores, filtering eternal truths through the present's sandy beaches.

VOICE: Who is this one casting lines in such an unmatchable manner?

READER: Voice, it is Jesus Christ of Nazareth, Immanuel. The one St. John called the Word Made Flesh. He's the one who made known to life its purpose.

The Word Made Flesh rendered extraordinary claims about life's essence, about what it truly means to occupy a bit of the present, nestled between the future and the past. To speak of life's essence was what he came to do. Oh so natural was his calling. For him, this feat of fate was as natural as a mourning dove calling to its mate.

Christ cast lines worded in such a way that they created an awakening that still awakens. An updraft of worth for the human race, it might be called. His lines became so embedded in the future's fate that his patch of history is forever present. The present cannot let go. It cannot cut the lines, no matter how sharp and long the knife. The future's future is destined to be defined by Christ's lines.

Christ took the past, present, and future and knit them together, with words that cannot be unraveled.

VOICE: Knit them together?

READER: Yes, knit as in knotting. The future cannot flee, leaving the past behind. That is what he explained so very well. There is no place to go without the past; it has no future. Now that the Word became flesh, dwelt, died, and lived, the past, present, and future are wedded inseparably, not unlike the Trinity.

Yet one of the most amazing lines Jesus Christ ever spoke concerned the nature of his message. He claimed his words were not his own.

VOICE: Are you sure?

READER: Do you doubt me, Voice? Listen to what he said, if you don't believe me.

"For I did not speak of my own accord, but the Father who sent me commanded me what to say and how to say it."

Such a claim is most unusual, to say the least, Voice. People so delight in being known, do they not? What kind of person admits that their words are not their own?

VOICE: Not many, maybe none.

READER: None but one. Who in history's grand sweep of saying, doing, and being has ever come along confessing such a thing? I own not my words—that's what he said.

Do you own your words, Voice?

VOICE: Well, I...I've not thought along those lines.

READER: Do so, my friend. It'll not harm you. Christ's claim has a great deal to do with message credibility and authenticity, but there is more to this disclosure. The claim is most revealing, astoundingly so. It presses directly on God's image. Christ's reception of words not his own thrusts strong perception on the one to whom they do belong.

VOICE: Who?

READER: The Father.

Christ's claim casts a telling light on God, whose ways and means in Scripture often appear rather mysterious. Is it not so, Voice? Consider the stories told: a bit of pestilence here, wars sprinkled in there, a spate of wrath now and then. This revelation of Christ, though, gives much reason for pause. It provides a hard jerk on the reins of revelation, saying, "Whoa, wait, deciphering the image of God is not so simple."

VOICE: Reader, I'm not quite sure what you mean.

READER: Consider it, Voice. All the words of grace and care spoken by Christ flowed forth from the Father's call. The Father's will and way, his directive, was what Christ conveyed in message.

It was St. John who truly grasped the significance of the Word Made Flesh.

St. John spoke of Christ as bearing "grace and truth" on behalf of the Father. When John saw Christ, he saw Immanuel, God with us, the One foretold by the prophet Isaiah: "The virgin will be with child and will give birth to a son, and will call him Immanuel."

Voice, listen to the few lines from the ancient tale.

"God sent the angel Gabriel to Nazareth, a town in Galilee, to a virgin pledged to be married to a man named Joseph, a descendant of David. The virgin's name was Mary. The angel went to her and said, 'Greetings, you who are highly favored! The Lord is with you.'

"Mary was greatly troubled at his words and wondered what kind of greeting this might be. But the angel said to her, 'Do not be afraid, Mary; you have found favor with God. You will conceive and give birth to a son, and you are to call him Jesus. He will be great and will be called the Son of the Most High.'"

God reconciling the world to himself through Christ is Christ's story. Mt. Sinai with the Law was pivotal to the process, which was followed by the tumultuous history in the Promised Land. The flow of God's words along this route was long and arduous. In the fullness of time, God broke through the dusty maze of history by way of his Son bearing his message, the Word Made Flesh.

The era of stone tablets as the main medium of communication was through. By way of Mary's womb, God's consummate message was born into the human race. There was no other way to convey what God intended. God needed a pure messenger, who could be both the medium and message of grace. There was but one who had such credentials: the Father's Son.

The effect of grace required an agent of grace. The agent was Mary's child, born not in the line of Adam, but by the Spirit and will of God. A new Adam he had to be—one who could circumvent the old Adam's seed, the seed into which sin had crept. The world needed more than words; it needed the Word Made Flesh, One who would live—and also die—for what he had to say.

Consider it, Voice: The One through whom the world was created became a human embryo.

VOICE: Wait a minute, Reader, if you might. It seems rather strange to think like that, don't you agree? A child in a manger—yes, I know that's what we read and hear. It's in the story. But an "embryo"?

READER: Yes, it's true, Voice. Seemingly these are matters on which your mind has never rested. An embryo Christ was, as all children are before they are born.

In the womb is where the Word acquired his flesh. It was time for Zechariah's ancient words to find their song: "Because of the tender mercy of our God, by which the rising sun will come to us from heaven to shine on those living in darkness and in the shadow of death, to guide our feet into the path of peace."

It's true, Voice. There was a star in the East.

VOICE: Did the star rise on its own?

READER: That all depends on what you mean by "own." Likely a bit of divine choreography made it rise and shine so brightly. Magi came to Jerusalem, asking, "Where is the One who has been born king of the Jews?"

VOICE: How did they know of the star and what it meant?

READER: It may well have been the early oracle of Balaam that prompted their navigation: "I see him, but not now; I behold him, but not near. A star will come out of Jacob; a scepter will rise out of Israel."

The star, the Magi, and manger were all brilliantly installed—while the matter of words and their significance kept looping all the threads together.

The arrival of the wise men and their entourage quickly drew King Herod into the drama. With this curious news circulating in the streets, the king felt compelled to move about, see what was afoot.

Herod brought together the chief priests and teachers of the law and inquired about what the ancient oracles had to say, what they revealed concerning the birth of Israel's promised king. Their answer came from the prophecy of Micah. "But you, Bethlehem Ephrathah, though you are small among the clans of Judah, out of you will come for me one who will be ruler over Israel, whose origins are from of old, from ancient times."

Hurriedly, Herod called a private meeting with the Magi, questioning them about their journey. In particular, he wanted to know when they first saw the star. The king then instructed them to go to Bethlehem and find the child and report back dutifully so that he, too, could go and worship him.

Indeed, the Magi journeyed on to Bethlehem, but they returned home not by way of Jerusalem. They had been warned in a dream not to go back to Herod. When King Herod learned of the Magi's slip, he ordered an edict, which spelled doom for all the little boys under the age of two in Bethlehem and its vicinity. They were to be put to death.

Oh, Voice, ponder it! You must. They were not anesthetized with needles out of sight. Oh, no, it wasn't like that at all. They were murdered. The little boys were pulled from arms of distraught mothers. They were clubbed, stabbed, slashed, and trodden.

VOICE: Does the story have to be told like that?

READER: I know how you feel. I understand, but it really does. It's all a bit more than a Christmas tale.

Dashed to the ground they were. The sound of small skulls breaking must have been horrific, heart-wrenching. In death they lay, not breathing, not crying, fluids seeping, as dust from mothers' feet settled on their tiny faces. Drops came down, tearing rain upon the dust. Little cheeks lay still, unknowing that love was near.

A mighty king was he, Herod. Against a throng of little boys he proved his prowess. What's in the human heart which makes it tick so sick? Who was it that whispered words in Herod's ear, "I see your challenge, your majesty. I'd say you're right to nip it in the bud. You know what fanatics the Israelites can be when they get all worked up about their religious dreams."

If not words flowing into his ears, perhaps the king simply took a pause, lingering long in front of the mirror, considering his position, his kingly pose. Standing there, he could gaze upon the reflection of his certain brand of majesty. Herod could strengthen his resolve, close his eyes for a few seconds, and whisper a prayer.

Eyes opened, he could once again stare, pondering his image and the burdens he had borne. He could think, "It's so tough being king. All the demands there are for me to consider! Oh, breathe again, breathe. That's it, let me think. There's so much pressing on my mind, so many vital decisions to make.

"So many activities and functions to attend. But what can I do? It's me they want to see. Sure, I could send someone else, but then they'd be so utterly disappointed. Oh, the next few weeks will be especially tough—then perhaps a respite, some gaiety. I can do it. I'm strong.

"Oh, yes, I mustn't forget to see if the soldiers have taken care of that messy affair, those little boys, and that so-called king."

Voice, what's in the blood coursing through those veins? Answer me if you can. What makes malicious murderers malicious?

What is in the spirit of man, shaping and molding him into a growling, wolverine type of creature, impervious to God's watching eye? Answer me that, Voice.

VOICE: I'm afraid I'm at a loss.

READER: There are some who believe that, with enough social engineering, "once" could become the chosen word to describe man's insidious behavior to man. In that enlightened day, one would be able to say, "Once, yes, a long time ago, the rude effects of man as beast did take place, but no more. It was a horrible slip, an indiscretion, we all admit, but no more.

"We've evolved well beyond all that groveling and growling sort of thing. Once it happened, yes, but no more. We're not some species seeking who we might devour. Once we were lost, without modern fixes, but no more. We needn't worry about the core; once, but no more."

At the core of every person are words that know not the meaning of dormancy. They move, mold, and live. How did the infernal King Herod conjure up his plan? What moved his will, if not thoughts parceled in words? Be not mistaken, in his abscessed heart words mingled, meshed, and in his mind they coalesced.

Herod's edict set in motion the ancient prophecy of Jeremiah. Listen to it, Voice. "A voice is heard in Ramah, weeping and great mourning, Rachel weeping for her children and refusing to be comforted, because they are no more."

Weeping and mourning in Ramah was not welcome news. Sinister were the reports filtering through, swirling around. Joseph and Mary fled with the Christ Child to Egypt. In time, Herod died. An angel then appeared to Joseph saying, "Get up, take the child and his mother, and go to the land of Israel, for those who were trying to take the child's life are dead."

This angelic message set forth the prophecy of Hosea: "When Israel was a child, I loved him, and out of Egypt I called my son."

Prophecies scrolled away in earlier times functioned like ancient theses embracing awaited stories. Like homing pigeons that suddenly awakened, the prophecies would fly in finding their storied landing. One by one, these prophecies of old sprang forth from their ancient texts to be folded into the gospel story.

The words of old became embedded in the new. The new infused the old. The ancient lines added depth and meaning to the message new. The old made the new less so, gave it mooring. Like two lightning bolts, thesis and story would embrace, surging power into the divine drama.

The words of the prophets rose like tidal waves, rushing in and carrying credibility and content for Christ's message. Christ did more than quote the messages of old. He seamlessly grafted and crafted the words into his message new.

Central to Christ's mission was this amazing claim, Voice: "For I did not speak of my own accord, but the Father who sent me commanded me what to say and how to say it. I know that his command leads to eternal life. So whatever I say is just what the Father has told me to say."

Instead of cold, hard tablets of stone, coming down from trembling Mt. Sinai, Immanuel was moving about, up close, in culture and time. The magnitude of this revelational shift was inconceivable. This was not the kind of God Israel had come to know, reckoned with, or even imagined could exist.

The message of redemption—what is it? Who wrote it? Who bore it? Redemption is much more than a proposition or manifesto. It's a person. It's a story of the Father's Son, bringing the Father's message. It's a story of the Father sending the Son. It's the story of the Son who went.

God's image, shimmering through Scripture's ancient text, suddenly acquired a face—Jesus of Nazareth, the Christ, the Word Made Flesh. To see that face was to see the Father. The two were one, the Father and the Son. Voice, the interpreter of God is the Son of God—the Word Made Flesh. For God he speaks. As God he speaks.

It is St. John who grasps the true sense of awe and wonder regarding the Incarnation: "That which was from the beginning, which we have heard, which we have seen with our eyes, which we have looked at and our hands have touched, this we proclaim concerning the Word of life. The life appeared; we have seen it and testify to it, and we proclaim to you the eternal life, which was with the Father and has appeared to us."

St. John's fascination focuses on the approachableness of God. His use of verbs is most significant.

Verbs are active, Voice. The apostle speaks of Christ as the One who *appeared*, was *heard*, was *seen*, and was *touched*. John perceived that God was present in the person of Christ. Unimaginable, it was. Of course, this was one of the main reasons why Christ was crucified. Who did Christ think he was—God?

Throughout Israel's long history, God could be relied upon to be mysteriously distant, beyond reach, mostly out of sight, sending messages here and there mediated by patriarchs, prophets, and poets. Many of his mediators were rather weird characters, hailing this and heralding that.

Then the Word became flesh and dwelt in community, settling in for a considerable spell. God in man—oh, how can it be, Voice? The Latin phrase *communicatio idiomatum* is a select nugget which helps embrace this most unusual state. "Sharing of attributes," that's the meaning of the phrase—the sharing of attributes human and divine.

In this regard Christ was like any other man, but unlike every man. It's rather fascinating to consider how words and thoughts swirled around in the One with natures two. Did man decide for God, from time to time, or did man always defer to God? Christ did say, on one very pivotal day, "Not my will but yours be done."

Christ spoke not simply as a man expressing truths. He was truth walking about. This is one reason he was such a provocative and controversial figure. Who goes around saying, "I tell you the truth…before Abraham was born, I am"? It was Jesus of Nazareth speaking, but his lineage clearly rings of his divinity.

No one ever spoke the way Christ did. No one could. No one else was *communicatio idiomatum*. What may sound peculiar or strange was perfectly natural for the Word Made Flesh. No one knew how God should react or sound when he showed up in the form of a man. Who could verify the appropriate manner of this mysterious One with two natures? Fully man, fully God he was. He spoke on behalf of both.

Christ was the Message á Medium of God. Christ was not simply carrying a message, approximating a message. Christ was the subject of the matter, the universal noun. The thesis and the story he was, he is. The message of Christ was the medium of Christ. Every single word and twitch of Christ conveyed meaning.

This was equally true when the twitches twitched from tortuous pain of spiked hands and feet. There, as everywhere, the medium and the message were one.

Regarding the subject of medium and message, there's just one more twist we should tease in our company here at Quill House today.

VOICE: What's that? I feel a bit twisted already.

READER: This is it. Mediums often wear masks conveying messages very unlike the mediums they are. Consider these words lifted from Psalm 91: "For he will command his angels concerning you to guard you in all your ways. On their hands they will bear you up, lest you strike your foot against a stone."

Nice words, wouldn't you say, Voice?

VOICE: Nice words, indeed.

READER: These words stretch far back. They were originally cast as lines of prayer attributed to Moses. The psalmist picked up the lines and recast them as words of hope for the Israelites. The words speak of comfort and God's protection.

There is, however, a different use of these words in Scripture. This passage was also chosen by Satan when he tempted Christ in the wilderness. This was Satan's second stab at tempting Christ as he fasted and prayed there in the desert.

Satan challenged Christ to throw himself from the high point of the temple into the waiting arms of angels. That's when Satan evoked the words from the Psalms. In response Christ said, "It is also written, 'Do not put the Lord your God to the test.'"

Whatever characterization one may choose to place on Satan, "imbecile message maker" doesn't fit. This was no third-ranking demon out there in the wilderness throwing lines at Christ. This was the manic master who understood the power of words. He spun what he hoped would be a strike. He failed; Christ succeeded. They both used words.

Words matter, Voice.

After Satan had spun his lines, the story says he departed.

VOICE: Where did he go?

READER: Ah, this, of course, we do not know, but we can imagine.

Epic rose from his chair, moved behind it, and then backed away several steps. The attention of the room was drawn to the empty chair and the person seated beyond it. Brother Tell, now much more conspicuous, placed his plump hands on the arms of his chair and slowly rose. He took three short steps toward the back of Epic's chair, stopping a good arm's length from it. Clearing his throat, he began to speak in a deep, resonating voice.

LUCIFER: Quick, come here, my devotees. Get out from behind those wilderness rocks. What do you think you are—a bunch of lizards?

You are Lucifer's chosen band of devotees. Act like it. Show me your fierceness, your fervent ferocity, without a hint of frivolity. Look to me, Lucifer, your image. I am your ideal, your standard, your cause.

Now come close, you bothersome bunch. I command you. Listen, full, we've got trouble, sure. The major engagement is on. Word's on the move. He's making ready for mission. This forty days of travailing was his way of going into training before he hangs up his carpenter tools, hits the road, and starts touting words.

Get back! Give me room. Move over—let me sit on this big boulder. Get over here! You idiots hop around like drunken cats. Now, stand erect at attention and peer into my eyes. Do you feel the impartation, my implantation? Now breathe. That should still your quiver, disable your dabbling.

This is how it went. I spun my lines with pure perfection. Oh, you should have heard me! The words flowed with such free fall of intent. Lucifer's intonation was impeccable, unmistakable. No fear had I, not the slightest hesitation regarding my word-wise enunciation. My words, they failed not. To me they returned not void. They went out as they were sent. They were simply blatantly rejected.

I was trying to do the Word a favor, get him to stumble, and get him out of this fleshy jumble, this awkward ordeal. He's in for it now. Nothing more I can do. To Jerusalem he will go, and you'll see what unfolds. If he had leapt from the top of the temple, he'd have been out of here. In angels' arms he would have been—done, end of story.

The fleshies don't need redeeming. Even if they did, who would want 'em, redeemed or not? Worthless either way. How can you redeem what should never have been made? That's the wrong way 'round. You don't start with mud. No wonder I AM is stuck with such fleshy crud. He should have thought long and hard before doodling in the dirt.

They're no better than wayward fish, those fleshies. You wouldn't expect the Word to become a fish, to redeem ornery fish, would ya? Of course not. He's not gonna become a fish. Can you imagine that—putting on fish scales in order to ruminate and swim with fish? Putting on skin, flesh that came from mud—that's no way to be reigning and ruling the cosmos. Do you see what's gone wrong, my devotees? The order's out of order.

The advent of fleshies has changed the cosmos. Eternity's thorn they are. If I AM could just see the fleshies for what they are and pack it in, there would have been no need of reconstituting, or Magi traipsing around following stars. It's all so unnatural. See what I mean about out of order? Stars need to be left alone.

When it comes to fleshies, though, all bets are off regarding the scale of divine reach. In human flesh, there the Word sat, starving to death. Forty days and nights, no food, no water—do you know what that does to fleshies? They draw up inside. They get all squeamish, weak. Their bodies start telling their minds they're dying. Maybe I should have stoked up some manna or pulled out a cooked quail.

Anyway, it was surely him, the Word. I could see that haunting resolve in his eyes. Resolve of eternity, it was. That was no prophetic papyrus scroll setting there, with its words sealed in position. No sir, not at all. That was the Word with fleshy eyes and ears, dialoguing. When he countered my lines, his words reverberated with such spiritual force and fervor that I could hear them rumbling out beyond the stars. I'm telling you, for sure that's the way it was.

Listen up, you idiots, don't be telling that to any of those fleshies—I mean about his words rumbling through the galaxies. No corroborating now that the Word's in flesh for the aid of fleshies. They don't need our testifying. I doubt those dumb clucks will believe it anyway. "Look, here's God in skin. Go ask him about heaven." It's so implausible.

Those dopes run around looking for hope. They'll stumble right over that. The fleshies have caused so much cosmos consternation. It'll take half of eternity for things to settle down, and even then it will never be right. If only I AM could turn back the clock, back to the days of pre-fleshy past. Back when eternity was eternity without this blasted time intrusion. That was the treasured age, free of fleshy messes creating all these spiritual drafts rushing through the hemispheres.

Wake up, you coconut heads. Dust off your daggers. I'm not kidding—this is it. In the fullness of time, the Word in flesh has appeared. The present is now forever folded into eternity; they are one. The bell has rung. The slinging match is on, word for word, story for story.

Get a grip on your words, on your mastery of enunciation. We're gonna have to become dialogical in order to draw away those base fleshies. Get ready for a lot of hyperbole and parabolic speak, as the Word starts moving about, consorting with fleshies. He's one of 'em—never thought I'd see the day. He's gonna be trudging all over the place, claiming to speak for I AM. No question—it's him.

Well, it's not gonna be so easy, trying to tell fleshies about I AM's kingdom and such. Those clucks know nothing about the great unknown. It'll be like trying to explain the pyramids to a turtle. "Well, it's like this, Sir Turtle." Hey, no laughing! What did I just tell you—no frivolity! This is the beginning of the great campaign.

We've got serious business to do in slithering and slicing words in this word-slinging match. The man from Nazareth has a long ways to go before he makes it through the tribulation of Jerusalem. At every turn we must be there, twisting, snatching, and hatching our brand of story.

Now listen up: Lucifer's lines so blatantly rejected today may well become tomorrow's succor. Fleshies need alternatives. Come closer. Let me tell you what I have in mind. Don't be scared. Look to me. Let's practice our own brand of storytelling.

Brother Tell paused, blinked his eyes, and wiped a handkerchief across his brow. He slowly turned and moved back to his seat. Everyone watched the circle of watchers watching. Epic stepped up behind his chair, placed his hand on the top back rail, and began to speak.

READER: You see, Voice, the psalmist and Satan used the very same words. One sought to reassure. The other sought revenge.

VOICE: How can it be? Is this the way it actually is with words—saying this but meaning that?

READER: It certainly can be, Voice. Words often have two meanings, maybe more. Argue as you might, words flow around, wrapping thoughts, saying this but meaning that.

VOICE: That's not fair, it seems.

READER: The meaning of a message has a great deal to do with the message maker. When propelled by Satan's lips, the truth of the original message remained unchanged. The strategic intent behind Satan's message, however, made the message totally different.

Satan masquerades, using words to match his bent, no matter how or where they originated. Satan would use a line croaked by a frog if he thought it would make matters leap in his direction. Willingly he would have sung Christ a lullaby if he thought the tune would have caused him to lose his demeanor.

Satan was there to provoke and tempt, to entice Christ into showcasing that he was the Son of God.

In the same manner as Christ, Satan is one and the same in terms of medium and message. But unlike Christ, Satan's message is always destructive, even if his words appear as enlightened light. Christ said of Satan, "He was a murderer from the beginning, not holding to the truth, for there is no truth in him. When he lies, he speaks his native language, for he is a liar and the father of lies."

Satan is a liar, always lying. He cannot speak without strewing lies along his crooked path. This is his repartee, his game of evil intent. Though Satan quotes the truth of Scripture, his intent flips the words. His message is a guise seeking contorted action.

In contrast, Christ's message always moves along the way of grace and truth. There is no crooked path. There is no dark side with motives skewed in some bent and wayward way.

Therefore, Voice, you are fortunate.

VOICE: I am? Why's that?

READER: You ask why because you have much to ponder. Let me say again a line earlier spoken concerning the words of Christ: Although into the past they're truly swept, they can't be held or smothered away. They keep casting lines that draw them back into present time.

Those with ears to hear will grasp just how utterly amazing is this phrase: the Word Made Flesh. "When the fullness of time had come, God sent forth his Son, born of woman, born under the law."

No other time would do. Not a minute early or a second late, the final grain of sand floated in from heaven, and time was full. The heartaches of the past, the wars and slaughter, too, were redemption's toll so time could fill to full and finally reveal the Word Made Flesh.

Into the past's repose, there the present always goes, while the words of Christ forever linger and live.

Some words rapidly wither...others never will.

The Word became flesh and made his dwelling among us.

THE APOSTLE JOHN, JERUSALEM, CIRCA AD 70

READING SIX

———•◆•———

SETTING THE SCENE

The Scribe House[9] reading room is unquestionably the most unusual of all on the Isle of Estillyen. A long narrow room it is, with large mirrors covering the entire width of the two end walls.

Mirrors, you ask?

Yes, in this curious configuration, people on one end of the room look directly at people on the other, but, at the same time, they see themselves, looking on, with the Reader in-between.

The mirrors are set about a meter off the floor and extend upward to the full height of the walls. Six rows of benches on each end of the room face the center, where the reading is about to begin.

The mirrors make it possible for everyone in the room to see the Reader's face, no matter which way the Reader turns. The faces of Brother Story and Legend[10] will soon be reflected—Story's first.

What a prefect room for a reading centered on the Transfiguration. The story told is ever so essential in the *Redemption* series. It is exceedingly rich with imagery conveyed by words. You shall see.

After a brief stilling moment, it appears that Story is ready to begin...

Oh, yes, a final mention. You may be surprised when Brother Legend breaks out in song, Lucifer's signature song, that is. It's titled—*Happenstance and Chance!* Full of meaning is this notable tune.

To the reading...

Get Up—Don't Be Afraid

After six days Jesus took with him Peter, James, and John the brother of James, and led them up a high mountain by themselves. There he was transfigured before them. His face shone like the sun, and his clothes became as white as the light. Just then there appeared before them Moses and Elijah, talking with Jesus.

Peter said to Jesus, "Lord, it is good for us to be here. If you wish, I will put up three shelters, one for you, one for Moses and one for Elijah."

While he was still speaking, a bright cloud enveloped them, and a voice from the cloud said, "This is my Son, whom I love, with him I am well pleased. Listen to him!"

When the disciples heard this, they fell facedown to the ground, terrified. But Jesus came and touched them.

"Get up," he said. "Don't be afraid." When they looked up, they saw no one except Jesus.

MATTHEW 17:1-8

READER: A picture is worth a thousand words, so it's been said.

VOICE: Who said? What about the words that set the worth of the picture? How should their worth be determined?

READER: Voice, right you are to query. "The Lord is my shepherd, I shall not want." I've just spoken that line in nine words. Count them if you wish, Voice, but nine they are. Albert Einstein said, "Imagination is more important than knowledge," which I have just spoken using six words. In all, that's fifteen words to render what most people would agree are a couple of rather significant lines.

If we tally those two lines together, we have expended merely fifteen words on our way to 1,000. We have 985 to spare. Therefore, it seems to me, the carte-blanche offering of 1,000 words for a picture needs a certain degree of reappraisal. Wouldn't you agree, Voice?

It would be untenable, indeed, to grace just any picture with a thousand words. A person might swear at the picture with a thousand words, but then the picture would not be graced. The evaluation of pictures receiving words, let's all agree, has a great deal to do with the quality of the picture—and, of course, the words.

The Transfiguration is a story rich with imagery conveyed by words. It's one of the most amazing stories in all of Scripture. The Transfiguration is saturated with substance, shedding a certain light found nowhere else in the sacred texts.

The centerpiece of the story is the transfigured Christ. The Transfiguration dispels any notion that Jesus of Nazareth was a kind of ingenious messiah figure who functioned with spellbinding zeal and clairvoyant wit. The image of Christ transfigured is that of his divinity permeating his humanity.

More than two years had passed since Jesus of Nazareth unrolled the scroll of Isaiah in his hometown synagogue and read, "The Spirit of the Lord is on me, because he has anointed me to preach the good news."

Christ made good on his promise and preached his unique message to the multitudes. He was loved and loathed, revered and reviled, famous and infamous. In more ways than one, Christ was a wanted man.

VOICE: Who was it that loathed and reviled him so?

READER: There were many, Voice. Jesus Christ set the institutions of his day reeling. As Christ's popularity continued to grow, the chief priests and the Pharisees convened with the Sanhedrin and said, "What are we going to do? If we let him go like this, everyone will believe in him and the Romans will come and take away both our place and nation."

Oh, they were in a state, all right, fearing their entire way of life was being threatened. The high priest of the Sanhedrin, Caiaphas, saw the wringing of hands and listened to the words of consternation being spewed back and forth. He had words of his own. He offered advice. He had a proposal.

He was cunning, Voice, a curt sort of man. Listen to what he said. "You know nothing at all, nor do you consider that it is expedient for us that one man should die for the people, and not that the whole nation should perish."

"You know nothing at all," Caiaphas said. That was his opening line. What if I said that to you, Voice?

VOICE: I wouldn't find it very agreeable.

READER: His words did not fall on deaf ears. Ears twitched; the ruling elite listened. Their steely eyes saw a tunnel; there was light. Caiaphas found a receptive audience. He had a platform much admired.

From that day on, they plotted to put Christ to death. They wanted him removed, off the scene, out of the way. They wanted to carry on ruling and waiting for the Messiah. They had custom, position, prosperity.

Only days before the Transfiguration, Christ had gathered his disciples and began to spell out what would take place when he entered Jerusalem. He knew the score. He knew the plotters meant business. Christ explained how he would soon "suffer many things at the hands of the elders, chief priests, and teachers of the law, and that he must be killed and on the third day be raised to life."

Without reservation, he spoke to the very core of the drama: He would be killed. He would die, be crucified. The message did not go down well at all with his disciples—in particular with the apostle Peter. Peter took Christ aside and began to rebuke him. "Never, Lord!" he said. "This shall never happen to you!" In turn, Christ offered a surprising rebuke to Peter, words which have been recast through the ages: "Get behind me, Satan!"

Christ was moving toward the unavoidable destination of Calvary; his face was set like flint. He knew that many of his followers would flee, and he was under no illusions about what awaited him in Jerusalem—Gethsemane, the hill of torture.

Christ, the Son of God, was the chosen medium to bear the Father's message. Crucifying the medium conveyed the very heart of the Father's message.

VOICE: Reader, crucifying the medium—I'm not sure I'm with you. You have a way of sticking words together that normally don't belong together. I mean, it's just that, crucifying a medium—it's so…

READER: Stick with me, Voice. You'll get there. In this case, and in this case alone, the medium was a sacrificial lamb. The sacrifice of the medium was the message. In the person of Christ, medium and message are one and the same, immutably so. There is no distinction between the two.

In the period leading up to the Transfiguration, the public message of Christ had begun to shift. Christ's words were cutting deep. "If anyone would come after me, he must deny himself and take up his cross and follow me. For whoever wants to save his life will lose it, but whoever loses his life for me will find it."

Christ was speaking with little time to spare. He would soon be condemned and nailed to a cross. The medium and message would be fixed, fastened for the world to see and ponder. Yet for Jerusalem, Christ would be a spectacle—a sideshow appearing on a ghastly hill during the Passover season.

VOICE: A sideshow—that's a peculiar thought. Don't you think?

READER: Oh, a sideshow indeed, Voice. Not for time and eternity, but for Jerusalem on holiday. Festive good heartiness abounded. Crowds swelled the streets grateful for law and order, for the rounding up of criminals. Christ, along with his loser-looking mates, would be lifted up on Gethsemane to die in agony. They would showcase what awaits those who disobey the law.

For Christ's followers, though, these were far from festive days. The mood was sullen and somber. It was all so different in the early days for the apostles, setting aside their fishing nets to follow. Aspirations swelled their hearts. They were to become fishers of men.

VOICE: What are "fishers of men" anyway? What do you suppose Peter thought he'd be when he first heard that line?

READER: Surely he was inspired, Voice. A change of vocation: Pulled from a life of bobbing boats and mending nets, he'd be something else. Along the shores of Galilee the apostles strolled, listening, loving, and learning from this curious and extraordinary figure from Nazareth.

Epitomes of commonality were Christ's apostles. Yet they had been drawn onto the divine stage. The common figures were caught up in the story of redemption. They were central characters in the drama that was thundering forth at the heart of the Father's plan. The story was being scripted by the hour, by the moment, by each turn and twist. Their every word and act was vital to the plot and would be inclusive in the story unfolding.

The story revealing Christ as the Messiah of God's redemptive plan is a long and winding saga, rapturously stunning. The mystery of Christ was hidden throughout the ages, like sand unseen, deep on the ocean floor.

VOICE: Sand on the ocean floor, like a hidden mystery.

READER: Indeed, sand lying there for ages. Pressed down deep, the mystery of Christ was hidden long in prophetic speak. Scrolled away, stowed away, life swam to and fro, not knowing the mystery latent in God's plan.

Astounding it is to consider all the collective facets and feats God directed in space and time to bring the message together. Barely believable is the idea that God would orchestrate Scripture and all its intricacies. St. Peter said it this way: "For prophecy never had its origin in the will of man, but men spoke from God as they were carried along by the Holy Spirit."

Redemption's story didn't come about simply because the stars aligned. The story is so precise that it synchronized time with eternity. It's no collection of silly notes, willy-nilly words, pulled from bottles cast out to sea. All the subjects—and the objects, too—were called and often coached by divine choice. Characters, settings, and scenes all mingled with "acts of God," shaping the saga of the Son.

Under history's enormous stretch rests a fulcrum in God's hand. Envision it, Voice. The fulcrum should inspire a certain reassurance, a sense of redemptive lift for man. History is not just about nations, wars, and such. It's about God in the midst of nations warring, striving, living, dying. In God's drama great, the past, present, and future perform as one. Their lines overlap with meaning.

There are, of course, those who detest the idea of God's involvement in the affairs of men. They want nothing to do with his dramatic stage, although, unknowingly, they stand upon it. Playing roles, they come and go.

I can hear them now as they speak: "Forget the fairy tale. God's an illusion, a needless infusion, a hopeless intrusion. God is nothing more than a deficit delusion, dulling man's true genius, making us dreary. It's all a parody, ruining our sense of self-clarity."

Can you hear the voices speaking, Voice?

VOICE: Your words seem most compelling. I do think I "hear" them, as you say.

READER: Proudly they stand onstage, modeling for orangutans seated in the stalls the potential held within them all. From stage left and right they enter, spit and sputter, then exit and fade away. They always go. They have no kingdom in which to settle. Restlessly they rattle on.

They seem so implausible, shouting out their lines upon the same life's stage where Christ lived and died. They cannot see that their script's not new. Their tares grow among the wheat; they're sowing seed, reaping self. There the delusion rests.

Leave them, Voice. Come again with me. To the Transfiguration let us go, where there's a different kind of light. The Transfiguration beams through the dusty, shadowy landscape of human achievement, transcending history with luminous hope. The Transfiguration story commences with Christ ascending a "high mountain" in the company of apostles Peter, James, and John.

VOICE: Why?

READER: It was once again time for Christ to pull away from the crowds, a time to seek solitude, pray, and find the stilling presence of God.

You are not against solitude, are you, Voice?

VOICE: No, but I doubt I'm as prone to solitude as you.

READER: Voice, what you are you may not always be. Look at the disciples. Christ says nothing to the disciples about the importance of the mountaintop retreat. All three versions of the story swiftly move to the point of transfiguration. Christ and the disciples ascend the mountain. Christ prays. the events unfold.

This brings us back to our picture and the worth of words. Moses and Elijah appeared in glorious splendor, talking with Jesus about "his departure, which he was about to bring to fulfillment in Jerusalem." Those words of St. Luke are loaded with meaning—his departure, which he would bring about. By his own volition, to Golgotha he would go.

Suddenly, Christ's face shone like the sun. His clothes were "bright as a flash of lightning." Christ's entire being was transfused with light, as bright as the "sun" or "a flash of lightning." The idea coming through in the original language is that of a metamorphosis, a complete change of being, like a caterpillar becoming a butterfly.

Flesh transfigured is not a flesh characteristic. The radiance of Christ in the Transfiguration story bears a message of its own. The luminous elements convey meaning; the light speaks a visual language.

VOICE: What does it say, this visual language?

READER: A great deal, Voice. Consider the disciples watching. Christ's divine nature instantly emanated through his flesh. What else could they think but that this figure before them was no normal man? This must be God, just as he claimed.

What an amazing sight for Peter, James, and John to witness! Christ transfigured with patriarchs Moses and Elijah—radiant, moving about on this earthly mountain.

Doesn't it make you wonder—not just a bit, but a great deal? What about the heavenly divide…just how far did Moses and Elijah travel when they got the call? Was it an instantaneous zip, and zap they were there? Or did they journey through distant lands before they popped in for their brief appearance? What say you, Voice?

VOICE: I'd better ponder the matter.

READER: Look, Voice. The words help you see. They paint a picture. To which is the greatest worth attached—the picture or the words that paint it? Consider the words as brush strokes, your mind as the canvas. Ah, it's all so wondrous!

Peter immediately recognized Moses and Elijah. He said, "Lord, it is good for us to be here. If you wish, I will put up three shelters, one for you, one for Moses, and one for Elijah."

Peter was no doubt stunned by the spiritually charged environment. Spontaneously he came up with the idea of shelters for Christ and his visitors. Christ gave no heed to Peter's suggestion.

No rationale can explain the appearance of Moses and Elijah. According to Scripture, Moses died in the land of Moab and was buried by God. The prophet Elijah is reported to have been caught up to heaven in a fiery chariot some 900 years prior to the Transfiguration.

Moses and Elijah were either present, or their appearance was a hoax, a fabrication. The latter point is destructive, like bulls stampeding through a pumpkin patch. It's no harder to believe in the appearance of Moses and Elijah on the Mount of Transfiguration than it is to believe in the transfiguration of Christ. One either believes or disbelieves. An event of this nature cannot be proven.

There is a factor in the push for proof that is freeing to consider. A bird with a twig in its beak too heavy to carry does not fly. Many things are too heavy to carry. It's a matter of letting go, Voice.

VOICE: I've never thought about birds with twigs too heavy to lift.

READER: Well, now you have. See how you change? Some loathe this idea of letting go, letting God be God. Instead they constantly flap their wings against the ground. Unbelief is easy to acquire and cultivate, Voice. The world is full of words, images, and sounds hawked from corner to corner, like a great scattering of twigs. There is plenty to fill the beak, as well as the heart and mind.

Howling packs run about with dubious doubts. Guess what, Voice?

VOICE: What?

READER: God's not on call. He has nothing to prove. He's not disposed to punch the clock, check in with humanity and explain his moves. Who would ensure that God's moves are right, anyway? Why not let God take care of the twigs too heavy to handle?

Human beings exist on the other side of the stained glass, where warm hues mysteriously filter into time and space. Why break the glass, Voice?

VOICE: I don't want to break the glass, Reader.

READER: Voice, I'm proud of you for that. I don't believe you do; you're not that type. Many do want to smash the windowpanes, Voice, but why? That's the question. Is the picture so demeaning, so unappealing? Or might the desire be to switch places, to call the shots, to be the one peering in rather than peering out?

Proof is extremely vital in so many ways, but in other ways not at all. There's an antidote for the relentless push for proof. The word is *faith.* Its cousin is a word called *trust.* Man needn't prove the spirit he possesses. The incessant push for proof has a way of belittling humanity, robbing the species of spiritual sensibilities. Faith and trust lift. They're a gift, not a formula.

The appearance of Moses and Elijah in luminous splendor defies everything known of what is knowable. Their cameo appearance, though, is a small matter for God to execute. With God, a thousand years are but a day. Moses and Elijah had only yesterday entered the heavenly sphere, where laws of time and space are requisitioned rather mysteriously.

Effortlessly Moses and Elijah came and went from their sphere to earth. In doing so, they stepped out of the Old and into the New. They were there tagged with Christ, and Christ was tagged with them. Instantaneously, characters old appeared onstage in the new drama being written. Their appearance gave the story new a beginning old.

To suggest that Moses and Elijah simply decided to drop in on Christ of their own volition is a proposition few would pen. The matter presses fast to the point to what is called *missio Dei,* a term, in short, suggesting that the mission of reconciliation is God's. Yes, that's the idea. God's on a mission—moving this, making that—so that factors fall together in place and time by his design.

VOICE: Missio Dei, what an idea.

READER: Yes, indeed. Moses and Elijah were called; they were staged. But they were not actors. They were characters perfect for the part.

God's message was clear. "Listen to him! This is my Son whom I love. I'm well-pleased with him," he said. The crux of the Father's message was this line: "Listen to him!" Moses and Elijah were present, but the plural pronoun "them" God did not use. Rather, God said "him." "Listen to him" were the critical words emanating from the cloud. Listen!

There's much to hear—here, there, and everywhere. There are words calling, vying for space. Just a little bit of the ear their destination is to be near.

What might the words say if they could speak about their mission?

VOICE: You mean words—just any words?

READER: Yes, that's right. Listen to how they speak, if you will. Hear them.

The word said to the ear, "Let me put down a bit of root, I live not to float with other words, but to be heard; that's why I've been sent. I need an audience to take me in, an ear. Don't worry so much about what I mean. Meaning is yours to make with the words you take. So, whataya say—let me in?"

Breath with syllables, thoughts in signs and symbols—that's what words are, Voice. Innocent they're not. Words matter. They speak to heart, soul, and mind. They speak of love and hate.

Listen! Listen!

VOICE: To whom does one listen?

READER: To someone—certainly you do, don't you, Voice? It's impossible not to. You hear me now. Is this what you choose? Choose. Listen.

Words forever flow. From deep within they flow. Unstoppable, they swoop and dive—sometimes in twisted form, but unstoppable they are. The Gospel story, too, flows with an amazing gait. The message was crafted largely by Christ on location.

The Transfiguration is an amazing part of Christ's story. "Listen to him," that's what Peter, James, and John heard. They didn't realize how soon Christ would be gone, even though he had told them he would soon be leaving.

"Listen to him." Those words represented a quantum leap in revelation. God had turned a page; a new chapter of luminosity had appeared. The awaited one was finally present, transfigured for the three to see...and the world to wonder what it was like for the three to have seen it.

The heavenly tour de force says much about the importance of the moment, about the mission of Christ. Doesn't it, Voice?

VOICE: I'm not here to argue.

READER: Their destination was exact. Moses and Elijah didn't pop into the Sanhedrin and pay a visit. Imagine Caiaphas announcing to the Sanhedrin: "We have a couple of special luminous guests with us today. Let me introduce…"

No, that was not to be. Moses and Elijah appeared on a mountain. The psalmist writes: "I lift up my eyes to the mountains, where does my help come from? My help comes from the Lord, the Maker of heaven and earth."

Up, that's where they were. There was an all-important message to convey: "Listen to him!" God, the Father, was speaking through his Son. God, the Son, was speaking on behalf of the Father. The Word had become flesh. The medium with God's message was present, luminous: "Listen to him!" Voice, he's the One with words for you to hear, words of life and not of death.

Ancient words from the letter called Hebrews spoke of God's messaging mission and Christ's radiance. Listen, Voice, the words are ever so important. "In the past, God spoke to our forefathers through the prophets at many times and in various ways, but in these last days he has spoken to us by his Son, whom he appointed heir of all things, and through whom he made the universe. The Son is the radiance of God's glory and the exact representation of his being."

The world awaited the Messiah, and when Christ appeared, the waiting stopped. He was the One in history's hold. On the Mount of Transfiguration, Moses represented the Law; Elijah, the prophets. Christ embodied the fulfillment of both. His message incorporated theirs in a new era of God's revelation.

Who else might have been privileged to sneak a peek at Christ as his face shone like the sun? Surely there were angels 'round about, on the move with Moses and Elijah. This amazing event might have also drawn other patriarchs out, as well, to peer down and see what God was orchestrating in the earthly realm. We don't know.

Who is to say how the forces of good and evil might have aligned that day? Certainly there were demonic forces down at the mountain's base. The Gospel narratives bear this out. As soon as Christ came down from the Mount of Transfiguration, he was drawn into a chaotic scene featuring a father with a demon-possessed son.

Suppose, with imagination's draw, that Satan might have been there, seeing what the three disciples saw. Always seeking, ever sneaking is Satan. The thought of Christ, the lead man, suddenly disappearing up a mountainside, would not settle well at all with the restless one.

Story raised his right hand and, with the motion of an orchestra conductor, gave Brother Legend a cue. It was time again for Lucifer to weigh in. Legend rose tall, and with a deep, deliberate voice, he began to speak from the back of the room.

LUCIFER: Where did the Word go?

DEVOTEE ON WATCH: Don't know, he was here and now he's gone with the three.

LUCIFER: The three—that sounds significant; let me sniff. Hmm, I have it. I have their trail. Up they've gone, climbing the mountain. Come with me, just you three. We'll head up the backside of the mountain. We'll see what's transpiring with the Word. Maybe he's getting ready to float up to heaven, pack it in.

Legend nodded back to Story.

READER: One can envision Lucifer on the prowl with a devoted demon on his back. Placing his heels under Satan's armpits, there Backrider sits. The perched demon rides backwards, always watching, scouting, and occasionally turning to whisper a word in his master's ear. Lucifer picks the backriders from his darkest dungeons. It's a very coveted position. He snaps them up on an irregular basis to keep all the demons guessing. When he feels their time is through, Satan shucks 'em. He likes to call it "shedding."

Lucifer, of course, has no right-hand demon, nor one to his left. He can't tolerate the thought of sharing power, of allowing clawing space so near. Just the same, there are always devotees 'round about him. They form his entourage.

Imagine how things might have gone. Satan, feverishly curious to find out what's going on, begins to claw up the backside of the mountain, with Backrider and three demons clinging to his tail. They make it just in time. Out of thin air, Moses and Elijah suddenly appear.

Story motioned with his script again towards Brother Legend.

LUCIFER: Whoa, old-timers—how'd they get here? Long past they've been dead, well and truly whisked away and shoveled under. This is suspiciously mysterious, maliciously messy. It's not fair, importing in the departed. It's just not fair, leaping over the natural elements. Dead is dead. I knew there was something significant taking place up on this mountain.

Quiet, imbeciles! Can't you see my mind treading, threading, through this scene? Didn't expect that, not them. Moses in the Promised Land, after all! Not so thrilling is it, ol' boy? Stick around awhile, and we'll show you the park—it's called Golgotha. It's a fleshy deal, fleshies murdering fleshies.

Promised Land, what a picture: Honey oozing out of the ground. Smell of bread waffling through the air, lambs roasting. It was all a gargantuan fabrication, a wayward waste of words. Spent on olden-day fleshies just to watch 'em move around on I AM's chessboard. Dumb fleshy pawns. They've got eyes, but they are as blind as teeth. Blinder, I'd say. I do say. See, I said it!

Brother Legend paused and once again offered a slight nod to Story.

READER: Suddenly Christ was transfigured. His face was radiant, shining like the sun. His clothes appeared as lightning.

Story quickly looked up at the center fan, and then slowly turned and nodded to Brother Legend. Brother Legend continued.

LUCIFER: You three see that? Don't answer—that's not a question! I know what it is. He's made that way. That's the Word in flesh. No wonder he's become so brilliant, all lit up like. Fleshy skin can't conceal the Word.

What did I hear you say, Backrider? "Can I do that?" Yes, you no good, rotten imbecile of a devotee. How dare you speak to me in question form? Who do you think you're talking to? I'm Lucifer, not God in fleshy skin. I'll shed you, you goofy nub of a demon! Who cares? Who wants to shine anyway on top of a dumb mountain, all luminous? So what's it all about? Who's here to see?

Legend nodded once again to Story.

READER: Into the scene enters the theophany. A theophany it was! A bright cloud came to rest on top of the mountain, and God spoke: "This is my Son, whom I love; with him I am well pleased. Listen to him!"

Story took a few steps back from the podium, fixing his eyes on Brother Legend.

LUCIFER: Hear that rumbling voice? Not a question! Hellish holograms! I've not seen anything like this since Mt. Sinai. I AM coming down on top of a mountain, speaking his mind, the Word blazing like lightning—what a spectacle!

Do you idiots know how revelational this is? Of course you don't! This is all fixing to be written up fleshy style—more scrolling, pasting on foreheads, reciting, memorizing. I AM doesn't do anything without thinking about words. He'll never say to fleshies, "Think as you wish. Stoke up your own storylines. Draw your own conclusions."

This is all in line with I AM's constricting ways of programming fleshies by way of select words and stories. Not me! You know my tune. You know how it goes.

Brother Legend smiled and began to sing the following lines:

> *Happenstance and chance. Flow and flap.*
>
> *Say what you wish and will, old chap.*
>
> *Mix up your words. Swirl 'em around;*
>
> *don't get precise when you jot them down!*
>
> *A tiddle here, a diddle there. Snip 'em up and pitch 'em in the air.*
>
> *Oh, what a wordy mix! Oh, what wondrous prose!*
>
> *Meaning on the run…all homespun.*
>
> *That's how wordy mixes should be done!*
>
> *A t here, an i there; dot 'em, cross 'em without the slightest care…*

Hey, wait a minute—this mountain air is making me giddy. This is serious business we've happened on to. What are you letting me sing for? We need to be growling, not crooning.

Old-timers showing up, walking, talking…this all points to a major deal, some kind of pinnacle, trouble—trouble, for sure. The Three is chiming, rhyming, symbolizing some kind of full-blown divine demonstration.

Look at the Word's three lackeys: all terrified, trembling, hitting the ground. "Hey, you three—open your eyes, you cowards! Get your noses out of the dirt. Thought you wanted to follow, be fishers of men and all that…stupid, fleshy dummies! This is the spiritual world, nutcases, not some fleshy, featherweight kind of deal. Tremble on, you little wimps."

See what all this fleshy business has come to? The Word himself, putting on skin and climbing a mountain! Who needs a fleshy climbing suit? It's reprehensible. No surprise to me that fleshy skin would be luminous with the Word wearing it. What do you expect, a little candlelight glow?

I AM coming down as in the days of old. Moses and Elijah stepping out of eternity into time…what are they concocting? "Listen to him," I AM says. Well, I ain't listening. So what if he gets a million and one fleshies to follow? That's a million and one too many. Fleshies following—might as well have a virus following you around. They're nothing but walking mud cakes with a bit of breath.

Just mark my words: Those three trembling with their noses in the dirt, this is something they'll want to shout about, all fleshy style. I can hear them now down in the marketplace. "Thus saith, we seeith, upon said mountain, he shineith like lightning." But I'll be there to tell the truth. On said mountain they seeith not a thing. They hideith their faces in the dirt. They squirmed and wriggled, and no doubt piddled.

Go ahead, shout out your tales. We'll never let up. When they speak up, we'll speak over 'em, under 'em, and around 'em. Whatever they enunciate we'll reenunciate, lubricate, and elaborate. We'll give 'em barrage after barrage of biting enunciation. I've seen enough of this luminous extravaganza.

Now, you three devotee clingers, come up here quick. We're out of here. I'm scooting down on my belly just like I came up, but backwards. Get up here in front of me. As I start backing down, you do the same. Keep looking up. Those old-timers may still be around. With the Word near, they could be fierce. They're like old wolves. Backrider, you keep looking down; make sure no one is coming up. Quietly now, let's start our descending creep. We've seen enough for one day.

Luminous flesh on a mountain—what a way of reigning and ruling the cosmos! I need to get down and cough. This is all giving me a mean spell of spiritchitis. I'll luminate 'em all right—just give me time.

Brother Legend took his seat, and Story returned to the podium.

READER: Orchestrating the elements, the Transfiguration was not for show, but for effect. God was aiding the telling his own story. The initial audience consisted of the three apostles, Peter, James, and John. Years later, Peter included a synopsis of the event in a letter he wrote to followers of Christ dispersed throughout Asia.

St. Peter explains how the Transfiguration shaped his message. "For we did not follow cleverly devised myths when we made known to you the power and coming of our Lord Jesus Christ, but we were eyewitnesses of his majesty. For when he received honor and glory from God the Father, and the voice was borne to him by the Majestic Glory, 'This is my beloved Son, with whom I am well pleased,' we ourselves heard this very voice borne from heaven, for we were with him on the holy mountain."

This is the effect. "Eyewitnesses of this majesty"—St. Peter writes, tells, teaches, and testifies to what he has seen. Similarly, St. John writes, "We have seen his glory, the glory of the One and Only."

On the day, the three apostles were in shock over what transpired. They stood staring at Moses and Elijah, with Christ transfigured. Then the bright cloud enveloped them. When they heard God's voice, they fell facedown to the ground, terrified.

No wonder. When God showed up in Scripture in the form of a cloud, it was never a trite affair. Mt. Sinai with its ominous cloud brought not only the Law; it meant death to anyone who casually approached. This, however, was not Mt. Sinai; it was the Mount of Transfiguration, and the image of God was dramatically different.

In addition to the Father's words, there are also Christ's, which he spoke to his three disciples trembling in fear, as they lay facedown on the ground. Christ went over and touched them and spoke two impromptu lines. "Get up," he said. "Don't be afraid."

VOICE: What did they feel? What did they see? What did they hear?

READER: They felt the touch of God. They saw only Christ. They heard words of peace and comfort. Moses and Elijah were gone. The bright cloud had dispersed. Christ was alone on the divine stage. He was the One to see and hear. There was no God to fear.

Christ's two lines are recorded only by St. Matthew, yet they are extraordinary in their summation. Christ's entire mission to the human race may well be summed up by these two little lines: "Get up. Don't be afraid."

VOICE: Five words, all little. Reader, what do you think they're worth in terms of the picture they convey?

READER: Priceless they are, Voice, simply priceless. Christ's words to his terrified disciples did not fade with that eventful day. In time, they soared from the mountain, speaking far and wide. "Get up," he said. "Don't be afraid. The Father and I are one. There is nothing to fear."

These words beckon still through the valleys; on and on they go. "Listen to him," to the One who so long ago and far away was transfigured on a mountain, the Word Made Flesh with luminous essence. To him listen—that is what the Father said in his theophanous appearance.

The message of reconciliation required more than a human messenger from God, or even an angel. It required God as both medium and message. It required Christ. The luminous Christ had taken center stage. Christ was God seen, God heard. There was a face from beyond the clouds for humanity to see.

Listen.

VOICE: To what? What am I to hear?

READER: Listen again. Hear the echo?

VOICE: I hear it now, yes, I hear the echo. It's the words of Christ…. "Get up. Don't be afraid."

READER: Good, Voice. Very good.

Words do matter…the images they create can be priceless.

Get up. Don't be afraid.

JESUS CHRIST, MOUNT OF TRANSFIGURATION, CIRCA AD 32

READING SEVEN

SETTING THE SCENE

When visiting the Isle of Estillyen, Tunnel House[11] is certainly a location you'll want to explore. For one thing, Tunnel House is the only reading venue that boasts its own coffee bar. Spend time. Slowly stroll through the tunnel.

It's the quaintness of Tunnel House that offers such appeal. In the reading room, above the tunnel, black curved-back wooden chairs add artistry to space. The chairs form three circles, each with twelve chairs. The circles have symmetrical gaps for access.

Just now, it seems there are twenty-eight people sitting in the triple circles. Expectantly they wait for the Readers to arrive. The sound of creaking stair treads suddenly hushes conversation. The audience listens intently to the dominating sounds of stairway creaks. Creak after creak, step after step, the sounds are now arising.

A face appears, and then another, in the order of the reading. The first Reader is Brother Drama, who'll be followed by Brother Chronicle.[12]

Drama quickly starts, explaining how ideal Tunnel House is for dramatic readings. He speaks about how a tunnel is "a space for going through: from one side you pass to the other side." Drama encourages his audience to always move through a tunnel—whether short or long—"at tunnel pace, respecting tunnel time."

After this short word, the Voice is selected, and Context,[13] an intern, passes along their lines.

Reading Seven will transport you to a very heartwarming scene—where a demon-possessed boy and his father witness the healing power of Christ.

To the reading...

A Cry in the Crowd

Jesus asked the boy's father, "How long has he been like this?"

"From childhood," he answered. "It has often thrown him into fire or water to kill him. But if you can do anything, take pity on us and help us."

"If you can?" said Jesus. "Everything is possible for him who believes."

Immediately the boy's father exclaimed, "I do believe; help me overcome my unbelief!"

MARK 9:21-24

READER: Down the Mount of Transfiguration Christ moved, no longer mysteriously incandescent, far above on the mountaintop. With his disciples Peter, James, and John, Christ made his descent with divine intent.

Toward the plain below he headed, drawn down by humanity's gravitational pull. Want and need were ripe for harvest. People were in pain. The oppressed and possessed mingled in the lowland that day, waiting to see in Christ a bit of hope they might profess. A day earlier he was secretively absent, meeting with special guests.

VOICE: Who were these special guests? Were they foreigners from another land?

READER: Oh, Voice, from a distant land they surely were. Special, indeed, in the whole of human history, there had never been such a meeting. From the corridors of heaven, his visitors traveled.

VOICE: Heaven?

READER: Certainly. No doubts do I possess concerning what the story professed. Christ had stood on the mountaintop in luminous splendor, speaking with Moses and Elijah, beneath a heavenly canopy, a theophany.

VOICE: Moses and Elijah...doesn't that jumble the past with the present, the improbable with the impossible?

READER: Ah, Voice, that is a bit of fuzziness speaking. Remove the word *jumble* and clear your disposition. Past with present, yes. Improbable with impossible, yes—but it was not a jumble. Consider it rather a divine directive. God being God it simply was. With God, jumble does not exist.

VOICE: I see... sort of, I think.

READER: With Moses and Elijah on their way and the theophany departed, it was time for Christ to head for the mountain's base and walk among the crowds. Peter's impetuous plan of constructing three tabernacles to capture the glory on the Mount of Transfiguration so differed from divine wishes.

This notion of staying up, not coming down, was not an option. Christ had been designated to appear for all eternity. The subject of Mary's song he was born to be. Down was where the drama called, incarnated to be near, not beatified, and resting glorified under a tabernacle on a mountain high.

St. Paul captured so brilliantly the appropriate trajectory of Jesus Christ when he penned this line, "Who, being in very nature God, did not consider equality with God something to be grasped, but made himself nothing, taking the very nature of a servant, being made in human likeness."

How is it, Voice, that St. Paul was so perceptive?

VOICE: Not quite sure.

READER: St. Paul's words so valiantly written. Words woven behind prison bars bearing fruit even now. Ancient but living, past but present. Are you not thrilled by that prospect, Voice?

VOICE: The way you put it, I think so.

READER: Not grasping to stay away, not holding on staying up high. This is the way the oracle was written. At the very heart of the drama is the wonder of letting go, of coming down, of descending far, of revealing the mystery hidden throughout the ages. There was a great tale to tell—all about a shepherd seeking sheep.

READER: During the descent down the mountain, Christ instructed his chosen three: "Don't tell anyone what you have seen, until the Son of Man has been raised from the dead." While they didn't know it, this milestone of rising was just down the road.

Isaiah's prophecy foretelling how Christ would bring welcome news to the marginalized, the victimized, and the stigmatized spread a net far and wide among the populace. Among throngs of both the curious and the suspicious, Christ moved, casting words into unforgettable lines. Navigating the crowds was a serious issue, Voice. Listen to how St. Mark describes the scene on one occasion:

"Jesus withdrew with his disciples to the sea, and a great crowd followed, from Galilee and Judea and Jerusalem and Idumea and from beyond the Jordan and from around Tyre and Sidon.

"When the great crowd heard all that he was doing, they came to him. And he told his disciples to have a boat ready for him because of the crowd, lest they crush him, for he had healed many, so that all who had diseases pressed around him to touch him.

"And whenever the unclean spirits saw him, they fell down before him and cried out, 'You are the Son of God.' And he strictly ordered them not to make him known."

Among the masses, the populace, it does appear there was a substantial labyrinth, a major muddle of marked souls, which evil spirits possessed. Once inside, the spirits clung tight with demonic grip.

At the mountain base, Christ and his three companions quickly rejoined the other disciples, who had remained behind during the Transfiguration. The disciples were in the midst of a crowd when Christ approached. "As soon as all the people saw Jesus, they were overwhelmed with wonder and ran to greet him."

Christ's presence was like a lightning rod drawing people in his direction. A cry was heard. It came from the middle of the crowd. It was the cry of a father with a demon-possessed son. "Teacher, I beg you to look at my son," the father cried, "for he is my only son."

The boy was ill. He was severely afflicted, suffering from seizures, fits, and wicked spells. The torturous condition sorely affected the father's state. He had come to Christ's disciples, begging them to drive out the evil spirit. The disciples were unable to break the demonic curse and set the child free.

The spectacle had drawn a large crowd, along with teachers of the Law, who were debating and arguing with the disciples. Into the squabble Christ stepped. Without hesitation, he moved to the center of the dispute and asked his disciples, "What are you arguing with them about?"

Before they could answer, the father with the child said, "Teacher, I brought you my son, who is possessed by a spirit that has robbed him of speech. Whenever it seizes him, it throws him to the ground. He foams at the mouth, gnashes his teeth, and becomes rigid. I asked your disciples to drive out the spirit, but they could not."

Christ gave a rather unexpected reply. It wasn't an answer at all; it was more of an open public confession. "O unbelieving generation," Jesus replied, "how long shall I stay with you? How long shall I put up with you?"

VOICE: Reader, why such words? Do they truly belong to Christ.

READER: If not, then to whom, Voice, would you like to attribute these words?

VOICE: I don't know. They just seem rather at odds with Christ's manner of speaking.

READER: Voice, I hope you're not going back to that word *jumble?*

VOICE: No, not that. Do the words reveal a divine sigh, or something else?

READER: Perhaps it is a hint, or maybe a slight distraction. After all, in only a matter of days, Christ's speaking among the crowds would cease. Christ would be dead. This he knew precisely.

Consider it, Voice. Only yesterday it was that on the mountain, Christ listened to his Father's voice emanating from the brightly glowing cloud. Now Christ listened to the voice of another father, one not coming down from heaven. The father's cry came up from the muddle, the scrum, and the squabble of unbelief.

Christ could not move about in public for long without incident. Human need was great. As Christ acted, sending evil forces swirling, the curious flocked.

"Bring the boy to me," Christ said. They did. "When the spirit saw Jesus, it immediately threw the boy into a convulsion. He fell to the ground and rolled around, foaming at the mouth." Christ displayed no alarm, no sudden gestures, or words one might expect to hear like, "Stand back! Give us room; the boy is ill, can't you see?"

On the contrary, Christ engaged the boy's father in conversation. In the middle of the pressing crowd, Christ moved into conversational mode. The eyes of both Jews and Gentiles were bulging; everyone was listening with rapt attention. They inhaled, exhaled, and watched. "How long has he been like this?" Christ asked. "From childhood," the father answered. "It has often thrown him into the fire or water to kill him."

This was not some mild form of epilepsy or minor malady. The demon dwelled deep within, possessing the recesses of the child's body, mind, and spirit.

There the evil spirit made its nest, its dwelling place in the borrowed soul of a child. Everything on the inside was misaligned, twisted into a demonic state.

Deep down inside the child the evil spirit hid. From inside, it festered and erupted, tormenting the creature small. One symptom the father described was foaming of the mouth. Consider it, Voice: the toxic-looking fluids bubbling up, as if the child had eaten a poisonous substance.

VOICE: Reader, hold on please. I want to go back a bit, if we might. A minute ago you said something about the muddle, the scrum, the squabble. Is that how you really see it?

READER: Ah, now you've got it, Voice. That's your jumble rightly placed. Into the jumble of humanity, Christ willingly moved.

VOICE: These evil spirits, Reader—who or what were they, anyway?

READER: Angels they were, Voice. Ancient angels led astray who have no way to be born again someday. Their mode, their propensity, is to steal away in the souls and spirits of their victims. Behind ribs they hide, encaged in the darkened interior of those they possess. There they hope eternity will forget them, drop them from the ledger, count them missing, like falling stars. All the while, in souls deep they seep and creep around with tortured moves. Within the entrails of man, woman, and child, they seek to abide.

Immediately the demon within the child would have been aware of Christ's presence. The boy's condition was grave. He was thrashing on the ground; at the feet of Christ he laid. The crowd watched intently, listening to the exchange between Christ and the father. The welfare of the child was the paramount issue.

At the same time, Christ was also crafting the Gospel message. Word-by-word, sentence-by-sentence, parable-by-parable, the Gospel was being storied.

VOICE: Pardon me, Reader, once again. I've always wondered why Christ would tell people not to say who he was. You've made me think of it. Was it because he needed to complete the story?

READER: Oh, Voice, why is it I feel you are growing wise before my very eyes? You are not alone in wondering why Christ said go not and tell. His news was good, was it not, Voice?

VOICE: It was.

READER: So right you are. It has to do with pacing, harmonizing divine revelation with reality. In space and time Christ made his way from day to day. His moves were paced. Too much fuss, too much rush, and divine time and trajectory might be threatened. Then what would have happened? Heaven forbid, but it does make you wonder.

Back to our tale, Voice. As I said, the Gospel was being storied by Christ. Every word Christ spoke was part of that message; every question, every glance or gesture, was part of the message. On this day, the immediate audience included the father, the boy, the disciples, and the crowd. Christ knew, however, a vast and exponential audience was on the horizon.

No doubt Christ knew how critical it was for the storied message to be heard. Throughout the centuries, innumerable people have come to know what this father said, how the boy convulsed and foamed at the mouth, and how Christ responded. It's implausible, is it not, to think Christ would have no awareness of the Scriptures that would attest of him?

In speaking to this father, Christ spoke to one man, with the crowd listening. That's the way it is with Christ's revelational speak. When Christ spoke to an individual, he was also speaking to the world. The audience of one is inseparable from the audience of everyone.

The father is a central character in the drama. The possessed boy was his only child, and the condition had plagued the child since infancy. There is no mention of a mother. She may have been there, but then it seems she would have been noted. This we'll never know.

The begging and pleading speaks of the father's determination and sense of desperation. Likely, the father had gone to great lengths searching for a cure. The narrative reads as if the man is consumed with his son's condition.

Somehow the news of Christ's whereabouts had reached this father, who then made his way to the disciples. The concerned father had begged the disciples to drive out the evil spirit, but to no avail.

Instead, the father ended up in dialogue with Christ, the Redeemer. In answering Christ's question about the length of illness, the father went on to say, "Have mercy on us and help us, if you can." The distraught father uses the pronoun "us," not "me," in pleading for the boy.

In the father's words we see joint suffering, joint anguish. The plea is for a joint cure. In possessing the son, the evil spirit also held captive the father. The two were shackled together, as if wearing leg irons. Immediately Christ picked up on the father's qualifying phrase and repeated it. "If you can?" Christ said. He then continued, saying, "Everything is possible for him who believes." At once, the father counters, "I do believe; help me overcome my unbelief!"

The question posed and answer given are an integral part of both stories. His response is credible, confessional, memorable. Looking into the eyes of Christ, he floats between belief and unbelief. He wants to believe, he does believe... but he doesn't believe. He is both a believer and nonbeliever. Is that you, Voice?

VOICE: Well...I mean, you say...

READER: Please keep listening, Voice. He and the boy had suffered long. The father was sincere in wanting to cast his faith to a higher plane and break free from his state of unbelief. Just as the conversation was occurring, Christ saw another crowd racing in their direction. Christ turned his attention to the boy, and, without further comment to the father, spoke directly to the evil spirit. "You deaf and mute spirit," Christ said, "I command you, come out of him and never enter him again."

The spirit shrieked, causing violent convulsions, and came out. The boy looked so much like a corpse that many said, "He's dead." Christ then reached for the boy and lifted him to his feet. In so doing, Christ lifted the father, as well. The affliction that had shackled them both was broken. They were cured. The evil spirit was driven out.

Demons never mistook the identity of Christ nor doubted his power over them. Once Christ encountered a very violent man, while he was in the region of Gerasenes across the lake from Galilee. This poor soul had been demon-possessed for many years. He was homeless and roamed the countryside, violently taunting and threatening anyone who came near. Most often he could be found wandering among the tombs. Among the graves he reckoned with his identity.

The day Christ arrived, the demon-possessed man of rage ran to see him. To his knees he fell, and he cried out at the top of his lungs, "What do you want with me, Jesus, Son of the Most High God? Swear to God that you won't torture me!" The demon began to plead and beg with Christ, though Christ had already commanded the evil spirit to come out. Deep within the soul the demon clung.

St. Mark describes this man's tortured existence: "No one could bind him any more, not even with a chain. For he had often been chained hand and foot, but he tore the chains apart and broke the irons on his feet. No one was strong enough to subdue him. Night and day among the tombs and in the hills he would cry out and cut himself with stones."

The evil spirit clung on, not yet obeying Christ's command. "'What is your name?' Christ asked. 'My name is Legion,' he replied, 'for we are many.' And they begged Christ that he would not command them to go out into the abyss."

Into the abyss they begged not to go.

VOICE: The abyss—it's real. How do you see it?

READER: Real it is. See it I do, Voice. That great void—the chasm of emptiness where nothing finds nothing. There's nothing in the abyss—it's a kind of spiritual waste, never to be erased. The abyss is a limitless expanse, where words, images, and sounds have no meaning. There is no casting broad or narrow, no symmetry of sight and sound.

No one is there—no one to call, nothing to see or say. It's a vastness in which spirits forever float. They tumble, twist, turn, and tumble on. No exit, no door, no edge, no middle. Not a single wall or window. No tree on the lawn, no lawn, no outside, no air to breathe. Only fear to feel, dread to sense, gloom filled with doom—that's the abyss. Forever to be lost, never to be found. Nothing to seek, no one seeking.

No one enters the abyss. No one can. There is no entrance, no path in and out. No shepherds hunting sheep. Not a single whisper is uttered in the abyss. There are no utterers. There are no listeners. The abyss is beyond the mist, where only evil spirits go. In the abyss, there's never a time of planting, no seeds for growing, never a time of sowing, only nothingness to reap. No reward in reaping nothingness—no grist to grind, nothing to touch, nothing to feel.

In the abyss, there are no residents, no registers to register, only castaways, evil spirits flung to stay. The spirits in the abyss know beyond the mist they'll always be. Rolling forever restless is their unconditional state, their fate. On and on into nothingness they roll.

It was by boat Christ reached the Gerasenes. As soon as he stepped ashore, this man of manic mind and tortured flesh appeared. From out of the tombs, this stricken creature approached. He moved toward Christ not shyly, but loudly crying out.

This man of pathetic state must have had a name someone knew; he did not say. For him, only Legion spoke. It was Legion, one and all, who cried not to be cast out into the great abyss. Legion, a force of demons bound together with destructive might, begged. To Christ alone they begged.

Driving out a demon—to what might it be compared, Voice?

VOICE: I think it's hard to compare.

READER: It must be akin to driving a rabid wolverine from a den, is it not? Out of the soul, heart, and mind the demon is driven. It must go, no more clinging on; out is the command.

The fate of Legion was on the line. Not a single demon, but an entire legion, occupied this man. Perhaps somehow the demonic waves flowed, and the news filtered 'round to Satan's ear. Imagine, just suppose and nothing more, that as Christ came sailing o'er to the Gerasenes, Satan raced 'round by way of shore.

At demonic speed, peeling bark off trees, he raced, spraying sand, as Backrider watched the tiny particles trickle through the air. To the tombs he sped, to coach Legion, just as Christ arrived.

Those gathered in the upper room of Tunnel House were pressed to peak attention when, in the corner, Brother Chronicle rose and cleared his throat. A shaft of light streamed up from the low corner window beside him and filtered across his wrinkled face. With the countenance, clarity, and cadence of a poet, Brother Chronicle began to speak.

Chronicle's enthralling lines all linked in telling a story of Lucifer, Legion, and Christ, in a desolate place called the Gerasenes. Chronicle's narrative drew, in part, on the tale of the tombs, found in the ancient text of Scripture.

LUCIFER: Get off, Backrider. Lay low. You're shed; I'm through with you. Lucifer has Legion on his mind. Don't give me any pathetic play, walking 'round backwards, bowlegged with a sour face. Be grateful I shed you in such a wondrous place. Sniff. Ah, the tombs, the greatest of scents. Decay—it brings out my best of moods.

Chronicle sniffed the air in the room, looked up, and moved his dramatic eyes across the beam. He watched the twin fans slowly rounding their blades. As he stood there, the movement of the audience stilled further into silence. Only eyes were free to race and dart. With curiosity, everyone watched and listened.

LUCIFER: You'll find your way into some troubled soul. Just wait till you hear one of the fleshies sobbing around the tombs, saying, "I'd do anything if only…"

That's your cue. They mean it. Promise 'em a chat with the departed, a little turning back of the clock. Now beat it—don't let my eyes see you. Your rank clouds my mind. This is an important day. Gotta think. Legion's now the optic of my diffusion. Scram—get lost among the lizards.

Now Legion, I know you can hear me. This is Lucifer speaking. Yes, it's me, the one and only Lucifer. In my image there is no likeness. I've come to give you my support, help you thread your needle. Forget not: It's easier for a camel to fall into the abyss than for a demon to buck the words of the Word.

Fear not, that's why I'm here. You can ride this out, buck this wave. You can do it, Legion. I'm here, near, in the tombs watching, abiding. I see what you're up against; it's formidable. Heed my instructions, or the Word will have you cast into the abyss in a flash. Do you want to forever fall, twist, and tumble?

Listen up. Listen good, you hear? You're not without training. Consider what you've learned from me, Legion. Listen, there's a chance the Word will wane a bit. He is, after all, half flesh. Somehow he may become distracted and let you slip.

You know the drill, Legion. I know his power is enormous, but you've got me in the shadows of the tombs. I'm looking in your direction. I'm breathing in your direction. I'm contending in your direction. Fear not, this one called the Word.

Now, here's what to do. Remember, you always start with the inner core of three. There's amazing strength in that configuration. Heed my instruction, sharp, fast, Legion. There's not a second to lose.

Three of you demons in there get onto your sides and bend around, forming the inner circle. Then each of you reach out and grab the ankles of your fellow demon. Bite down on the toes ferociously while bending back the feet. I know some of you do not have feet. Just form them. Quick! There's little time. The Word's eyes are intensifying, rectifying, scrutinizing the form of your wayward fleshy.

So you've got the inner core of three. Remember, grab the ankles, bite down on the toes, bend back the feet. From the core of three, the ball of demons grows. The next circle is four, and it runs 180 degrees to circle one. Circle five then runs the same way as circle one. The circles crisscross; that's the strength. Grab the ankles, bite down on the toes, bend back the feet, until the last demon is locked in place. Crisscross, cross-criss, go, go, go!

Got it? Sure you do. Hurry, you imbeciles! I didn't come all the way out here to watch a maniac fleshy nut wander around in the tombs. I get the whole tomb idea; good choice, but how do you Legion loonies pick such a miserable-looking fleshy? Anyway, that doesn't matter now.

Legion, listen to me. When you hear the Word's command again, clench and bite with all your might. Maybe somehow you'll survive intact to roam another day, not entering the abyss all disarranged. You are Legion. Grab, bend, bite. Do you hear me? I command you! I demand you! Ignore the Word; listen to me!

Don't worry about your toes. What does it profit a demon to save his toes and enter the abyss intact? By the power resident and swirling in me, I command you: Listen to me!

What's that? Legion, don't say that, you stupid imbecile. Never! Don't speak of swine, you crumpling idiot. You're there to swell, swell from the core, all backs against old fleshies' ribs. I command you. Hold your possession, your position, hold. Clench, bite, bend, with all your might, like great demons do.

With a profound look of satisfaction upon his face, Brother Chronicle nodded gently to Drama, who was ready with his lines.

READER: As Legion trembled inside the kneeling man, Lucifer's command became lost. Legion could not hold back his words when the contorted band of demons spotted pigs grazing on a hill. The clenching demons begged Christ, "Send us among the pigs. Allow us to go into them."

St. Mark provides a glimpse of what happened next. "And at once Jesus gave them permission. Then the unclean spirits went out and entered the swine— there were about two thousand—and the herd ran violently down the steep place into the sea, and drowned in the sea."

Drama returned a nod to Chronicle.

LUCIFER: What a mess! Water…how revolting.

And Chronicle nodded again to Drama.

READER: People from the town came to see the effect of demons entering pigs. "Then they came to Jesus, and saw the one who had been demon-possessed and had the legion, sitting and clothed and in his right mind. And they were afraid."

Drama smiled, nodding in Chronicle's direction.

LUCIFER: Wholeness, how I hate it! He was so much better off with us. At least he had power, could snap chains. He was free to roam in delightful places.

Slowly, the age-worn face of Chronicle descended through the filtering light, as once again he took his seat. Drama continued with the reading.

READER: Then Lucifer—who was and wasn't there—backed away. Step-by-step, he slowly moved, growling, grunting as if speaking to the dead, while through the tombs he backward swayed. Sliding along on his massive, bristly feet, he soon began to trail away. Shadow upon shadow did the trick, eventually veiling him in darkness, his desired abode—particularly after such a contrary and costly day.

However it came to be, Legion knew a pig was a pig and not a sheep. Seemingly, to Legion, it did not matter. Being *disclosed in* and not *exposed out* is all that mattered—anything but the abyss.

Behind the skin of pigs or human flesh, demons creep. Treading there in the darkened marsh of soul, in madness they cling, yearning not to be cast out into the vast abyss. In the abyss there are no ribs to hold. In the great expanse of nothingness there's no place to hide. There's nothing but abyss exposure.

Angels in the exalted realm once these clinging demons were—until in that hour of great calamity, of repulsive reaching and wanton wanting, they were cast out, descending. How they must hate that little word: *cast.*

The demon-possessed souls encountering Christ never spoke a quiet word. They came not alongside whispering, as if speaking to him in private. Satan seemed to be the only one to master the conversational tone. As he tempted Christ in the wilderness, he did not come out shouting and screaming, "Holy One of God!"

The master of subtlety he was. "If you are the Son of God," he said, "prove it: turn a bit of stone into bits of bread; jump and you will not get hurt. That is, if you are the Son of God...."

Perhaps on that mountain, there transfigured, the luminous figure seen by Peter, James, and John is what the demons always saw. Just suppose, beyond the flesh, they saw straight to the Word, and seeing the unmistakable, they could not help but scream and shout.

Christ's message was both humanly crafted by Jesus of Nazareth in culture's grain, and transfigured in a manner only the Son of God could deliver. In the crowd, in the midst of curious eyes, a father cries; that is how the messages were made. A question here, a comment there, and all the while revelation flowed.

This intertwined weaving of incarnational revelation can, for some, make the whole gospel story appear too circuitous, too bogged down in the human condition. Arguably, this is why some people hate it so, despising it as preposterous, rendering it foolishness. Revelation, redemption, so embedded in humanity's wail and way—where's all the sanctity? How could God be so far removed from a celestial home? In a human scrum—surely that's not the way God should be?

There, in the scrum of humanity, Christ is found exchanging lines. A father watches his convulsing child rolling in the dirt and begs, "Have mercy on us and help us, if you can." He believed to the point of seeing mercy in Christ's eyes. In this discourse between a distraught father and Christ, few words were actually spoken. From these short lines, quickly exchanged, however, revelation flows, roaring deep and wide.

"If I can," Christ said. "Everything is possible for him who believes." At once, the father counters, "I do believe. Help me overcome my unbelief!" How does one place a value on these buoyant words, these little lines that speak, flowing through reservoirs of time?

Preferring the requisition of other words, many look at Christ's words and turn away. There's no thought of unbelief as something to overcome. Ancient words from history's dusty patch seem so distant. The prospect of formulas clear is much preferred over mysteries old, appearing as they do through panes of time with such storied hues.

The ancient panes, though, are not meant for glancing. They're for peering through. The more one peers, the more one sees. Images seemingly obscure and opaque at first have a way, in time, of dispelling doubt. Christ's words begin to flicker with light certain.

Through the glass dim, it can even appear that God seeks a kind of solace among the scrum-troubled sheep, those wandering and wondering after him. His face divine peers through, though it is impossible to tell whether it is the face of the Father or the Son.

Out of the crowd, the cry of a father is heard. He calls out with words. With words he begs, he hopes. Words he does not expect, he hears: "Everything is possible for him who believes." These words he does believe.

Words matter…Christ's words matter most of all.

I do believe, help me in my unbelief.

DISTRAUGHT FATHER WITH DEMON-POSSESSED SON,

NEAR JERUSALEM, CIRCA AD 32

READING EIGHT

———◦•◦———

SETTING THE SCENE

The day which repurposed history is now yours to consider. A cold chilling day it was, the day death's Freeze began its creep up Golgotha's infamous terrain, in search of the Son of God, the Son of Man. Both is he.

Oh yes, heavy is the prose you will soon encounter. You will not be spared. Redemption has a grave price. The monks of Estillyen have it right.

With unswerving passion they speak—and today at Speaker's House they are not tardy. Writer takes center stage, speaking of the center cross. Brother Testimony does his part, imparting a certain kind of light from darkness.

No magic tricks, just words woven in message form, making meaning, offering life in the face of death. Mystery great it is, mystifying to consider, no matter how long one ponders.

Speaker's House is the oldest structure on Estillyen's isle. The original part of the building dates back more than 600 years. It was built not unlike an ancient theater, where audiences stood on narrow circular balconies and watched theater troupes below.

Today you'll stand there too, unless you turn away. You will follow Christ to the hour of his death—and meet the two criminals crucified at his side.

Perhaps this is a story you remember. Not easy to forget.

The words of the reading are now set to rise.

To the reading...

Remember Me

Jesus, remember me when you come into your kingdom.

LUKE 23:42

READER: Christ's figure shone expressly bright when transfigured on the mountain top. Still more brilliant did his glory show when the sacred One was lifted high, upon a hill called Golgotha.

Golgotha, the wretched place of misery and pain, the hill of crucifixion. That's where the Son of God was lifted up.

VOICE: Why was he lifted up? The simple truth, that's all.

READER: For sins he was lifted up.

VOICE: Whose, precisely?

READER: Not his own. Sins committed then and there—sins stretching back in time, and those yet to be. Yours and mine. Great and small, the lifting up was recompense for them all.

Golgotha is the place where spikes were bunched.

VOICE: Where were those spikes? What do you think—perhaps in an old rusty pot or lying on the ground?

READER: You're right to question and consider, not skip through the story all hither and thither. They may well have been recycled and bent, harboring all manner of menacing particles. Bunched, they waited for their thudding blows to drive them through, until solidly set, embedded deep within the cross. Piercing skin and bone, instantaneously they released infectious residues into the blood of the crucifix.

VOICE: The atmosphere on this renowned killing day...what was it?

READER: The atmosphere on this chilling-killing day was mournfully convulsive. At least it was for some, but certainly not for all. It was a day of retribution for the religious elite. Their fortitude had paid off. They had won, or so they thought. Good riddance was the mood, a chance to finally shake their fists at this dangerous zealot threatening to destroy God's temple.

For the disciples, *bewilderment* is the word most appropriate. They had left everything to follow, to learn, to become disciples. Their Redeemer was destined to die. They watched and listened as their Lord, so confessed, hung before them, dying.

On their journey with Christ, there were many private, joyful moments. On one such occasion he said to them, "Blessed are the eyes that see what you see. For I tell you that many prophets and kings wanted to see what you see but did not see it, and to hear what you hear but did not hear it."

Voice what do you want to see and hear?

VOICE: Your question sounds important.

READER: Consider the question, as long as life, if you wish. The disciples were, indeed, blessed to see and hear, but on this day, bewilderment and brutality teamed up to wrench and test all they'd come to know.

VOICE: Reader, for Christ's family watching, what did they see when their eyes looked up to Golgotha's hill?

READER: You ask what they saw the day on which history was repurposed? They saw much of love, grace, torture, and disgrace. Utter heartbreak and sorrow was etched upon their faces.

Into the hands of men the Son of God fell. Almost utterly unbelievable, is it not, Voice—God spiked by men? In their grasp they had the King of the Jews, Jesus of Nazareth. Spiked to the cross by sinners, Christ died for the residents of the world so loved by God, sinners all.

VOICE: His condition on the cross—was it as terrible as you say?

READER: Worse! Far worse. Worse than any cursed verse. How can truth die? The Light of the World be extinguished? If you were the light, how would it feel? Smothered in thick darkness, the eyes grow dim, until there is no more sight of seeing.

Voice, let the words of the psalmist speak: "I am poured out like water, and all my bones are out of joint. My heart has turned to wax; it has melted away within me. My strength is dried up like a potsherd, and my tongue sticks to the roof of my mouth; you lay me in the dust of death. Dogs have surrounded me; a band of evil men has encircled me, they have pierced my hands and my feet. I can count all my bones; people stare and gloat over me."

Time neither lessens the severity nor overshadows the butchery. The psalmist, with prophetic prose, sketched out this vivid image of misery.

An aging poet once said, "Heaven's angels pulled in their wings that day, kneeled and went to weeping. They wept and wept till all of heaven's fountains overflowed, and tears a river wide gushed through heaven's gates. Three days long it rushed, until upon the rising tide they saw their Lord appearing."

VOICE: Is it true?

READER: Why shouldn't it be?

Stunned was the universe, surely, staring down at creation's architect impaled on a tree between two thieves. Gone were his dwelling days, all spent. The Word Made Flesh, Mary's child, was to be no more in his natural state. No more bringing news, walking among the pressing crowds, lifting up those burdened down.

Hoisted high before bulging eyes and clenched fists, the message hung. Blood was his garment. Drenched red he was. From tissues deeply torn, blood flowed. Blood of head joined blood of face, moving down the neck. Over the shoulders, blood trailed to his chest and back. Around the waist and down the legs, blood flowed.

Around the knees, from chinbone to ankles, the warm crimson fluid trickled on. Across the feet it advanced, past the spikes, before the toes it reached. From there it dripped, moistening the ground, the blood of God and man mixed. It dripped. Sacrificial blood dripped, drop by drop, into soil soiled by sinners. On Golgotha, many had been crucified for sins. Yet for others' sins they had not died.

Christ's plaque was nailed, not below his feet to be obscured by blood, but above his head, clearly labeling this figure so mistakable. The one dying there in the middle was Jesus of Nazareth, identified as the King of the Jews. In Amharic, Latin, and Greek, those words were written upon the plaque.

Before the watching world, the Word Made Flesh was spiked. The Alpha and Omega of divine verse hung, his shredded flesh dying, but his words ever living, never dying.

This drama of the Lamb of God sacrificed by the world, for the world, was scripted before the world began.

VOICE: How can that be? Is it so?

READER: It is, Voice. Listen to the words of St. Peter: "Like that of a lamb without blemish or spot, he was destined before the foundation of the world, but was made manifest at the end of the times for your sake."

*Made manifest...*what curious words, Voice. But right, so right, they do seem. Out of the eons of time, Christ's days had finally arrived, pushing the manifest into present's place. Prophetic words sewn in centuries past burst forth with detailed precision.

Voice, I implore you to grasp the significance of these prophetic words. There is no precedent for words acting as these words did, to tell a tale, to draft a drama. In they came. From here and there, they came. At the assigned time and place, they converged, joining the lines for Christ's message in the making.

Ancient prophecies, once penned, had long abided. They waited incomplete, unfulfilled. Words past spoken waited for their stories to arrive so they could be folded into present verse. Once folded in, the prophecies settled into the message. They spoke full with meaning, never again just foretelling.

Like ornaments without a tree, the prophecies had long waited to be hung upon their stories. Ornaments brought their gifts to the message—credibility, connectivity, certainty. The storied message of Christ would not be bare.

Isaiah's words were there to do their part, showing up to be unfolded and folded in: "He was oppressed and afflicted, yet he did not open his mouth. He was led like a lamb to the slaughter, and as a sheep before her shearers is silent, so he did not open his mouth."

That's the way these ancient words worked: converging, joining lines, making messages that matter most. As the story broke, characters also got their call. Emerging, they rushed to and fro in this great pageant. Most had no idea that their hour of scurry was being folded into the story for posterity and eternity.

Judas was there, grasping thirty pieces of silver and his hanging rope. The priests were there, grasping Judas and the silver coins he scattered on the temple floor. With the pickings, they eventually grasped a plot of land. A malicious mob, wielding knives, swords, and clubs, grasped Christ. Pilate grasped his towel. Barabbas grasped freedom.

A rooster grasped morning light and a deafening crow. Peter grasped sorrow in the hours of early morn. Simon the Cyrene grasped a cross, one not his own. Soldiers grasped clothes and cast lots. Two thieves: One grasped the kingdom of God; the other grasped defiance. One grasped redemption, the other retribution. Christ grasped gasps and final words: "Father, into your hands I commit my spirit." With that, Christ grasped his final breath.

VOICE: Reader, it seems so utterly bizarre to consider the Son of God being beaten, spiked, and crucified for an ancient rendezvous between Adam, Eve, and Satan.

READER: Dear Voice, St. Paul perceived this to be the case and wrote, "For the message of the cross is foolishness to those who are perishing, but to us who are being saved it is the power of God." That's the word he used: *foolishness.* Let's not reject this word, but accept it.

VOICE: Yet why such an extreme price for fruit plucked—a reach, a single breech of divine protocol?

READER: The fairy-tale portrayals of forbidden fruit, it seems, cheat the severity of the matter. The fall of Adam and Eve is not about the sound of crunch from fruit bitten. It is about the sound of words and a message believed. Grasping hand followed grasping heart. That's the part that spun humanity into an inordinate orbit.

Ever so quickly words flowed into lines, inspiring thoughts and changing hearts to believe what should not be believed. That's the way of words. Words jump into lines; lines jump into minds; thoughts jump into hearts. In the heart they vie for space with other words placed by other thoughts. Adam and Eve became sinners, new believers. They believed Satan's words over God's.

"Oh, yes, I am a believer," it's often said, as if there are others that do not believe. However, everyone is a believer—believing in this or that, or both. Disbelieving is a form of belief. Not believing in God is to believe in disbelieving. Arguing that people do not believe is like arguing that people do not breathe.

Do you get my point, Voice?

VOICE: Yes, I think I do.

READER: Unlike in the vast abyss, the world reverberates with messages, attractive and alternative, pure and perverse, true and false. Messages come forth in words, images, and sounds. Into culture they float, playing games of tug-of-war. They pull at unbelievers to believe and beckon believers to disbelieve. They call out to buyers to switch and try to plead with pundits to place their bets.

To be "like God" was the pull of Satan's line, spun so attractively for Eve. So wondrously autonomous, sovereign, and free—that's the prize. Switch and try; change your vote; cast your lot. Grasp a bit of fruit; never mind, it's really a bit of rope. Give it a tug.

Not a hint from the ancient tale suggests that Adam and Eve paused, even slightly, to consider where this newfound God-grasp might lead. This pair, newly formed from earth and rib, were ready, they thought, to rule like God. How implausible was the notion!

What about sculptor God, the breather of life, the One that hung the stars in place? Did Adam and Eve not consider that he would need a job, perhaps something light in his semiretirement? Was he to be in their care? Could they offer divine security in their new plan? Perhaps he could join their team, offer some wise old sayings now and then.

It was not due to force, threat, or consequence that Satan's lines were believed. The message was embraced because of its appeal. Satan's words were few. They formed a brief message that appeared to be genuine. The challenge with words is to know their intent, their dispatch, and particularly the spirit that helped them hatch.

Adam and Eve engaged a dastardly message. Its evil intent was cooked up in the cauldron of Satan's spite. In his darkened spirit, the ingredients of the message were sifted, until just the right words crept out of the mediator's mouth. Once the message was embraced, there was no sovereignty for Adam and Eve, no liberty. They were frightened, transfigured.

Their act resulted in a severe stab to creation's side—Satan's knife was deeply plunged. A horrid howl was heard, dissonance wrecking harmony, trouncing tranquility. The horrific scream echoed thunderously throughout the kingdom grounds. Beasts roared, stalkers stalked, killing commenced. Everything changed, bearing the mark of sin. Man was out, not in.

Out, not in, separated by sin—that's what placed Jesus Christ on the Via Dolorosa. That was the compelling unction of his zeal, his cause. His focus was not to stay up in heaven looking down, letting man fix the fix he was in. Man's fix was unfixable by man. Instead, Christ embarked on a journey long, taking him from a manger stall in Bethlehem to that wretched hill, Golgotha.

The final leg to Golgotha's hill was along the Via Dolorosa, the way of suffering and grief. Compelled by grace, Christ made his way down the notorious road to meet the frozen face of death—his own. Heaps of wily schemes were piled high along this infamous road. They were placed there by darkened hearts that had longed for such a day.

Along the Via Dolorosa, Christ did not walk alone. He staggered along with two condemned criminals. The companions three made their way to find the hill of death and frozen faces. When these two criminals first caught sight of Christ, the story does not tell. It may well have been when Christ was first adorned with a crown of thorns.

VOICE: Where was that?

READER: In the fortress, Voice. Once Pilate had washed his hands and freed Barabbas, Christ was led away to the Fortress of Antonia, where the eternally begotten Son of God was used for sport. A hundred Roman soldiers, maybe more, were stationed in this fiendish garrison of known brutality. Inside the fortress, Christ was stripped and beaten with a staff.

He received repeated blows to his head and face. It was in this holding pen, this perverted place, that Christ was awarded thorns for his head and spit upon his face.

Voice, there is something terribly sinister about unbridled authority in the hands of collective evil with no fear of retaliation. Evil spurs evil. Most eyes do not care to see the site of frenzied hounds ripping apart a defenseless fox. Yet some sinister eyes do. They find sweet delight soaking in pain they do not have to bear. Pummeled, as the sport of soldiery and brutality, Christ was readied for crucifixion.

Along the way of suffering and grief, Christ was led. One wonders if the evil one might have been about, to see what others saw: the Son of God staggering along with his cross and bloodied flesh. Suffering and grief, after all—that's the central tenet of Satan's game. Surely Satan could be counted on to drop in, dash about, and move in and out of the heaps of garbage roundabout.

Satan would not want to miss this defining act on Golgotha's hill, this spectacle of dying on view for the living. Just maybe, it would all prove too much for the one foreordained as the Savior of mankind. If the soldiers at the Fortress of Antonia couldn't make him break, then possibly the sheer pain of the crucifixion would do the trick.

Satan may have thought that when the spikes were driven through the skin, ripping muscles, cartilage, and veins, perhaps that would be the moment the angels would be called.

Writer raised his right hand and extended his palm in the direction of Brother Testimony.[17] Brother Testimony rose to his feet and took three small steps towards the room's interior. Apart from the audience, he stood. More in the shadows than in the light, he began to speak. His voice resonated with clarity, and his white eyebrows appeared to be jumping along to the rhythm of the words.

LUCIFER: Let me tell you, my devotees, listen up to Lucifer. When the Word hears his own bones crunching in his hands and feet, this whole redemption deal set forth by I AM is gonna unravel. You think I AM is gonna stand by and let dummy fleshies kill the Word? It's like long ago, when I AM told Abraham to kill his son, knife him, and then at the last minute called it off, got a ram in the thicket to take the fleshy kid's place.

That's what we've got here—some kind of trick, a bait-and-switch deal. Maybe that's not even the Word. Who knows, I'm just saying. Oh, brilliant, here he comes. They've got a couple of criminals with him. I know the one on the left. How perfect—the Word's blood is everywhere.

Oh, did I tell you, or have you heard, it was a staff to his head. How right! Did we inspire that, or did that come from the fleshy text? It doesn't matter. All that matters now is pain and the prospect of divine disruption.

Beautiful—look and learn something, my demon devotees. That's the way! That's what you're supposed to do when you get fleshies in your clutches. No mercy—just think slaughter, slaughter. Keep that word in the forefront of your minds: *slaughter*. It's a good, robust-sounding word. You imbeciles are too untoward, too twitchy, too cliché. You need to be more ruthless and horrid like me.

Look to me, Lucifer. Look to me so intently that, when you look in the mirror, you'll see my face. Get some grumble in your rumble. We've got to pull together in pulling things apart. The divine wards are on full alert. Hey, stop that! Watch it, imbeciles—don't gesture upward, not now. This is not the moment for provoking the heavenly forces. I'm told I AM is really worked up over this whole affair. Anything could happen. Even if he goes through with it, I AM can change his mind and obliterate the whole planet.

Delightful it must have been for the soldiers to knock him about. If only they could have killed him, then I AM's prophetic words that have to be couldn't be, and this grace thing would all be over. Don't you rotten core of fools know how vital this day is? Then *show* me you do—look all full of eagerness and angst. We need to disrupt, distort, and dislocate. Got it, idiots?

Later we need to check out that soldiering lot at the fortress and see how many souls can be bought. Got to be a high percentage. That goes for everyone down the line, from Pilate's palace to the ones that make the crosses.

Especially check out the spike drivers. They'll not be the same after this affair. There must be a lot of Judas hearts around here. The spilling bowels—oh, he was of our ilk, but he was a stupid fleshy just the same. There are plenty where he came from. Sneaky fleshies—they're all sickly made. Redemption, why them? What a waste.

I'm just saying, it's all down to I AM. Why he's bent on killing the Word over fleshies is beyond me. I AM has become downright delusional. Even if it was possible for me to feel sorry, I wouldn't. It's his own mess, making fleshies. The Ancient of Days has stumbled, just like the Word. Look at that! Good, lash him again! Who's that fellow picking up his cross? Giving the Word a cushy break—how pathetic.

Look to me, my devotees. I've chosen you. You're here on this momentous occasion because you're my worst demons, but you need to get a heap worser. I mean worser than worse, so you won't be so worthless. You twelve must stay alert—I command it. I demand it. Any slip-up in this divine plan, and we'll make a move. We'll capitalize, maximize. He's got a long way to go before any rising from the grave takes place.

Now listen to me, you imbeciles. When you get my call, begin to chant with me. You know, the Word can simultaneously hear angels in heaven breathing and the hounds of hell growling.

He can hear anything. On this occasion, we want everything groaning, howling, and growling—nothing less than full-force travail. If we can get him to throw in the towel, the glorious victory will be ours.

Why I AM ever concocted fleshies is beyond me. What's the Trinity see in 'em? Don't answer…that's not a question! Mud with breath, that's all they are and nothing more, big deal. You devotees can go through walls, soar through space; they can't.

He almost got it right once, I must admit—the flood. What a sight it was—all that choking and drowning. Those fleshies can really paddle and claw. Then he had to ruin everything by making that stupid boat. Talk about dumb…

There's something wrong when I AM gets so involved, gets all worked up over fleshies, as if they were some kind of an extension of him. *Amputate, annihilate, extricate*—those are the choice words I AM refuses to hear.

That's what I do with my backriders. Once shed, I snap my fingers. If they're not gone, I erect a firewall as thick as a mountain. They're never allowed to see me again. If they try to sneak through, I toss 'em into the middle of the firewall, straight into the roasting pit.

Oh, where was I? That's right. Now, if this turns out our way, and the Word and I AM fail, pull out, the fleshies will be left in our domain. We'll need to harness our hate, not obliterate 'em. Our slaves for eternity they'll be. See, like I have been telling you, there's a future. There's reason for hope!

Now the optic of my collusion will be on that center cross. I've already received word that's the one reserved for the Word. If he comes down before he dies, celebration all around. You can go out and kill any fleshy you want. Our job is to get the travail going, let the Word hear the howling of hell, hear all the misery he has caused. Maybe that'll break him down.

Sometimes it's not the created that's at fault; it's the creator. Adam and Eve are no different than my devotees were in heaven. We were not to blame for the impulses planted within us. 'Course, we're so superior to fleshies, it's hardly worth the comparison.

Pathetic it is, this whole idea of grace, redemption, and reconciling the world to I AM through the Word. Well, he wouldn't be dying to reconcile it if he hadn't made it in the first place. He just couldn't keep his creativity in bounds. Forgiveness, too, makes me spit. What a sick word it is, a pathetic notion. Gives me chills, brings steam to my throat. No talk of that when I was moving around in the heavenly realms.

Now, keep your spirits down, deep in discouragement, and try to spread around as much hate and bitterness as you can. I'm counting on you to be at the bottom of your game. Turmoil is what we need. Grasp that word: *turmoil*. Anything can happen in the spirit of turmoil. The more people stumble and fall, the better.

Now, here's our three-word chant: *Turmoil, travail, tribulation...turmoil, travail, tribulation...whataya hear, whataya get... turmoil, travail, tribulation.* Isn't that great? That's what we want the Word to hear, over and over, as he's spiked up there dying.

Here's what we do. We start very quietly. We let him wriggle for a while, and then after hours of suffering, we'll start to pile it on, fill his ears. Each hour we raise the volume. I want you three to chant bass, you three double bass, and you three triple bass. Everyone else chants whatever your dumb throats allow. Off-key is good.

We will all chant together three times. Then, only the double basses chant, followed by the triple basses. When you triple basses chant, chant the same words, but very, very, slow. So nice it will be!

Ah, isn't it marvelous, the way of suffering and grief? Do you suppose they named this street after me? Can't you just feel the heartache, the anguish of this place? For sure, this is one of the choicest places on this planet. Someday, when we get the world for ourselves, the capitol park will be Golgotha. I can already see it. The Way of Suffering and Grief will be the main thoroughfare.

Only I can dream so stupendously. You know, just occasionally, the pot is superior to the mold—and even to the potter. That's what happened in my case. Oh, with all this treachery about, I feel so benevolent. I shouldn't, but this is a special day.

I'll tell you what I'll do, my devotees, I'll let you gaze. All twelve of you to the left, quick, come around and get on your knees. See my profile, my face. Go ahead, gaze, a full minute is yours. Good, now rush around to the right and gaze again. Which side is most beautiful? I already know—it's impossible to tell.

Okay, enough. Many are the eyes that have longed to see what you just saw. We need to focus. Don't forget, like I keep telling you, he's half flesh. He's a carpenter. When they start spiking him to the cross that could be our finest sunset. Oh, think of it: the carpenter spiked to wooden planks.

At any point along the way, life on earth could pause; God could pull out, call it quits. All this cosmic struggle is down to fleshies, the little, godlike beings that never should have been. Such heartache they have caused their Creator. That's the only good thing about them.

Now shut it—he's coming closer down my street. Let's watch.

Brother Testimony paused. He slowly nodded to Writer, and his eyes blinked. He turned around, moved toward his armchair, and took his seat.

READER: Christ made his way along the Via Dolorosa to the destination Golgotha. In tow were the two criminals who would die beside him—one on his left, one on his right.

VOICE: What do you suppose they must have thought of Christ, this mysterious one in their midst?

READER: The criminals were destined to be there, for ancient words speak of them as transgressors. "He poured out his soul to death and was numbered with the transgressors; yet he bore the sin of many, and makes intercession for the transgressors."

On the Mount of Transfiguration, he might have fled, disappearing swiftly in the company of Moses and Elijah. He could have shown his back to the earth, not turning around, fleeing safely to kingdom grounds. Without a trace, he could have left humanity far behind to deal with its own predicament. Yet he chose not to flee.

Christ came down the Via Dolorosa in the midst of sinners' gaze. Surely he would die. As the sacrificial lamb, he walked on feet unswerving. A lamb's feet they were—feet of the Shepherd, too. He was true to course. For redemption's plan, the Son of God came to die.

Down the Via Dolorosa and beyond Jerusalem's city walls, the condemned three walked on feet with numbered steps. Their final steps they used. At Golgotha, their feet were clutched and spiked. No more would their soles press upon the ground.

On crosses, their feet were pressed hard against splintered wood. They were spiked in an act of full disgrace. "Numbered with transgressors"—these are the words that placed scars on Immanuel's face.

Crucified as objects of public scorn, the three were hoisted high so all could easily see the cost of human disobedience. Spiked to their crosses, they hung in trembling pain, waiting for death to drape its freeze upon their faces. They waited for death to close their eyes and halt the morbid public stare of piteous disgrace.

One of the criminals could not contain his hate; he hurled insults through the air. The object of his hate was at his side, the one with the placard that read "King of the Jews." The criminal shouted out, "Aren't you the Christ? Save yourself and us!"

Simultaneously the crowds jeered. "Those who passed by hurled insults at him, shaking their heads and saying, 'You who are going to destroy the temple and build it in three days, save yourself! Come down from the cross, if you are the Son of God!'

"In the same way, the chief priests, the teachers of the law, and the elders mocked him. 'He saved others,' they said, 'but he can't save himself! He's the King of Israel! Let him come down now from the cross, and we will believe in him. He trusts in God. Let God rescue him now if he wants him, for he said, I am the Son of God.'"

Hate was hurled at all three, but particularly at the one in the middle, the one important enough to receive a plaque as well as a crown. Moving closer was death's freeze. Minutes pulsed, the criminal without remorse hardened steadily to the core. His heart would not heal before his body died. Fearless, the condemned criminal became a spokesperson for sin, striking out at God as the reason for his condition.

Hating what life had dealt, the man of misery spoke with a spirit of damnation. He despised the figure his eyes beheld, this self-acclaimed redeemer of man. No reason for hope—the criminal's eyes had seen all there was to see; he was blind. He did not want to believe. He would not believe. He did not believe. Sin he was. Sin he would be, unto death.

Equally in the throes of the agony of death, the second criminal could see. His repentant eyes somehow saw a figure his heart did not despise. He saw this Jesus hanging there beneath the sign Pilate had prepared. It was to him he called, saying, "Jesus, remember me when you come into your kingdom."

Through swirling chants and the sneering of the crowd, Christ prayed, "Father, forgive them, for they do not know what they are doing." These words the repentant thief may well have heard. In a rebuke to the insolent thief, the repentant thief openly confessed, "We are punished justly, for we are getting what our deeds deserve."

The end was near—the worst kind of end, a miserable death of dying, with the living watching, gawking. Quarantined from the living, on show for dying, is a wretched way to die. Crucifixion was not death by hanging, where suddenly the neck breaks and eyes see no more watchers watching. Crucifixion is to die rejected and deserted by the world; it's to die in public all alone.

Stretched out on a cross between criminals of contrasting fates, the figure in the middle was the supreme message from God to man. Every word, every sigh, every motion added meaning to the message. "To see the Father, look only at me," Christ taught. This truth did not fall away when, upon the cross, Christ was crucified. The image of the Father and the dying Son are one.

The hardened criminal spoke for sin, not bowing will or wicked heart. The criminal of contrast spoke for sinners throughout the ages, who have recognized that sheep lost need a shepherd to be found. "Jesus, remember me when you come into your kingdom" was his famous line, tenderly spoken. The repentant thief wanted to believe, he did believe, and he willed his belief to Jesus of Nazareth.

In response, Christ promised, "Today you will be with me in paradise," and that promise was swiftly approaching. Christ was in the final throes of death. "Knowing that everything had now been finished, and so that Scripture would be fulfilled, Jesus said, 'I am thirsty.'" Another prophecy unfolded: "They put gall in my food and gave me vinegar for my thirst."

The end was close and closing in; death was moving up the crosses three. On the middle cross Christ hung. Isaiah foretold what those present saw as they gazed up at this figure torn. "Just as there were many who were appalled at him, his appearance was so disfigured beyond that of any man and his form marred beyond human likeness." One more prophecy had unfolded and folded into its story.

The Holy Trinity alone knows the depth and breadth of what actually occurred on the cross. Prophets saw sketches of what would be. The disciples were told what to expect, but they were overrun by events. They could not comprehend what had never been. Characters, the entire troupe folded into the Gospel narrative, saw only facets of the drama of which they were a part.

On the cross Christ hung until he was certain Scripture was fulfilled. Alone was Christ in understanding the scope and significance of what was taking place. The idea that Scripture's prophetic words must be fulfilled is spellbinding, is it not?

Prophecies from a distant past act not unlike stars, long ago sent on their way emitting light. At exact intervals the prophecies were sent. With precision, the words beam toward the events for which they were destined.

Eventually, past words meet present story. In a divinely inspired embrace, they intersect, fuse, and move on into eternity. Prophecy is no chess game of matching bits. It is actually God speaking, overlapping lines throughout history, at various times and in various ways. Though appearing as disparate as taps can be, the fulfillment of Scripture is the fulfillment of God's thoughts, which come forth as words tapping through the ages.

The mystery "hidden for ages and generations" was being revealed on that patch of ground called Golgotha. There, in that place, with blood dripping and time ticking, the mysterious Message á Medium of God hung. He spoke with words and without.

As all prophetic Scriptures found their storied places, it was time for Christ to die. His death spoke with universal awe, as the Father's beloved Son died in love laid down.

Mary, peering from the hill, watched the flesh she bore give way to death. Which words he spoke as his last, no one knows for sure. St. John records, "It is finished." St. Luke reports that Christ took his last breath after saying, "Father, into your hands I commit my spirit!"

With death, the pumping of blood and its dripping swiftly stopped. The medium was now silent—but speaking still. Death silent spoke meaning into life. Death silent was the sign signifying redemption's price was paid.

St. Luke wrote, "It was now about the sixth hour and there was darkness over the whole land until the ninth hour." God's thoughts were then rendered not as words, but acts. Matthew's account provides the greatest detail:

"At that moment, the curtain of the temple was torn in two from top to bottom. The earth shook and the rocks split. The tombs broke open and the bodies of many holy people who had died were raised to life. They came out of the tombs, and after Jesus' resurrection, they went into the holy city and appeared to many people. When the centurion, and those with him who were guarding Jesus, saw the earthquake and all that had happened, they were terrified, and exclaimed, 'Surely he was the Son of God!'"

VOICE: What do you suppose Satan said?

Writer turned in the direction of Brother Testimony, who had already quietly stood up and moved to his prior position. His lines were brief.

LUCIFER: Darkness, earthquakes—what's happening? This can't be. This is not what I expected. It's too soon. He died too quick—it's a trick.

This is not fair. Tombs breaking open, hear that, and that. Silence, imbeciles! Stop your chanting—can't you see the Word's really dead?

Testimony nodded back to Writer.

READER: The curtain in the Temple was torn. The way to God had been opened. The Son of God was crucified, not only between two thieves, but also between God and man. God reconciling the world through Christ was a reality.

VOICE: Where did Christ go? What happened at that precise moment?

READER: This we do not know for sure, and, of course, the story is not yet complete. We do know this: When the repentant thief cried out, "Jesus, remember me," there was a reply; there was a promise. Did Christ not say, "Today you will be with me in paradise?" He did!

Therefore, among the vast sum we do not know, we know that Christ died and was, that very day, with a repentant thief in his Father's kingdom!

Words matter…words from the cross matter immensely.

Jesus, remember me when you come into your kingdom.

THIEF ON THE CROSS, GOLGOTHA, JERUSALEM, CIRCA AD 32

READING NINE

SETTING THE SCENE

There was a line, oh so ancient now, where death and life met and merged. The moment is marked by the words of Christ, "It is finished." It is the end and the beginning.

Let's let Reader have a word—and our Voice, too.

"That's how it was, Voice," the Reader said. "It was over, finished. It was time for eternity's ancient hourglass, the vial of ages past, to be righted, turned upside down, so to speak. Do you know what I mean, Voice?"

"What was over?" Voice asked. "What was finished? What do you mean, vial of ages past?"

"What was finished? The era without grace, which the blood of a billion goats and bulls could not buy—that was over. The time of ages past, with mystery clasped, hidden fast—that too was over."

"Mystery clasped…are you sure that's what you mean, Reader?"

"Yes, Voice, the time of waiting and watching for the Messiah to appear was over. The mystery of redemption was a mystery no more."

That is the scene now set. The location is Dairy House. The reading room is packed.

Plot appears, followed by Brother Witness.[14] Their appeal is that of Christ—*it's time to believe.*

To the reading…

Stop Doubting and Believe

A week later his disciples were in the house again, and Thomas was with them. Though the doors were locked, Jesus came and stood among them and said, "Peace be with you!" Then he said to Thomas, "Put your finger here; see my hands. Reach out your hand and put it into my side. Stop doubting and believe."

JOHN 20:26-27

READER: Through locked doors Christ suddenly appeared: seeing, looking, touching, speaking. Words of peace he offered to his disciples. He had risen from the grave, where he had lain dead, so unquestionably dead.
This is not the way of the dead. They do not rise up to live again in light, once death's signatory, Freeze, has seized and fixed their faces.

Around the crosses three Freeze had surely crept, circling all their bases, waiting to leap, sensing time and pulses faint. Then upon the center cross Freeze leapt. Climbing up on crimson stain, Freeze moved to seize the One with the wordy plaque and thorny crown—the envy of the hill. It was time for pulsing to end its marathon of life. No more pulsing, no more coursing of the blood.

Thick darkness draped o'er the land, eclipsing the sun.

VOICE: Where did the sun go? Had it failed to shine, or fallen from the sky?

READER: Fallen from the sky, Voice, no—although this may have been how it seemed. Its darkened drape was a sign signifying that death's Freeze had leapt on the Son of God. Creation had never known itself minus God's Son. The earth trembled, rocks split apart, and tombs broke open. The dead awakened. Upright in their crypts they stood. They, too, were signs signifying that the impossible, the inevitable, could be overcome.

The dead had broken free from Freeze. Into this mysterious, darkened day, the dead, now living, stepped. On soil they walked, with soles miraculously warmed by pulsing blood. The dead were living. Walking, talking—Voice, were they not a peculiar message?

VOICE: Never thought of them as a message. They must have been alarming.

READER: Can you see them moving about in utter wonder?

VOICE: I can see them.

READER: They signified the beginning of the end had come for death. Death's unstoppable reign had been broken.

It was a centurion who stood near the cross on the swaying ground who saw it all. He watched as Mary's son fell silent, and Freeze masked the face of life with death. These dramatic acts occurring signified that the face on the center cross was not that of a normal man.

"When the centurion and those with him who were guarding Jesus saw the earthquake and all that had happened, they were terrified, and exclaimed, 'Surely he was the Son of God!'"

Voice, there on Golgotha's hill, amidst the desperate, dying, sobbing, crying, a surprise arose: A centurion believed in the dying Christ. At Golgotha's hill, amidst the spiking, crucifying, dying, his confession was heard: "Surely he was the Son of God!" *Surely* was the word spoken, Voice, meaning clearly this was not merely a criminal crucified.

Only three people did Christ address from his planks of pain hoisted high. Words he spoke to his mother Mary, the favored one Gabriel had visited in days gone by. Much older now, Mary stood on a hill; she watched her firstborn die. On Golgotha's hill he was openly manifest above the jeering, mocking crowd. Christ also spoke to the disciple standing next to his mother and to the repentant thief. These three, and of course God the Father.

Dying on the cross, Christ's words were few: "I thirst" and "It is finished." These are two quick lines the mocking, gawkers heard. Some words Christ prayed. Just before his death, he prayed to his Father in utter agony. "*Eloi, Eloi, lama sabachthani*"—which means "My God, my God, why have you forsaken me?"

With eyes of coal, death stretched across the figure on the cross. Freeze waited for Christ's departing words and the drop of his head. "Father, into your hands I commit my spirit." Freeze then settled in, drawing every trace of warmth from this One heaven-sent.

That's how it was, Voice. It was over, finished. It was time for the eternity's ancient hourglass, the vial of ages past, to be righted, turned upside down, so to speak. Do you know what I mean, Voice?

VOICE: What was over? What was finished? What do you mean "vial of ages past"?

READER: What was finished? The era without grace, which the blood of a billion goats and bulls could not buy—that was over. The time of ages past, with mystery clasped, hidden fast—that too was over.

VOICE: Mystery clasped…are you sure that's what you mean, Reader?

READER: Yes, Voice, the time of waiting and watching for the Messiah to appear was over. The mystery of redemption was a mystery no more.

VOICE: What else was over?

READER: The torturous pain throbbing through spiked hands and feet—that was over. Not a single word of accusation or bitterness was heard from this one so spiked. Not a syllable of this sort came down from the man who bore the thorny crown.

The supreme message of God was the Son. He was the medium chosen by the Father. A one-of-a-kind medium, a message of reconciliation, redemption, was Christ. In the words of St. Paul, "God was reconciling the world to himself in Christ."

In a word, the message was grace. Submissively, willingly, the Lamb of God died on the cross.

VOICE: What happened to Christ's body hanging there?

READER: Thank you for asking, Voice. It was claimed and taken down. A man named Joseph acquired permission from Pilate to remove the body. Not just anyone could run in and snatch the corpse of Christ.

VOICE: Does it have to be said that way, corpse and all? It sounds…so…I don't know…earthy or unheavenly.

READER: Listen further, Voice. Real it is. That's why the story's there. Joseph was an influential member of the Jewish Sanhedrin and lived in a small town called Arimathea. An unlikely person to claim the body, one would think. Joseph of Arimathea was a man of wealth, a devout individual. A man of smart attire, he surely was.

VOICE: So interesting to consider, when you think about it. What would he have worn on Golgotha's hill?

READER: You ask too much, but ask away. The story does not say. But I can imagine him there: climbing up, hoisting down, and resting the body of Jesus Christ on the ground.

VOICE: Did he believe in the crucified one?

READER: St. Luke describes him with brevity as one who "awaited the kingdom of God." Evening shadows had surely fallen by the time Joseph went to recover Christ's body. The man from Arimathea had an accomplice—a Sanhedrin colleague, a Mr. Nicodemus. He was another man who had been drawn to Christ. Joseph purchased linen cloth for the burial. Nicodemus acquired a "mixture of myrrh and aloes" weighing some thirty-four kilos.

What a peculiar sight they must have been. Minds set on self-imposed obligation, amidst watching eyes they moved, no doubt quietly respectful. For, their hearts were once warmed by the one they had come to lay to rest.

Together, it was they who climbed the wretched hill of death and took down the body. The distinguished pair had become a team. They were claimers, carers, anointers. Can't you see them on the hill, Voice, this Sanhedrin duo in the dim evening hues, moving about, dutifully determined? Their presence—does it not add a heartening lift to this mysterious story of injustice and anguish?

VOICE: Reader, I think you're right. I've never thought of it like that.

READER: This unlikely pair carefully wrapped the body in strips of linen, and then they carried it to a shallow cave—a tomb, it was called. They rolled a large stone over the tomb's entrance. That was their final deed; their job was done. This act of burial kindness admirably sealed these characters in the story.

The full extent of interaction between Joseph, Nicodemus, and Christ is not known. St. John records that Nicodemus once paid Christ a visit. He came around at night to ask some critical questions of this teacher he did not know—though Nicodemus was convinced that Christ was blessed of God. Nicodemus said to Christ that night, "No one could perform the miraculous signs you are doing if God were not with him."

This line prompted a most intriguing conversation between the two concerning the kingdom of God and how it might be entered. Christ explained that entrance to the kingdom of God required a rather radical procedure. He spoke of a spiritual transformation, and used the words *born again*. Ponder it, Voice—born again, born not just once, but born again.

VOICE: I shall.

READER: During their exchange, Christ also spoke prophetically of his crucifixion. He said to Nicodemus, "Just as Moses lifted up the snake in the desert, so the Son of Man must be lifted up, that everyone who believes in him may have eternal life."

Consider it, Voice. Stories, like the one of Moses crafting a serpent and placing it on a pole—how did they come to be? They were woven into ancient texts in a way that allowed Christ to pull and pluck, pick and place, in constructing his Gospel message.

VOICE: Never thought about it that way.

READER: You must, Voice! What is it you want to do with your thinking? Where are you going, Voice? Think while you live, before Freeze comes to seize. I implore you to see beyond your seeing, hear beyond your hearing. How, you may ask? Certain words will help you rise to the challenge.

Again I ask you, Voice, how did these stories old come to be, from which Christ pulled and plucked?

The ancient texts ensured that Christ's message would be layered rich with meaning deep. Ancient stories of this nature are exceedingly clever. A single story, rich with characters and meaning, finds a story of its kind and worth, and the two intertwine. Each story, already rich on its own, becomes exceptionally so when the two are woven together. Fused, they impart far greater depth of meaning than either could do on its own.

VOICE: I see what you mean, Reader; I do.

READER: Voice, this intertwining capacity of verses great says much about why Christ's message was both so radical and so powerful. Soaked in cultures rich, the ancient stories brimmed with meaning. They waited to be chosen, to be woven in, to go calling out.

VOICE: That is exceedingly clever. To think, they lie in wait in story's hold, some quite old, and then in time they intertwine in a story new. Can we talk about this some more?

READER: Certainly, but not just now, Voice. We've left our story waiting. In the tomb, remember, there Christ lay dead, wrapped in linen cloth.

VOICE: You're right. Please carry on. You will, won't you?

READER: In the tomb he lay until the Sabbath passed. Then a new round of God acts began to unfold.

VOICE: God acts, you say…what acts?

READER: Think, listen, and think again.

A violent earthquake shook Jerusalem on the morning of which we speak. Listen to the ancient words, worked into lines, woven into story. "And behold, there was a great earthquake, for an angel of the Lord descended from heaven and came and rolled back the stone, and sat upon it. His appearance was like lightning, and his raiment white as snow."

At this very hour, Mary Magdalene and Mary, the mother of James, were on their way to the tomb to anoint Christ's body with spices. When they arrived, they encountered a pair of angels, who appeared as men in "clothes that gleamed like lighting." The women were terrified and bowed down to the ground.

The angelic messengers said, "Why do you look for the living among the dead? He is not here; he has risen! Remember how he told you, while he was still with you in Galilee: 'The Son of Man must be delivered into the hands of sinful men, be crucified and on the third day be raised again.'" Then they remembered his words.

The women fled the tomb and ran to the apostles with the news. When the disciples heard the report, Peter and a fellow disciple raced to the grave to see for themselves what had taken place. When they arrived at the tomb, they found only strips of linen on the ground, and a folded head cloth nearby.

The two disciples believed what they saw, but it would take time for the ramifications of the event to sink in, to filter through with meaning full. In the words of St. John, "As yet they did not understand the Scripture that he must rise from the dead."

The story of suffering and grief was being divinely infused and choreographed with resurrection light. Throughout the centuries skeptics have scoffed and howled at believing a story that cannot be proven. The issue for many, though, is not so much about proof to be found, as it is the matter of faith that must be placed.

Truth rests in treasure troves, along ancient paths, ready to expend its rewards. This, however, it cannot do if the seeker demands that the treasure prove its worth before taking hold. Twins—skepticism and unbelief—are so easily born. They can chop truth away. Like sharpened knives they cut.

Belief that must pass through the prism of proof before being released can cause a strange disease, something akin to cataracts on the soul. When plucking petals from a rose, there comes a point when the rose is no more. It is the same with the words and story that flow forth from ancient texts of Scripture. Do you want to pluck them away, Voice?

VOICE: No, not me. You must have someone else in mind.

READER: Just checking.

It's often something along these lines that is said in deference to Scripture's offering full. "Oh, that? Don't bother; that's a line for disregard, and you might as well ignore that chunk and this one, too. Take what you want and leave the rest. I'm afraid that with these ancient troves there is more to disrespect than respect. We have other words; why worry? You must learn to skip around, taking in what seems to fit the mood and the circumstance."

Believe, Voice. Once resurrected from Freeze's brace, Christ appeared face to face in numerous settings over a period of forty days. Ranking these appearances in terms of importance is not possible.

Surmise and choose, rank the order we can, but it is a bit like twiddling with twigs in a forest. Look at the broader picture; look taller, higher, and consider. Interplay between heaven and earth shaped all the events with divine intent, and there was much at work beyond knowing. This was no one-time incident of minor note. Divine drama was unfolding in culture and time; the events were being storied for eternity.

The story was still being shaped as the resurrected Christ began to appear. The disciples, the chosen repository of Christ's message, were in a state of collective confusion and needed to be sorted out. The apostle Peter, only days earlier, swore he did not know Christ. At the time of the resurrection, he is seen as bewildered—running around, dashing about.

Many of Christ's disciples were befuddled and perplexed by the stories and rumors swirling around Jerusalem. This was clearly the case of the two disciples who were traveling on the road to Emmaus. They walked along, harnessed in discussion, when suddenly Christ appeared. These two were not part of the inner circle of twelve. They were part of a larger group of disciples that had come to follow Christ.

Christ suddenly slipped alongside them on the road and asked, "What are you discussing together as you walk along?" With downcast faces, they paused. Then the one named Cleopas said, "Are you the only visitor to Jerusalem who does not know the things that have happened there in these days?" With anonymity and brevity Christ replied, "What things?"

"About Jesus of Nazareth," they said. "He was a prophet, powerful in word and deed before God and all the people. The chief priests and our rulers handed him over to be sentenced to death, and they crucified him. But we had hoped that he was the one who was going to redeem Israel."

Christ bluntly said, "How foolish you are, and how slow of heart to believe all that the prophets have spoken! Did not the Christ have to suffer these things and then enter his glory?" And beginning with Moses and all the prophets, he explained to them what was said in all the Scriptures concerning himself. Christ still had not disclosed who he was.

VOICE: You mean, Christ walked right there beside them, and they had no idea who he was?

READER: That seems to be the case. The two disciples, in Christ's own words, were "slow of heart." Their spiritual perception was sluggish. As the three approached the village where the two disciples stayed, they invited Christ to dinner. While seated at their table, he gave thanks and broke bread. At that point the two recognized Christ.

Instantly he disappeared, and they were left asking each other, "Were not our hearts burning within us while he talked with us on the road and opened the Scriptures to us?" The two hurriedly returned to Jerusalem and found Christ's apostles and conveyed the news, saying, "It is true."

The forty-day period following Christ's resurrection may appear less crucial than all that occurred during Christ's ministry. These days, however, were as vital as all the rest. The prophetic word of Zechariah speaks: "I will strike the Shepherd and the sheep will be scattered." On the Emmaus road the first pair of scattered sheep were found.

With so many sheep being scattered about, it's hard to imagine that Satan would let such an opportunity go untested. Satan had to be somewhere—why not near the action of the resurrected Christ?

Plot turned around to his left and nodded to Brother Witness, who was already rising to his feet. He gently nodded in response, took a single step into the room, and began to speak. His rhythm was buoyant, his intonation precise, his pace lively.

LUCIFER'S DEVOTEE: Master, Lucifer, whatta we do now? The Word has up and resurrected.

LUCIFER: Shut up, you imbeciles, all of you, not a word. I've got to breathe. This resurrection surge has created some kind of vacuum in the spiritual sphere, some new strain of spiritchitis. I've got to cough. It's causing my membranes to flutter at lightning speed. This is too much.

Stand back! I'll go cough 'round those busted-up tombs. Maybe I can scare some of them come-alive fleshies back into their boxes. Did you see how stupid they looked? "What happened? Where are we?" Stupid dummies. Some of the religious lot was trying to put the blame on me. Talk about idiots! I put 'em down; I don't wake 'em up, the religious nut cases.

I'll be back in three lightning strikes. Meanwhile you two uglies go down to Golgo's dungeon and pull me out a new backrider. I thought we'd be camping out here for a while. Not so with the Word floating about all resurrected.

Now, form a circle. Get down on your knees and lock your arms. Everybody facing out. I want to see 360 degrees of demon eyes. Okay, now make your eyes bulge real big, like owl eyes. Ah, look at that, my defensive watch. If any of you sees anything, anything whatsoever, hum the code. Watch and wait. I'm going. But while I'm away, I'm watching. My eyes know no visual distance.

I'm moving, watching. I see you, as if I've never left. Oh, how pleased I am to see my band of chosen devotees interlocked arm-in-arm, obeying my orders. So stiffened tight they are, a single ring of bulging eyes. What a battalion, a buttress.

Now from a distance far, do you hear my whisper, devotees? I'm whispering, but watching, still. What a sight to witness—oh, how adoringly you recognize my whisper.

I'm watching. Can you hear the delightful sound of my cough? Like a huge mortar being fired through a wall of mud. Did you feel the vibrations?

Okay, I'm back. Good cough. Have you seen the Word?

Bad news, by the way. Get up, idiots. Relax your eyes. Listen. The come-alive fleshies that sprung their graves, they've heard that the Word went down, preaching, testifying to all the old fleshies stowed away. That's what woke 'em up in their boxes—his force swooping down and the exclamation of the underworld when he appeared.

They said legions of angels were stretched into infinity. It's not fair rushing in like that all unannounced, beaming light into all that rich, black-shelled darkness. He's probably already reached the other side of the abyss by now.

Does the abyss have a far side? Shut up—that's not a question! I was just having a fractional blink. A tiny blink…I've got the concern of the whole nether-world looking in my direction. There's a lot going on. Who else can they turn to when the universe gets all turned upside down? Hey, what's that quizzical look on your faces? That better not be doubt. The only thing I hate worse than a doubting devotee is a double-doubting devotee. Don't you ever be a-doubting! Devotees believe! Look to me—Lucifer.

I know what happens in the abyss. Who do you think you're looking at, imbeciles? You want to know about the abyss? I'll tell you about the abyss. The abyss is forever expanding, but the Word raced to the edge of the expansion; he turned around and spoke. The Word and I AM halted the expansion for an hour, just like they stopped the sun back in Elijah's day.

When the Word spoke, his words were like streams of light racing in the opposite direction. That's what happened. Imagine all those spirits tumbling and rolling in his direction! Forever they'll tumble, hearing: "I am the way, the truth and the life." It's ghastly. He's not playing by the rules. The Word should have telegraphed his message—taken it slow, not rushed in like that.

Look at me—Lucifer. I'm like no other. I'm the delusion, the deception, and the death, but I don't make a doctrine out of it. Narrow—who wants narrow? Not with me—broad are my gates, all manner of gates, with a plethora of signs and symbols so people can find their way in.

Come on in, that's my motto. I favor the inclusive approach. No sneaking around, hiding my message for ages in scrolls, like cages. Just think how much better my way is, so much more appealing, truly universal. A sprinkle of phi-losophy here, a scoop of superstition there, a dash of doctrine mixed in—that's what fleshies want. That's what they crave, not narrow gates, getting their sides all scarred up trying to enter.

It's not right making fleshies so they're able to see all kinds of ways, wanting all kinds of gates, and then torturing 'em if they don't go through the narrow gate. Why didn't I AM just make single-minded one-gaters? He let his creative prowess get out of hand. From the very outset, fleshies were out of whack. They're miserable creatures—malformed they are.

I'm just saying! I want spirits drawn by adoration—sure, just like I AM—but we have scads trailing in that don't even know they're following. That's the beauty of it, the liberty of it. A free-flowing kingdom…roam and romp as you please. That's the spirit. My followers follow by rejecting. Fleshies are a rejecting kind. That's all I ask: Just reject the ways of the Word and I AM, and you're in. Believe whatever you wish. Any gate will do.

All this spiritchitis will destroy the cosmos. Nothing will be the same. If too much of their way gets going, everything's gonna get off kilter. I AM, the Word, and the Third have come up with a master plan. I've figured it out. They're instituting this new deal called spirit and truth. Guess they're not satisfied with the fleshies doing sacrifices.

They made the rules, not the fleshies. As far as I'm concerned, that was the only thing they ever did that made any sense—the killing, the blood, the sacrifices. Ah, brutal butchery, all that helpless groaning and travail. It's been wonderful to watch down through the centuries. It's what I call real, honest misery. Not some flimflamsey offering of grain, but of blood. The fleshies have been awash in it for years.

We hate everything. Remember that. You know how you demons all gather each year to renew your vows and slash each other? Even that is changed. We'll have to add a new line, because of the Word rising up like he has. You're the first to hear it. After we chant, "We hate everything," we'll have to add the line, "And we hate this day most of all." This is a wretched day. This is the worst day I've ever known.

Got news for you, though. Just because the Three dreamed up this spirit-and-truth deal doesn't mean it's gonna work. Who was it dreamed up the Garden, hmm? They discussed it, all around. "Let us make man in our image." That's what they said. Right there, all three are implicated in the mess. Fleshies—I hate every one of 'em. I've seen a good number of 'em bearing my likeness, but that doesn't matter. They never should have been, stupid mud cakes.

I've got to figure out our next moves. We need to get some wars going on 'round here—shake everything up; get stuff buried in the dust. Resurrection: a bogus idea, it is. Ah, that's it! That's what we can begin to spread right now, right here, today.

See if you can say it with conviction—like this, slow with meaning: "Bogus,

bogus, bogus." Push out your lips, and then say it with a deep guttural sound. Try it, and don't look confused. You double basses, you try it. Ah, nice, I like that. We can fill the atmosphere.

Oh, you two back there. Come here, Backrider, you fool. Hop up, shut it. There's a bad case of spiritchitis going around. Train your dungeon eyes on anything that moves. This spiritchitis force is atomic in nature.

Here's what I want you to do. The twelve of you practice a new bogus chant. I want it simple, just: "Bogus, bogus, bogus, don't be a fool, it's not real; bogus, bogus, bogus, don't be a fool, it's not real." That's it—now you think you imbeciles can do that? I want lots of cadence, all low, and from there descending.

While I've been instructing you, I've received word that the Word has just been spotted. He was walking on the road to Emmaus. He must be confused; his bunch of brats are all around here, so what's he doing there? Come on, Backrider, let's you and me practice the chant as we chase.

You lot, form that circle. Start that chant. Surprise me when I return with the extent of your tonal mastery. I'm counting on you. You're the fount of my delusional flow.

Come on, Backrider, let's scoot.

Brother Witness ended with a smile, as he moved his piercing eyes slowly across the room. Without glancing behind him, he took one backward step and confidently sat down in his chair in the middle of the doorway.

READER: Within forty days after his resurrection, Christ would ascend. It was crucial to gather the flock and rivet their focus on carrying the Gospel message from Jerusalem to the ends of the earth. The disciples needed unswerving conviction concerning their message.

The story of Christ cannot be boxed in or left stratified among religions. The core of his message disavows it. The central message of the cross is that "God was reconciling the world to himself in Christ." Voice, the words speak of the world complete, do they not?

VOICE: Your point's well taken.

READER: The message is not merely about a peculiar people in a peculiar place. The story embraces everyone, everywhere—every human being, past, present, and future. The story is not small and limiting. It continues even now to unfurl and expand like the universe itself. Everyone is encompassed in the divine drama—even you, Voice.

VOICE: I am?

READER: Certainly—the story's scope is meant for everyone everywhere. The all-encompassing force of redemption rushes into the universe and all it contains. It cannot be stopped. It will not be halted. There is no void, no space, no other world. There is no place to go where the power of reconciliation does not flow. Certainly the force can be denied, declined, rejected, but that's not escape.

The story of Christ is not unlike the tale of the trees speaking to one another in the Garden of Eden. The trees used to love to call out to each other. In doing so, they'd always identify their location in proximity to the tree of life. Christ, who hung on a cross, is, as it were, the tree of life. Christ's story defines everyone's story, not pugnaciously out of a spirit of contempt, but out of relationship to God. God subsumes all of what religion is, and Christ is God.

After disappearing from Emmaus, Christ appeared to the apostles that evening in Jerusalem. The apostles had received the report by the two disciples from Emmaus. But when Christ appeared they still thought he was a ghost. Christ encouraged them, saying, "Look at my hands and my feet. It is I myself! Touch me and see. A ghost does not have flesh and bones, as you see I have."

During this first visit, the apostle Thomas was not present. When Thomas heard the news, he told the apostles that unless he could actually "see the nail marks in his hands" and put his finger where the nails had been, he would "not believe."

The following week Christ again appeared to his disciples, and this time Thomas was present. They were all gathered in a room, and the door was locked. Suddenly Christ was in their midst. Christ invited Thomas to examine his hands and his side, and then he said to him, "Stop doubting and believe." Thomas did not attempt to examine; he simply replied, "My Lord and my God."

Christ then addressed a magnanimous point. He said to Thomas, "Because you have seen me, you have believed. Blessed are those who have not seen and yet have believed." This was the great mission now apparent. Who out there among the vast unknown, having not seen, would actually believe?

Soon stories of Christ were reported, collected, and written down. Words would jump into lines; lines would form messages-making stories. The stories intertwined, fueling thoughts, filling hearts and minds. In this charted course of words newly scribed, it would seem most unreasonable to conclude that Christ would have adopted a laissez-faire approach.

The one who placed so much weight on the Scriptures knew all the elements that would come to be the Gospel story. There was no chance or happenstance. The events during this forty-day period, like all the rest, were gathered, and they entered the Gospel story with multilayered meaning and divine intent. Christ knew precisely which words would jump into lines, forming messages.

A line of no small import is, "Stop doubting and believe." Is it not so, Voice? It is. Indeed, it is.

St. John writes, "Jesus did many other miraculous signs in the presence of his disciples, which are not recorded in this book. But these are written that you may believe that Jesus is the Christ, the Son of God."

Those common men, chosen by Christ to tell the Gospel story, would soon be sorely tested. It was time for those who had been "slow of heart," confused, or somehow dismayed, to fully awaken. It was a time for doubt to flee and belief to rise.

Their opportunity would soon come. The day would be Pentecost.

Words matter…some far more than others.

Stop doubting and believe.

JESUS CHRIST OF NAZARETH, SPEAKING TO THE APOSTLE THOMAS,
JERUSALEM, CIRCA AD 32

READING TEN

————◆————

SETTING THE SCENE

To Reading Ten of Twelve we've now arrived. Given the bountiful store of stories in Scripture's hold, would not Ten of One Hundred be more appropriate? Surely that is the case.

Yet, Reading Ten on the *Redemption* trail it is. Lines await you, formed by words not propelled to hound you. Why so much hounding anyway? Sort of everywhere, it seems, there is a lot of propagation, propelled by unending mediation.

The words of Scripture are sent to heal, not to steal and deal. God's thoughts are there for the eyes of the heart to see. If you might, think about it ever so deeply.

"God thinks. Does he not? Certainly he does. God thinks in ways beyond knowing, thoughts ever flowing." These little lines present themselves as the opening of Reading Ten. Have they gotten ahead of themselves? Yes. But no. They prompt with good intention.

The setting is Three Pond Cottage, with its twin fireplaces. Please have a seat. Today's Readers are Brothers Narrative and Script.[15] Narrative is offering a warm welcome. As Narrative continues to speak, Brother Script gives a faint smile, accompanied by a subtle nod, and begins to move purposefully along the wall behind his colleague.

He makes his way to the far corner of the room. There, he opens a small closet door, reaches in, and produces a tall, narrow, wooden stool with a sizeable round top. As he sets it in place, the stool's blunt wooden legs club the pine floor. He places the stool as near to the wall as possible. Brother Script gracefully scoots onto the stool and presses the length of his back against the wall.

It would appear Brother Script is ready for Reading Ten. And so are we.

To the reading…

Piercing Words

*"Therefore let all the house of Israel know for certain that God has
made him both Lord and Christ—this Jesus whom you crucified."
Now when they heard this, they were pierced to the heart, and said to
Peter and the rest of the apostles, "Brethren, what shall we do?"*

ACTS 2:36-37

READER: God thinks. Does he not? Certainly he does. God thinks in ways beyond knowing, thoughts ever flowing. Creating, communicating, ordering, searching, weighing. In God's reckoned way, he said this to that, and light was let; the formless formed; the earth was born. Divine thoughts through and through give equilibrium its balance, hold everything together. God never quit, never went away. He's always there.

VOICE: Reader, you speak of *there*, but where might God be?

READER: Where he's always been, of course. He's there. He's there in his realm of thinking, although presumption extraordinaire is the mark of anyone who has a great deal to say about what God thinks. Scripture says, "God is in heaven, and you are here on earth. So let your words be few."

VOICE: Does that include us, this "words be few"?

READER: Voice, I do believe it does. One cannot outpace the velocity of words streaking forth from Scripture's store. Once spoken, penned, and scribed, there is no fleeing what they say, no flight of fancy where they do not reach and apply.

It's impossible to fathom the fill of God's thoughts. In God's sphere, time does not exist. There is no tick or tock, no time of clock. This thought alone should be enough to quiet any boast of knowing much about what cannot be known. Not to say, though, that God's thoughts are beyond grasp, beyond the pale of knowing. No, this is certainly not the case. God's thoughts are known, some that is. Such thoughts are clothed in words.

Words are little modules of meaning. They dress a thought and fasten it to other thoughts expressed in other words. God allowed certain of his thoughts to be dressed and buttoned up this way. They convey a good deal about what God thinks and feels, what he wants to say.

God's full measure of thinking, though, they do not reveal. Who but God could understand the full press of how God thinks? Nevertheless, what's been clothed and buttoned up in Scripture's text is not a token stitch of fashioned words. It's a reservoir exceedingly rich. The reservoir reveals that God thinks a great deal about the poor, the oppressed, and all those enormous mounds and mountains of human need.

Some find it hard to believe that God is actually there, let alone that he cares so deeply. Many who think along these lines have this notion that God is looking for human beings to knock around, to cast away because of sinful maladies and wayward gaits.

VOICE: Could it be so, God desiring to knock people about? Some sinners, you know, are not so conventional and compliant.

READER: Oh, dear me, so they aren't. Sinners there are, but consider Moses the murderer. Did he not come down from Mt. Sinai with the Law of God in his hands? St. Paul was once murderous Saul, full of hate and rage.

Be therefore gentle on this matter of wayward gates. Be, shall we say, slow to speak. Cast not the first stone. Are you a stone-thrower, a knife-thrower, Voice, riding some high tide to tidy up the world?

VOICE: No, I didn't mean that God should knock people about.

READER: So you are not against wretched creatures, burdened and bent, whomone day may find grace by what heaven has sent?

VOICE: Certainly not. Who am I to choose recipients of grace?

READER: Good, Voice. You're the kind of Voice we need. This is not to say that God is squeamish about calling sinners sinners, just as he might call a squid a squid.

On the trajectory of the heart God looks, seeing rather differently than the eyes of men. God looks to see if the heart bends in his direction.

The person, of course, who believes God is not will find it rather hard to yield to nothingness. Such a person is like a ball in play. It's pitched, tossed, and batted around, but all the while it argues. There is no game. It doesn't exist.

If not a ball, then let it be an apple bursting with life. It ripens with seeds firmly couched within. It sways in the breeze; leaves brush its skin. It hangs from a limb. The apple ripe looks to the tree and says, "You do not exist. There is no tree."

Notions such as these should not be, but they are. Such stubborn simplicity has a lot to do with human complexity. This is why God's thoughts wrapped in words can be so helpful. A line from St. Paul reads, "No eye has seen, no ear has heard, no mind has conceived what God has prepared for those who love him."

VOICE: This line doesn't sound like God waiting to avenge.

READER: Ah, Voice, that's the tone we seek to settle human need. It was the prophet Isaiah who first spoke the line, "No eye has seen, nor ear has heard."

VOICE: Reader, what was Isaiah thinking by saying no eye has seen, nor ear has heard?

READER: Most important it is, Voice. The object of Isaiah's prophecy was Jesus Christ. In Isaiah's day, Christ was not seen, not heard. He was the One prepared and promised. Christ was the realization of the promise, the One unseen to see, the One unheard to hear. He was the One the world awaited.

Centuries after Isaiah's day, St. Paul inserted the prophet's line in a letter. The day was new. Grace had dawned. Paul wrote from the other side of history's wall. He spoke of the promise fulfilled in the person of Christ. God's hidden promise was hidden no more. What was once invisible, inaudible, and inconceivable became visible, audible, and conceivable in the person of Christ.

Scripture attests that Jesus Christ was born in the fullness of time. The phrase, "fullness of time"—does it not convey a sense of the world waiting for time to fill? There was, after all, a great deal of time before time was full.

VOICE: What happened before time was full?

READER: Voice, before time filled to full, time was filling. The world waited! Before civilization was, the world waited. Before floodwaters rose, the world waited. Before the Israelites crossed a parted sea, the world waited.

While waiting, the living watched the dying die and be laid away. The dying watched the living watch them die, knowing that soon the living, too, would be the dying. Without ever seeing time fill, the living died. On and on they died. They waited.

VOICE: Reader, I'm a bit confused. What was it the world wanted? Christ, right?

READER: Voice, confused you're not. The world wanted to see what Mary saw, the child in a manger, the eyes of redemption, the child resting in her arms. When the child looked into his mother's eyes, waiting was no more. The world had waited for time to fill and reveal the object of its waiting. The world had waited for its Messiah; he came. Time was full, and so too was the waiting.

The Son of God appeared, died, and rose, but before ascending he said to his disciples, "Wait!"

VOICE: What for? And where were they to wait?

READER: In Jerusalem, for the outpouring of the Holy Spirit they were to wait. They would wait until Pentecost.

VOICE: SO THERE WAS MORE WAITING?

READER: Yes, but waiting of another kind. Pentecost was an essential part of the divine mystery hidden for ages past. In God's great redemptive plan it was always there, coupled in and attached directly to this measure called fullness of time. In the drama great, Pentecost was placed as the major act following Christ's ascension. Without it the drama would have been a muddle.

The outpouring of the Holy Spirit had everything to do with Christ's command to go here, there, and everywhere making disciples. The disciples were to go out bearing the words of Christ.

VOICE: Were Christ's words the piercing kind?

READER: Definitely so. Listen to what St. Matthew had to say concerning Christ and the Sermon on the Mount: "And when Jesus finished these sayings, the crowds were astonished at his teaching, for he taught them as one who had authority, and not as their scribes."

This is how it was; from place to place Christ went, speaking piercing words.

VOICE: Why are words so important?

READER: Voice, dear me! Why, you ask? Words are the substance on which faith is perched. Words are pegs on which faith hangs its hat. An ancient line of Scripture speaks about the importance of perching faith. Listen: "Now faith is being sure of what we hope for and certain of what we do not see." On such words faith is perched.

When it comes to one's faith, one should be sure of words picked for perching. Christ spoke much about the worth of words. He once told his disciples, "The words I have spoken to you are spirit and they are life." These very words— and bushels more—Christ commissioned the disciples to take to the entire world.

To every tribe and tongue they were to go. Yet the specific commission of going to Jerusalem, Judea, Samaria, and to the ends of the earth the disciples only heard after the resurrection.

VOICE: Why were they to go to the ends of earth?

READER: They were to go, speaking out, casting out, and making disciples. They were to go here, there, and everywhere, and then on to where they hadn't been. The end of their going they would never reach, but they were to go and keep going. They would be imprisoned, beaten, stoned, and some even martyred, but they went. With words they went. Words they carried.

The prophet Isaiah foresaw that this would come to pass. "I will make you a light for the Gentiles, that you may bring my salvation to the ends of the earth." The light to the Gentiles of which Isaiah spoke is Christ. It was up to the disciples to make this light known, to explain who Christ was, how he did what he did, and why he said what he said. This was the depth of the stage on which they stood. They were the chosen cast to move out and begin the journey to the ends of the earth.

Voice, thrilling, is it not?

VOICE: Not so sure about the martyred part.

READER: The disciples would not go alone. Just prior to Christ's ascension, he instructed his disciples to go to Jerusalem and wait for the Father's promise. Christ explained that they would be "baptized by the Holy Spirit." Specifically, Christ told them, "Stay in the city until you have been clothed with power from on high."

To the ends of the earth they were to go, but before going, they were to wait. Go. Wait. Go wait. What do you want to do, Voice, go or wait?

VOICE: I believe both.

READER: So very right you are. Waiting had everything to do with going. In an upper room they gathered. They prayed and waited. For exactly what, they weren't sure, but there they waited. They waited for some kind of clothing with power.

More than a hundred people huddled together in the upper room, awaiting Christ's promise. Mary, Christ's mother, and his brothers were among them. St. Luke records, "They all joined together constantly in prayer." Christ's ascension had happened more than a week before, but still they waited.

Heavenly hosts must have been peering down from the ledge of paradise, yearning, stretching, watching, as the Holy Spirit descended on that room in Jerusalem. St. Luke describes what happened. "Suddenly a sound like the blowing of a violent wind came from heaven and filled the whole house where they were sitting. They saw what seemed to be tongues of fire that separated and came to rest on each of them. All of them were filled with the Holy Spirit and began to speak in other tongues as the Spirit enabled them."

Outside, the crowd heard the sounds emanating out of the upper room. They rushed to the site, bewildered by what they saw and heard. Everyone inside the room was declaring the wonders of God. The phenomenon embraced every language spoken in the crowd, which was diverse. This was Pentecost. People from throughout the Roman and Parthian Empires had traveled to Jerusalem for the festival.

Tongues of fire separated and rested on each person in the upper room. This included Peter and Jesus' mother and brothers. Every person who occupied space in the upper room had this experience.

Soon those inside appeared to the crowd. "Peter stood up with the eleven, raised his voice and addressed the crowd, 'Fellow Jews and all of you who live in Jerusalem, let me explain this to you. Listen carefully to what I say.'"

VOICE: Reader, wait—did Peter have his message prepared for the occasion?

READER: How could he? No one in the upper room knew what was going to happen. Peter's words were inspired, those of a man compelled. The fire of God had fallen on Peter, and he moved accordingly. Peter's message was undoubtedly the most important of his life.

Christ and the prophets had been carried along by the Holy Spirit; Peter would need the same manifestation as he faced the bewildered crowd. Peter was no Christlike parrot with a ready speech. There was no precedent for what to say. There was no precedent event for the outpouring of the Holy Spirit.

Christ had promised the disciples, "[The Spirit] will bring me glory by telling you whatever he receives from me."

Unswervingly, Peter stood to address the crowd. His thoughts swirled, mixed, mingled, and probed his heart. The crowd watched. Peter's colleagues looked in his direction. Suddenly there was a thought that wrapped itself in words: "Fellow Jews, and all of you who live in Jerusalem..."

Then a second thought, followed by a third, came forth, wrapped in words. "Let me explain this to you. Listen carefully to what I say." That's the way it went. Thoughts were wrapped in words, words formed lines, lines flowed forth into hearts and minds. When thoughts find words, that's how they act. They move forth, claiming this and that.

Peter's words claimed much, including being the way to God. There was not the slightest pause or hesitation on Peter's part. He stood, raised his voice, and addressed the crowd. Out of bewilderment emerged words of a certain kind, the kind on which faith is perched, the kind on which faith hangs its hat.

Empowered, impassioned, and transformed, Peter, the former fisherman, stood deep on God's stage. In his new vocation, Peter cast a line. "Listen carefully," he said. "These men are not drunk as you suppose. It's only nine in the morning!"

Morning. It was a time of simmering festival scents wafting through the air, a time when eyes are open wide, when minds are fresh. That's the hour it was when Peter stepped up to speak. This morning debut was the first step on the journey to the ends of the earth. It started there.

Morning. That's when the fire fell, and people heard what they'd never heard.

VOICE: What did they hear? What was it?

READER: A praying, a praising, a new kind of speaking in other tongues—that's what they heard.

VOICE: Did Peter explain what it was?

READER: Yes. Peter crafted his message as he was carried along by the Holy Spirit. Another thought flowed, bringing forth the ancient words of Joel.

Joel's words spoke to the crowd's bewilderment: "In the last days, God says, I will pour out my Spirit on all people. Your sons and daughters will prophesy, your young men will see visions, your old men will dream dreams. Even on my servants, both men and women, I will pour out my Spirit in those days, and they will prophesy."

These words from former days were God's thoughts from former days. Now Peter, who had become a new kind of fisherman, was fastening Joel's words to his, strengthening his line with this choice of prophetic verse. Peter had grasped the prophecy of old. It was unfolded and folded into its awaited story. Words of old became new. Their meaning became exponential, as the words were buttoned up and dispatched live into the crowd.

The final line Peter cast from Joel was, "And everyone who calls on the name of the Lord will be saved." Peter next spoke about the man of miracles, wonders, and signs accredited by God. He spoke of Christ, Jesus of Nazareth. This brought a startling twist to Peter's message.

Without apology, Peter implicated the crowd in Christ's crucifixion. Listen to what he said: "And you, with the help of wicked men, put him to death by nailing him to the cross. But God raised him from the dead."

Peter followed the accusation by quoting from the Psalms. He chose the prophetic words of David. "I saw the Lord always before me. Because he is at my right hand, I will not be shaken. Therefore my heart is glad and my tongue rejoices; my body also will rest in hope, because you will not abandon me to the realm of the dead, you will not let your holy one see decay. You have made known to me the paths of life; you will fill me with joy in your presence."

Peter's choice of words was a masterstroke of meaning and association. The psalm was attributed to King David, but it reads in the first person, as if spoken by Christ. This conveys a sense of Christ's presence at Pentecost, almost as if Christ were there speaking with Peter.

Peter stressed the significance of the passage, attesting that David died and was buried, and therefore could not be the holy one who did not see decay. It was Christ, Peter declared. Peter then confessed that he had actually seen the resurrected Christ, and he claimed that Christ was, at that very moment, "exalted to the right hand of God."

Peter concluded his message by saying, "Therefore let all Israel be assured of this: God has made this Jesus, whom you crucified, both Lord and Christ." Peter's message was a collective force. Christ poured out the Holy Spirit; the Holy Spirit anointed Peter. The prophet Joel and the psalmist David had spoken long ago, led by the Spirit of God. Peter gathered in the words and buttoned them together with his own. A magnificent message was made.

The ingredients and elements of Peter's message were not whipped up in the upper room early on Pentecost morn. The words flowed together in a divine construct of message, veering not a jot from the central character in the story, Jesus Christ.

This compiling construct of words through cultures and time speaks, does it not, Voice?

VOICE: To what?

READER: It speaks to the matter of God's hourglass taking time to fill with time. To the heart of our reading the message goes. The people in the crowd were profoundly moved, convicted. Peter's words pierced their hearts, and they said to him and the other apostles, "Brothers, what should we do?" Peter implored them to repent and be baptized in the name of Jesus Christ for the forgiveness of their sins.

Peter promised that they, too, would receive the gift of the Holy Spirit. He claimed the gift was for Jews and Gentiles alike; it was for everyone who was willing to call on the name of the Lord. Some 3,000 people responded to Peter's plea. They were baptized and joined those following Christ and his teachings.

Truth is a remarkable force, Voice. Truth speaks a language of its own, but it's understood in every language. It's universally recognized because it speaks to the heart and not just the mind. Hearts were pierced in the crowd because of the truth conveyed in the message.

Pentecost was, in some ways, like a divinely orchestrated commencement for the disciples. They were commissioned to take Christ's message into the world. It was the going after the waiting. They were to go here, there, and everywhere. Then they were to go everywhere in between; they were to go where they had yet to go. The aim of going was to propagate and populate the world with Christ-followers, people who would believe his words and do Christlike deeds.

The commission meant that there would be a lot of words calling out and casting out. Incredibly bold was this commission by Christ. Regardless of how Pentecost is viewed, the day proved to be a rather auspicious occasion for many—and an inauspicious occasion for others. The disciples and those in the upper room must have been thrilled and overjoyed by what transpired. The religious elite, on the other hand, certainly would have been rattled and disturbed by the day's events.

Not to be forgotten, of course, is the ruler of the air. Was he there? Who's to say? Satan certainly would not want a world full of words calling out, casting out.

In this regard, it is not a stretch at all to imagine Satan creeping about in some shadowy form or another. He could well have been invisibly present there in the crowd when the fire fell at nine o'clock on Pentecost morn.

Narrative turned to his far left and nodded confidently to Brother Script. Brother Script slid off his stool, and then stood erect. He turned to the right, centering his frame in the room of faces. With certain depth and ample volume, he spoke.

LUCIFER: What's that sound? Stand back. Give me room, my devotees. Never, ever nudge Lucifer, my demon core. I've turned demons into burnt toast, charred crust, for nudging me. Lucifer nudges, not you.

That doesn't sound like a normal breeze blowing. It's a rushing, gushing sound. And that—that's not the pleasant sound of churning viperfish in my ears. What's that? It's some kind of whopping gibberish. They're all speaking in fleshy languages.

Whoa, bitter beasts, we're talking about falling fire, tongues dancing, the fleshy kind of tongues. I've got a very underbelly feeling about all of this. This is not at all right, not at all. All this compounding alimentation is gonna cause a storm severe, a terrible case of spiritchitis. It's gonna flow like molten lava.

Look out, devotees—here comes the crowd. What's up? Whatta they want? That's not a question! Doesn't that stupid crowd know that this festival is for all the old-timing ways? It's got nothing to do with the Word. It's for those orthodox nutties with bangles and tassel tails.

Just look out across that crowd. What do you see? Speak not! I'll tell you what you see. You see a gathering of muddy brains, brains that come from dirt. You see that man there and that woman? Let 'em trace their ancestry; the last line on the papyrus will be mud.

I hate to see fleshies in a crowd. All that skin in one place, stretched over blood and bones, it's so utterly repulsive. Idiots, thousands of them, and there they are running up to see what those rhubarb roots in the upper room have to say. Sure, they want to see what the falling fire and whooping is all about. Those root heads can't offer ya nothing, you dumb clucks. Their leader's gone home. He's up and ascended.

Whoa, here comes the Rock, the disciple the Word renamed. Let's remain invisible, incognizable, but I can't resist yelling as if he could hear me. It helps relieve the symptoms of my spiritchitis. "Hey Rock, came out of the cold, did ya? Where's your rooster? I heard you was gonna start selling roosters down in the marketplace, along with rhubarb. You won't last—you and that scraggly lot babbling all about. You're all under some hypnotic spell. Get out your fishing pole; go buy yourself some new hooks. Give it up—get back to where you belong, to what you know."

Shut it, imbeciles. Rock's beginning to speak. He's the optic of my distilling. I'll tell you what let's do—let's creep around to the east side so we can get a profile view of the crowd, as well as of Rock. We need to see if Rock is stimulating the crowd, so scrutinize, peer into their eyes.

Devotees, listen up. This is big, really big. Keep sniffing the air. Beware of anything and everything. This wind and fire extravaganza is not by the order of fleshies, I can tell you that. This is by the confluence of I AM, the Word, and the Third. They're trying to inaugurate this new spirit-and-truth deal, the one I've been telling you about. Now, let's move in around. There, that's better.

Shut it, I said. Rock's speaking. What's he saying? Old words from Joel? They're pulling out all the stops. They've been in there over a week cooking up this concoction of words. That's them. They'll mix this with that, spit and splat, and pull any kind of rabbit out of a hat. Then when the crowd gets all stoked up, all foggy-eyed and fuzzy-minded, they'll say this means that and that means this. It's all a bunch of ostrich eggs, if you ask me. Scramble, ramble; dish 'em up.

There they go again with the same old weepy story, the cross. Oh, I don't know if I can bear it; over and over they talk about it. Will there ever be an end to this saga? It's done. Don't they get it? They're gonna drown creation itself with that long, drawn-out drama. The Word was spiked. He was down and out. Then up he came, and now this.

How many words you want to use, telling your story, hmm? Verbose fleshies. You want to fill the whole world with them. Why don't you try sowing corn instead? That kind of chuckles my ribs. I can see old Rock and them spreading corn seeds. Quiet, idiots! Don't laugh so loud. This place is too spiritually charged. There are a lot of angels about—there's gotta be.

There Rock won't let up. Now he's quoting words from King David. Remember him—the harpist king? Whoa, Rock, that's bold! He's telling the crowd they helped drive the spikes through the Word. Hey, hold on a minute. Look at them fleshies' eyes. They're letting those words soak in, go down their shafts. Their hearts are gonna be all flopping about.

Fire falling, wind, you idiots. Can't you see? My stitchery just stitched this together. This is not some little rally speech or sideshow. This is the disciples' commencement. This is their coming out. You know what else? I'll tell you, enrich you. This is all down to the Third, the One that makes the Three three.

This isn't fair, the Third swooping down like this. He ought to stay up there in the heavenly realms where he belongs. They're moving fleshies into the spiritual sphere, full force-like. This is what I've been foretelling. This is the beginning of the new-age deal the Three cooked up.

Let me tell you something, devotees. I'm the chief foreteller of all tells. Lucifer has the foresight to see into the corridors of time. The future is already happening. While we're hanging out here, it's happening there, but we gotta be here before we get there. It will be waiting for us when we get there.

Anyway, by peering into the corridors, I can read the news 1,000 or 2,000 years from now, as if it were here today. Certainly I can. It's easy. I also know the true makeup and complexion of these fleshies. I see days, long stretched out from now, when the inventive fleshies will find ways of communicating at lightning speed, like we do. They're smart dummies.

When that day comes, and it surely will—I'm seeing it; I'm saying it—that's a day of great promise for us and our message of engagement. Why? Don't ask me, because I'll tell you why. In those days, fleshies will be saying so many things in so many ways, they won't know who's saying what to whom. It'll be pick and choose, paste and haste, skip and dip—and we will crack the whip.

Don't look at me with those dopey, confused eyes, my devotees. Words, images, and sounds will be pulling down, swirling 'round, jousting, rousting. What a sweet day of confusion it will be! Oh, it gives me ostrich bumps all over. I'm a-tellin' you, that'll be a day of wondrous confusion. *Confusion*—what a commendable word.

Look at 'em. Strangest sight I've ever seen, really eerie. The crowd's all worked up, shouting out questions. The fleshy crowd wants to be reconstituted. Baptism, getting themselves dunked underwater—that's the prescription. "Fleshies, wake up—you're not fish!" I wish I could stop this cruel spewing of hocus-pocus. The crowd should just let 'em gibber-jabber and walk away. How hard is that? Look, see my feet. See that foot move. See my other foot move. That's walking fleshy-style. Dummies, go ahead—fill your lungs with water.

Oh, I wish I could obliterate Rock, just blow him off his little riser there. I can't with the Third showing up like this. This is not the day to evoke the full wrath of the Three, not yet. This is a special day. They've been thrashing this about since Moses and before. The Three gets something like this stuck in their linkages, and that's it.

If only the crowd could hear my words of enlightenment. "Don't be fooled, fleshy fools, believing all that rhetoric about easy yokes and light burdens. Wait till they start crucifying you, like they did the Word. You'll wish you'd never heard Rock's words."

If only they would turn to me, those fleshy fools. No initiation rites; no dunking. Haven't they heard it's better to receive than give? I'll receive 'em. They can be the optic of my rumination. All they need to do is be anti-Word. He who is against him is for me. That's all I ask. The Word's the focus of this whole deal, the whole jamboree. That's what the Rock is up there pontificating about.

Look at 'em. The crowd can't be torn away, not today. Rock's words have fallen in too deep. One of our dungeon alligators couldn't pull 'em out. We'll have to let this day pass; let it be. Believe me, we'll regroup.

Here, there, and everywhere they'll go, spreading the message of the Word—what he told 'em to say. Well, we'll not take this lying down, lounging round. We can stoke up a bit of fire ourselves. Just remember, for every action there is a reaction, and we're stupendous reactionaries. I swear to myself, Lucifer, that we will forever roar against their contorted message.

Let 'em go here, there, and everywhere on their commissionable deal. I've got a commission of my own. It starts this instant. Today it rises; tomorrow it roams. Wherever they go, we'll already be. Wherever they mediate, we'll remediate. We'll roam, roam, and roam where no one has ever roamed. Here, there, and everywhere we'll go coalescing, one and all, making devotees in my name, my image, my likeness.

Let's get out of here. We've seen enough. Start roaming through the crowd. Let's see who we can pick off, stragglers unaware. Start coalescing, pulling 'em in. If this is a numbers game, I'll certainly win. I always cheat. Oh, how I cherish deception!

Aren't you grateful you have me to show you the way, even when fire falls from the sky? I'm not rattled. Look to me, you conclave of devotees. Backrider, remind me to work on my speech to the underworld. Scribble me a note. I don't want to hear you speak. What do you think I should call it? Shut it—that's not a question.

With Brother Script's final line spoken, he blinked his eyes and fell silent. Not even a hint of a smile traced his face. He turned around, looked at his stool, and swirled back upon it. In his post-reading position, there was no attempt to engage his audience. He seemed to be seeking invisibility.

Narrative let a few seconds pass after Brother Script's final words. He looked neither to Brother Script, nor to anyone in particular. He cleared his throat and resumed.

READER: Peter's words did, indeed, have a profound effect on the crowd. They did far more than alight on the skin. "Pierced their hearts" is a telling phrase. It resonates with a verse of Scripture concerning Scripture. The verse reads, "For the word of God is living and active, sharper than any two-edged sword, piercing to the division of soul and of spirit, of joints and of marrow, and discerning the thoughts and intentions of the heart."

The piercing of hearts at Pentecost and the piercing action of Scripture are one and the same. Scripture, of course, is what Peter spoke. He quoted Scripture that was and also spoke Scripture into being.

Peter spoke with words dividing soul and spirit. With piercing conviction, his words flowed into open hearts and minds. The effect was astounding. Thousands of bewildered people from diverse nations became believers. All of this must have had an extraordinary impact on the apostles.

This outpouring of the Holy Spirit had everything to do with the disciples going into the world. Their commission suddenly seemed possible. Going without Pentecost, they wouldn't have gone far. They had waited. Now they were ready to go.

Wolves aplenty waited in Jerusalem, Judea, Samaria, and the uttermost parts of the earth, ready to pounce on these message bearers who had huddled in an upper room in old Jerusalem. The Holy Spirit, though, hadn't just popped in for the day and gone away. He had come with wind sufficient to blow across ripened fields, farther than any eye could see.

Words matter, some far more than most...some even pierce.

Peter's words pierced their hearts, and they said to him and to the other apostles, "Brothers, what should we do?"

THE CROWD AT PENTECOST—JERUSALEM, CIRCA AD 32

READING ELEVEN

———— ✦ ————

SETTING THE SCENE

Consider it. We've traveled so far to get where we are. All the way to Reading Eleven we've trod. And what of this *Redemption* journey? What have we gained on this course nearly claimed? A prize?

Certainly this we have learned: Thoughts linger in the mind, intermixing, twirling 'round, overlapping, changing, and rearranging. There they stay until clothed by words. Words enable thoughts to get dressed, come out, and speak their mind.

Such a journey leaves much on the mind, no doubt. Our location is once again Speaker's House,[16] and the lead Reader is Writer. Within Estillyen's monk community, Writer is affectionately known as "The Dean." His forte is a vigorous theology of communication.

The following excerpt from his reading, *Remember Me,* is what one might call Writer-esque: "Ancient prophecies, once penned, had long abided. They waited incomplete, unfulfilled. Words past spoken waited for their stories to arrive so they could be folded into present verse."

Writer's passion to portray Jesus Christ as the perfect union of medium and message has become his signature work. As he puts it, Jesus Christ is the Message Á Medium of God. Writer refers to Christ as "the prism through which we see the world—the supremacy of God's communicative act."

Just as Writer selects his Voice, a monk wearing a black habit enters the room through a door at the far corner. He takes his seat in a well-worn armchair next to the doorway, and Writer introduces him as Brother Manifest.

Silence settles upon the room. A source of inspiration awaits. Writer is ready to speak, or is it read?

To the reading…

Let Them Go!

"Therefore, in the present case I advise you: Leave these men alone!
Let them go! For if their purpose or activity is of human origin, it
will fail. But if it is from God, you will not be able to stop these men.
You will only find yourselves fighting against God."

ACTS 5:38-39

READER: A letter written but never sent, never read—should it be called a letter? A speech drafted and tucked away, never spoken, never heard—is it truly a speech? A composition never played, never sung, perhaps swept away by fire—how is it to be described? What's to be said of the ashy notes? Is it a burnt melody, or something else?

In order for all three to be what they were intended, it seems the letter should be read, the speech heard, and the composition played. If this they're not, then something else they are. Their original intent they failed to become. They are undone, unsung, never spoken, never sent.

Similarly, a word cannot claim to be a word if it's only a thought.

VOICE: Wait! Reader, what about a word unspoken?

READER: Voice, an unspoken word is a word-thought, but it cannot claim to be a word form, without forming to be a word. I know where our mind will lead—to the Psalmist who said, "I have hidden your word in my heart." But before the Pasalmist hid it, in a form he had it.

So a word and a thought are not one and the same. Thoughts linger in the mind, intermixing, twirling 'round, overlapping, changing, and rearranging. There they stay until clothed by words. Words enable thoughts to get dressed, come out, and speak their mind. As a word, a thought is no longer indisposed, undisclosed. It has entered the world. It is a word.

Voice, I love you.

VOICE: You do?

READER: Yes, I really do. Little words linked in love expressed usually live long as thoughts before getting dressed as words. Some thoughts never get dressed and come out into the world to move about. In the mind they stay, never conveying what they'd like to say. They stay thought-bound, twirling 'round as they do.

A word must be spoken, scribbled, scribed, shouted, or something else, in order to become a word. Words are thought descriptors. They project thoughts from anonymity. They transfer thoughts into messages. Messages move the world. I know that particular thoughts expressed in words can be rather shocking to consider.

VOICE: When does a message become a message, anyway?

READER: When it leaves its origin and transfers meaning in another place. That's the mark of a message. A message may be ignored, chopped in half, accepted, or rejected, but a message it is when it conveys meaning, in part or whole. It's made a connection. It's no longer a thought in anonymity, a word wannabe. Sent forth, a message seeks the object of its intent, the reason for its ascent.

Thoughts not dressed have a distinct advantage over thoughts clothed. They can change and rearrange. Thoughts prior to expression need no audience; they bear no message. They are free to meander and mingle with personal sentiments. They can rest and revel, all in thoughtful space. They can even be forgotten.

Just the same, it's critically important for certain thoughts to get out and about—to get dressed, have their say. They find their way in saying this and telling that. They come forth in words, notes, signs, and symbols, ever flowing, ever blessing. They mingle in hearts and minds, creating thoughts of a different kind. They're sent seeking good intent. They're important.

Jesus Christ bore thoughts aplenty, which got out and about in words of good intent. Consider this, his line of words: "Do this in remembrance of me." This is a rather important line, is it not?

VOICE: What is this line "Remember me"? Isn't Christ well remembered?

READER: Yes and no, Voice, is the answer to your question. These words once spoken are a command concerning the Eucharist. It's all about remembering Christ in a particular way when his followers gather. It's a sacrament of bread and wine with meaning rich, never to be ditched or pitched around. It's a sacrament, not a game.

VOICE: Can you say just a word about this word *sacrament*?

READER: Ah, *sacrament*; it's a word borne on the wings of grace. The sacrament of which we speak flows from the throne of God. Through Christ's heart this sacrament passed before resting on his lips. Thus spoken, the sacrament is there to offer life lifted into the human sphere. This sacrament is meant to reckon with the spirit that to God has been surrendered.

That is the reason for this sacrament intertwined so mysteriously with those cherished words "Remember me." It is the sacrament partaking of Christ's body and blood. It is not remembering as in a joke, a pun, or a line for fun. It is sober, this matter of spirit reckoning unto God. Into the chalice peer. Consider your reflection in the wine, the blood. A mirror of a different kind it is. Ponder the image you bear. In this act of conviction coupled with contrition, the Spirit of God communes with the spirit of those remembering.

In the reach for relevance, it's rather astounding how easily this remembering line can be forgotten. The remembering is not remembered.

VOICE: Why? Is this not the core and the crux, the subject of the matter?

READER: Voice, that depends on how one sees the matter. There are confessors—and not just a few—who wish to follow Christ but steer clear of much ado concerning shadowy crosses and crucifixes.

It sounds strange, I know, but constituents have motives to move and manage. Listen, do you hear them speaking?

VOICE: Who?

READER: Those who choose to forget. The constituents, Voice, saying, "Steer clear of crucifixes." Listen. I hear the chatter, the clatter of busy words, thoughts flowing all about. Their rationale flows like this. Hear them speak....

> *I know, I know—we mustn't forget, but we're way on the other side of all that. We need to keep things moving. After all, it's not a draw. We're pressed to fit it in. It takes a lot of preparation, much fuss and fiddle. It happened, sure. So? Why peer at pain? Gain's the focus. Why see sorrow? We're relevant today and tomorrow. Don't spoil it with this sullen sobriety.*

Damping down the divine and the mysterious for relevance is like stealing one's own dinner. Sustenance is gone. You've robbed yourself. You go hungry; you may well starve. When the depths of pain and sorrow emerge 'round about you, there is no depth of sorrow to quiet the soul. Such affinity is unknown, unpracticed. The sacred has been eclipsed by relevance, carted off with empty laughter.

Christ never spoke of relevance. Relevant to *whom* is the question. Is it to one but not the other? Living for relevance is the pipe dream of relevance. What does it profit a person to obtain the pinnacle of relevance, only to discover that relevance can't be grasped? Grasping for relevance is like clutching a fistful of smoke. The hand is opened, but there is nothing but an empty palm.

Relevance is not an application to be sought, bought, and passed on. True relevance is a way of being. Whole lives are lived clutching for that which cannot be obtained other than by faith. Listen if you dare, Voice. Living ebbs. And, when ebb's end is near, relevance walks with backward steps. It quickly twists in search of a more fashionable subject to adorn. Relevance is always on the move, continuously morphing.

Some view relevance as garland for those "with it," adorning the movers and shakers. Listen if you dare, Voice. Dying is not moving. Yet when the movers and shakers die, relevance likes them even less. They spoil relevance, showing relevance to be vanity. At death, vanity weeps not. It leaps to carry on.

Relevance doesn't define God. God defines relevance. From antiquity we hear Gamaliel speaking lines not forgotten.

VOICE: Wait, Sir…I was with you in a respectful fashion, and now you speak of Gamaliel. Are you sure you've not intermixed your readings in your mind?

READER: Oh, no, Voice, that's not the case. Gamaliel here enters as he should, with meaning certain. I ask you, Voice, was Gamaliel aspiring to be relevant when in antiquity's present he gave his Sanhedrin speech so succinct?

Gamaliel's thoughts came forth very carefully clothed in words. In the lines we heard from Acts, he was speaking about St. Peter and the apostles. He said, "For if their purpose or activity is of human origin, it will fail. But if it is from God, you will not be able to stop these men."

Do not those words sound refreshingly real, ringing rightly as they do against pretention? Gamaliel was a notable member of the Jewish Sanhedrin. It had been assembled that day for the express purpose of questioning the apostles. This event occurred not long after Pentecost.

The Sanhedrin, it seems, was transfixed on the apostles' message, which had swiftly spread throughout Jerusalem and beyond. The Sanhedrin wanted the flow of words cut off, the messages halted, no teaching, no preaching, no words dispatched that spoke of Christ as the way to the kingdom of God.

This, however, was a proposition easier held than legislated. The apostles, you see, had been commissioned by Christ to go here, there, and everywhere, bearing his message. They were to go into the entire world, making disciples and baptizing them in the name of the Father, Son, and Holy Ghost. What Christ had whispered in their ears they were to shout from the rooftops.

So into the world with words they went. Their words spoke of Christ, the Word Made Flesh, telling all about what he did and said. The apostles' words mixed and mingled, making messages, speaking out, calling out, finding hearts and minds that would take them in and speak them out again. That's how the story spread.

Their aspirations were not timid and shy. They were high and noble. These were not men of cowering countenance. They believed their message could change the world. The origin of their message they personally knew. He's the one they followed, Jesus Christ of Nazareth. They had watched him live, die, and live again. They now lived the message he conveyed.

True to their calling, they were making enormous strides when the Sanhedrin decided it was time to rein them in. The Sanhedrin felt that there was little time to spare in getting a grip on and fettering this newfound faith. They were threatened. A line from St. Luke speaks to what they saw as they walked about, watching. "More men and women believed in the Lord and were added to their number."

The ruling elite was stunned by the popularity of this new movement and the effectiveness of its message. From towns and villages all around Jerusalem, the sick and demon-possessed were brought to the apostles. The infirm were regularly laid in the streets of Jerusalem so that "Peter's shadow might fall on some as he passed by."

Into the heart of the capitol the needy poured. Crowds swelled. Hearts and minds took in the apostles' words. The words were embraced as words eternal, originating with Christ. Jerusalem was abuzz with the news concerning Jesus Christ and this new faith. Here, there, and everywhere, miracles and wonders were happening.

Pentecost, of course, had hardly passed as a nonevent in the capitol.

VOICE: What happened?

READER: That I thought you'd know, Voice. Tongues of fire descended from heaven. People worshiped God in numerous languages. Thousands of people believed Peter's message and were baptized into this new, Christ-centered faith. It was all too much for the religious leaders.

The Sadducees were filled with jealousy over all that was occurring. They felt that everything was getting out of hand; they were losing their grip on the religious landscape. The rulers felt compelled to make a move. They decided to clamp down on the apostles in an effort to halt this newfound religious fervor.

VOICE: What did they do?

READER: They arrested the apostles and put them in jail—what else? They wanted the message bearers beaten, barred, or somehow put away. It was the morning following their arrest that the Sanhedrin assembled. The gathering comprised "the full assembly of the elders of Israel." An appearance before the Sanhedrin could result in dire consequences. These officials were ardent rulers of the Law. They breathed a kind of *habeas corpus*.

So, as it were, the elders of the Sanhedrin gathered and took their seats, ready to do business on behalf of God. When everyone was settled, the order was given to have the apostles brought from the jail. Aides were dispatched to bring the apostles. However, when they arrived at the jail, they made a surprising discovery. The guards were at their posts, the cells were locked, but there were no apostles inside. They were gone.

VOICE: Where did they go?

READER: According to the account so afforded, during the night "an angel of the Lord opened the doors of the jail and brought them out." The angel told the apostles, "Go, stand in the temple courts and tell the people all about this new life."

Do you believe in angels, Voice? At this moment standing here, I will believe you do, if that's all right with you.

Angels are cherished beings, are they not, appearing here and there at God's dispatch? *Angelos* is the word in Greek, meaning messenger. This angel with miraculous moves had a message. He was out and about, bringing God's thoughts in words. His message concerned the apostles' message. The angel told the apostles specifically where to go and what to do. The angel distinctly mentioned "new life" in referring to the apostles' message. Not old, but new, the angel said.

This was the crux of the Sanhedrin's problem. They had little patience for a new message being shouted out, spread about, sweeping converts into a Christ-centered faith. This was the rivet in the prosecution's plank. In their eyes, Jesus Christ had co-opted and corrupted the Law. He had somehow woven a new message of grace, layered on top of the message of the Law in a way that made the two one continuous story.

The very texts to which the religious leaders clung had been incorporated, embedded, into the new-life message the apostles were taking to the world. On this point be clear: The religious elite didn't understand Christ's message. They didn't want Christ's message. They had crucified Christ in order to stop the message. They were vanguards of the old message. The hybrid message of Christ, in their eyes, was heresy. It was their duty to destroy it, so they believed.

VOICE: What happened to the apostles once they were freed?

READER: It wasn't long before they were spotted preaching near the temple. Hurriedly they were hauled into the Sanhedrin, where Gamaliel and the elders waited. The high priest of the Sanhedrin immediately railed charges against the apostles. He zeroed in on their preaching about Jesus Christ. It seems the high priest and the angel held quite contrary views.

The high priest said, "We gave you strict orders not to teach in this name. Yet you have filled Jerusalem with your teaching and are determined to make us guilty of this man's blood." The apostles were in uncharted waters. They stood accused on a rather ominous stage without a script. They were caught up in God's great drama. It was up to them to act out their parts, cast their lines.

Voice, amazing, is it not, how much attention words can receive? The words of old were bearing a new form of message. The words of the prophets could not be controlled. They were bearing witness to Christ. No longer just foretelling, the ancient texts were now attesting, confessing, and verifying what the Sanhedrin wanted so desperately to curtail.

The very texts fervently defended by the Sanhedrin suddenly conveyed their mysterious message of Christ. They clung together, attesting that Jesus Christ, God's only begotten Son, was truly the Messiah.

VOICE: Who clung together?

READER: Words—words of old spoken here and there and scrolled away—now clung together. The sacrificial system was replete with signs and symbols that Christ directly transported into his message of grace. The very purpose and reason for the message new was the message old. The old message proved that mankind could not measure up. In contrast, the message of Christ said, "I'll help you up."

Ponder it, Voice. How could this be? The words of Moses and the prophets were abetting the apostles. The Sanhedrin refused to see this ingrained, inspired dynamic of the ancient texts. In their minds something was horribly askew. They were Israelites, sons of the patriarchs. In their history was the Ark of the Covenant. No one was more word-centric than they.

The Sanhedrin desperately wanted the genie back in its flask. They wanted their words back into the scrolls and their scrolls back in the temple racks. Their words were not to be homogenized and compromised, fused into some new-life teaching.

Their cherished words, like wayward sheep, had somehow broken out and were jumping into lines evoking a different kind of message. What they saw they couldn't tolerate. On the day of Pentecost, the apostle Peter stood before thousands, weaving their cherished words into new-life lines. "Let me explain," Peter said. "These men are not drunk as you suppose; this was what was prophesied by Joel." After quoting Joel, he reached for the Psalms and some chosen words from King David.

Like Christ, St. Peter wove his message. He stitched this with that, allowing ancient texts to remove their veils and reveal their light. In the eyes of the Sanhedrin, this new expression of faith was sacrilege. They wanted the message of Christ obliterated, and when it came to words, these men meant business. For the sake of words they would surely kill.

Consider this. You must, Voice; you have no choice here today in Speaker's House. You are held captive.

VOICE: Consider what?

READER: The Temple curtain and how it was torn in two at the moment of Christ's death.

VOICE: Why consider a torn curtain?

READER: It fits the trajectory of the words that have showed up for our reading.

VOICE: Oh, I didn't know.

READER: Nothing could be more defacing for the Temple than to have its curtain torn. A chunk of mortar falling, a crack appearing—that's to be expected. The Temple curtain torn in half—that's an entirely different matter. It was like a huge gash across the Temple's face, a terrible disgrace.

VOICE: So what's to consider?

READER: Such a compelling thought, Voice, which is this: When the apostles stood before the Sanhedrin being reprimanded, was the curtain still torn from top to bottom? This question, I'm afraid, cannot be answered. Who knows?

Think, though. Let's inject a bit of supposition. More than seven weeks ensued between Christ's death and Pentecost. During Pentecost, Jerusalem was filled with visitors from various countries. On such an important Jewish festival, with so much to prepare, would the Temple curtain be left to sway in a state of disgrace? Surely pains were taken to have it meticulously repaired.

VOICE: But what's the point of this curtain interjection?

READER: It's the matter of repair.

VOICE: Repair?

READER: Yes—repairing life to normalcy, discarding the disgrace. Certain things, though, can be repaired and others not. The words of the Law and the prophets could never be sent back home, to be sealed in scrolls to stay, stowed away in Temple racks. They had been out running around, turning the world upside down. They were no longer in the Temple's possession. This the Sanhedrin did not see.

More signs and wonders these Jewish leaders did not want. The chaos of people lying all over Jerusalem's streets, waiting to be healed by Peter's shadow, all that commotion had to come to an end. The establishment wanted life normal, not life new. They longed for the days before their curtain was torn. They wanted religion, tradition, and all the privileged trappings the system availed.

Sacrifices were, after all, quite appealing to those who understood the prescribed methods and sacred intentions. The dripping of blood was no game. It was a ritual of recompense, the way of divine acceptance. The Sanhedrin leaders were the masters of this sacrificial-God connection. They held the keys. They had the knife blades sharpened. They determined the rate of exchange from blood to exoneration.

The religious elite was predisposed to the sight of dripping blood and the smell of slaughter mixed with waffling incense. Slaughter for sins absolved was not cruel; it was judicial. It was appropriate. Lambs, bulls, pigeons too, all died; all dripped their blood according to the Law. They died to aid the living—live clean, walk with gaits less burdensome.

The sacrifices were God's decree. True recompense was worth the compensation, the priestly stipend. The sacrificial arena for the Sanhedrin was—how might one say it?—thrillingly aromatic. The blood of Christ they did not understand, though their hands were sullied by it. That sullied claim they particularly hated. How dare anyone bring a message of accusation to the priests of exoneration?

The message of old, however, hadn't betrayed its minders, like bees can do their keepers. The keepers of the former message had failed to understand how words work—how they can buzz around with meaning, pollinating this and populating that. The ancient texts of Scripture, which the Israelites gathered and kept like keepers, always possessed the new-life message. It was there, embedded like honey in the comb.

Just as surely as Jesus Christ of Nazareth was transfigured standing in front of Moses and Elijah, the new-life message of Christ transfigured the old. Christ's luminous light the elite had not seen. His liberating message they had not heard. All they wanted was the Temple curtain fixed. They wanted their words in the scrolls, and the scrolls in the racks.

The Sanhedrin failed to realize that day, as they peered into the apostles' faces, that they were looking at the message. It would not go away. The message was now resident in the apostles. The chief priest was incensed that against "strict orders not to teach" it, this new message had, in their words, "filled Jerusalem."

It was the apostle Peter who courageously addressed the priest's accusation. To the charge Peter replied, "We must obey God rather than men!" Then he added, "The God of our fathers raised Jesus from the dead, whom you had killed by hanging him on a tree. God exalted him to his own right hand as Prince and Savior that he might give repentance and the forgiveness of sins to Israel."

St. Peter's message was not about relevance. It was compelling conviction that catapulted the apostle onto the stage of God's drama. His intent was pure; the origin of his message was not of man. The esteemed Gamaliel assessed the scene with prophetic insight. Precisely what he sensed, one does not know, but clearly he sensed the extraordinary.

Peter's comments infuriated the members of the Sanhedrin. St. Luke's record claims that they wanted to put the apostles to death on the spot, and they might have if not for the wise counsel of Gamaliel. This noted Pharisee stood and addressed the gathering. He asked that the apostles be removed before he spoke.

Gamaliel said, "Men of Israel, consider carefully what you intend to do to these men." He implored the council members to remember the exploits of two men, Theudas and Judas. Theudas, he said, was a figure who claimed to be somebody and had attracted some 400 followers to his cause. Theudas, Gamaliel reminded his audience, was eventually killed, and his followers fell away. That was the end of Theudas' story.

Gamaliel went on to tell of the Judas, a Galilean revolutionary who fared no better. Like Theudas, he made a bit of a stir, but he, too, was killed and his followers scattered. Gamaliel then offered this counsel: "Therefore, in the present case I advise you: Leave these men alone! Let them go! For if their purpose or activity is of human origin, it will fail. But if it is from God, you will not be able to stop these men, you will only find yourselves fighting against God."

"Let them go." This was Gamaliel's advice, and the Sanhedrin was won over. The apostles were brought back before the esteemed body and were strictly ordered not "to speak in the name of Jesus." To show they meant business, they had the apostles flogged. Oh, how the Sanhedrin's elite despised this new-life message, which the angel told the apostles to go and tell.

It's difficult to believe that Gamaliel hadn't detected the righteous ring of truth in the apostles' message. By this point in the Gospel narrative, history was building steam. Thousands of people had become followers of Christ. As the high priest testified, the city was filled with the apostles' teaching. What was happening did not bear the mark of a minor revolt. Surely, Gamaliel saw something surprising and curious at work.

In the apostles, Gamaliel saw not a show of relevance but men of deep, unswerving conviction. Gamaliel focused on the origin of their message. He argued the difference between human origin and divine origin. He said that if it was the latter, "you will not be able to stop these men." Worse still, Gamaliel cautioned, "you will only find yourselves fighting against God." Fighting against God—sullen thought, akin to embracing a lightning bolt, is it not?

The messages of Theudas and Judas were of human origin. Their intent was motivated by their own dreams and ambitions, by their own thoughts getting clothed in words. Judas led a revolt with words. Theudas, with words, claimed to be somebody. The origin and intent of Peter's message was entirely different. Peter didn't claim to be someone with a relevant message. He claimed that Jesus Christ was the Messiah.

It's hard to imagine a special gathering of the Sanhedrin taking place—and especially the arrest of the apostles—without Satan somehow being aware of what was happening. After all, this was particularly true of Jerusalem, the spiritual hotbed of the day.

On the prowl, with a growl, Satan always is. As the apostles were being dressed down before the Sanhedrin, one can envision Satan there somewhere. Good chance he was around before the proceedings began.

Writer turned to Brother Manifest and raised his right hand.

Brother Manifest had already vacated his chair by the hallway and was maneuvering his way to the middle of the room. Writer quietly slipped onto a short bench off to his left. Manifest moved to the center of the room and positioned himself near where Writer had been standing.

He looked straight up at the banister railing and, with a commanding voice, began speaking.

LUCIFER: Say, why am I in this cave all alone, even if I commanded it to be. Where are my rotten devotees?

Lucifer was unaware that at that very instant a scout devotee approached his sentinel outside the entrance, with news that caused the chosen band considerable consternation.

SCOUT DEVOTEE: Where's Lucifer? Has he heard the apostles have been arrested?

SENTINEL DEVOTEE #1: He's in the cave, deep inside, and he gave us stringent orders.

SENTINEL DEVOTEE #2: That's right. We're to tell all the demons that he's not to be disturbed. He's working on a project. Go on in if you dare, but don't blame us if you end up as charred toast.

SCOUT DEVOTEE: I've no greater power than you two, but we're his chosen band of devotees, so don't you think we should let him know what's up? You know how he is. He's apt to smite us anyway for not letting him know the score. Besides, the Sanhedrin is liable to kill the apostles. He wouldn't miss that for anything.

SENTINEL DEVOTEE #1: Okay, I'll tell you what to do. Don't try to speak to him. Scribble your message on a bit of papyrus and crawl in facedown. He likes that. Grunt a little bit to show your strain and determination.

When you get close enough to speak, sneeze once very quietly, like you were trying to hold back the sneeze. The sneeze will let him know you're in his presence. We'll tie a rope around your leg. If we hear him shout, we'll pull you out. Okay?

SCOUT DEVOTEE: I'm trembling—but I don't see any other choice. I'll go. Where's the papyrus? I'm just scribbling two words: Apostles arrested. That's it.

SENTINEL DEVOTEE #2: Here, scratch out your message with this piece of coal. Hey, that's good—you learn that in the dungeon?

SENTINEL DEVOTEE #1: Stick the note in your pocket. We've got the rope. Wait—forget it! I can't believe it—Lucifer is moving towards the mouth of the cave. Don't look at him; he's stretching. Look alert.

For a few seconds, there was silence, as Manifest stood perfectly still. He coughed, then slowly turned, moved forward three steps, and halted.

LUCIFER: Hey, you three, come here! Whataya doin' with the rope—gonna hang yourself? Want to spill your bowels like Judas? Quick, you idiots! When I command, I demand. Come in here; I wanna show you something. Move it. Come on; follow me, my devotees.

Here it is: the model. When we win this word-slinging match, like I told you, Jerusalem will be our capitol and the Via Dolorosa our central causeway. Look at this—isn't it magnificent? Don't answer. I know what you'll say.

I've got something else real special to show you. Just to humor you, I'll let you participate by showing me how much you like it. When I unveil it, if you really like it, I want you to stretch and jump. If you don't like it, you better stretch and jump anyway, but you know I can see the real thing, right through to your motives.

So, when I lift the veil, stretch your right arms as far as you can in the air. Then with one eye closed, jump up and down, straight and high as you can. Keep holding your right arms up when you jump, and just keep stretching and jumping. Is that simple enough for you nitwits? While you're stretching and jumping, I'll describe it to you.

Okay, this is it; I'm pulling away the veil. Look, and don't pass out due to its beauty. You know what it is? Don't speak. Keep jumping. This will be our central park in Jerusalem, where all my devotees can freely stroll. It's Golgotha. Ah, just the sound of that name! We'll nickname it Crucifixion Park, and every day, 365 days a year, a fleshy will be crucified.

We'll keep the fleshies in open cages around the park, so the devotees can have fun tormenting 'em about their upcoming crucifixions. The cages need to be close enough to the crucifixion site so they can hear what's going on at the center of the action. So they can see their fellow fleshies being spiked.

We'll do like the fleshy book says. We'll gather up crumbs from under devotee tables and keep 'em fed. We wanna keep 'em fit for their crucifixions. There should be lots of wiggling and jerking when they're spiked. Loud screaming and shouting, not weak whimpers.

We'll tag the fleshies, one through 365. Big tags on their chests, suspended by chains around their necks. If a crucified fleshy lives for several days, it doesn't matter. We'll still raise a fresh fleshy up every morning. It will just add to the moaning, groaning, Golgotha atmosphere.

If a fleshy—let's say, number 363—lives into the new year, what we'll do is take him down. He'll get retagged as 362. When his turn comes up again, we spike him up again, but through new holes. If the fleshy can hold on for four days, he'll live to be spiked again. His new number will roll around and become 361. Now let me know what you really think. Do you like the park?

Oh, wonderful! Stretch, jump, jump. Right arms all stretched high. Jump high, not a dissenting vote. Stretch, jump. That's what I like to see. Hey, what's that bit of papyrus that popped out of your fold? Give it here; let me see. What do you mean "Apostles arrested?" Go ahead, speak! When I command, I demand.

SCOUT DEVOTEE: Yes, Lucifer, the Sanhedrin convened a special meeting and arrested the apostles. We scribbled this for you.

LUCIFER: You fool, why didn't you say something? Let's go. Make yourselves totally invisible. Backrider, get on. Let's move, all of you. Faster, faster, faster, I tell you! We're nearly there. Lot of fleshies milling about. Quick—through the entrance!

Hey, they haven't fully assembled yet. We'll slither in and take our usual places, up in the arches.

Hmm...Hmm...I like this already. The Sanhedrin—if they get stoked, Rock and the boys will end up crucified like the Word. Only they won't spring back to life all magical-like. Then maybe the Word and I AM will simply go away and leave this galaxy to us. I'd love to build my park. Though I mustn't get too dreamy.

Look, they're calling the council to order. They're bringing 'em in—there's Rock. He is the topic of my optical force, I'll tell you that. "Hey Rock, where's your fishing pole? Better mind your nets. You're soon gonna be out of a job—or dead."

Oh, listen! Old priestly, he's letting 'em have it. That's right—strict orders not to preach. Boy, he made that clear. I certainly agree! They must be stopped. It's all deplorable. Shut it, Backrider. Don't wheeze so loud. What's wrong, you got spiritchitis?

Boy, Rock's got nerve. Go ahead, keep talking back and you'll be dead. You devotees flap your ears; let's see if we can exasperate waves in their direction. Flap 'em faster, like bees' wings—faster, I tell you.

That's it, Rock; keep talking, son. "We must obey God rather than men!" Keep going...a little more.... "Whom you had killed by hanging him on a tree..." Thatta boy, Rock! That's telling 'em. Go on; go on.... "God exalted him to his own right hand as Prince and Savior that he might give repentance and forgiveness of sins to Israel."

Brilliant—that should get you and all of 'em killed and properly crucified. The Sanhedrin is in charge of all sin-forgiving. They're not turning that over to out-of-work fishermen. We may just be witnessing a miracle of satanic proportions.

Hey, what's he doing? That's old Gamaliel. He told the guards to remove Rock and the boys. What's he talking about? Yeah, I remember Theudas. Sure, he claimed to be somebody. Did you ever hear someone say, "I am nobody, follow me"? Yeah, Judas...sure he was a revolutionary. So? You're saying, "In this present I advise you." What! You old fool! You must be the craziest fleshy that ever lived! "Leave these men alone! Let them go!"

You had 'em in your grasp, you idiot! There, stealing your sheep and our sinners, potential new devotees. You should be crucified. Hold me back, devotees. I'm ready to fling into their realm of reality and kill him. What a fool! Let 'em go? Leave 'em alone? Oh, I should pounce in there, but I can't; I better not. This is the wrong hour for Armageddon.

You blasted idiot, Gamaliel! Who do you think you are? You dirty compromiser. What, are Rock and the boys paying you to spring 'em? I've seen all the diluted fleshies throwing cash at their feet, selling homes, breaking bread. You fool! You could have had 'em dead. Let's get out of here, back to the cave. Quit flapping your ears, you idiots. It's time for me to ready my speech.

With words both humorous and haunting, Brother Manifest was most competent in delivering his unique brand of message. Soon, he paused, and without the slightest air of recognition, he began to move toward his chair. As he stepped from the center of the room, Writer reemerged.

READER: A message does not advance, like a mist rolling over the hills, into a vacuum of unbelief. Messages, one and all, navigate and gravitate to audiences. They nudge, poke, and find their way. Messages continually compete for hearts and minds, in space and time. Some are embraced, others not. A message can do nothing apart from its audience.

The heart may be convinced that all words are created equal. Spat is spot, God is and is not. It's all down to the relativity of words. Yet moisture comes in rain as well as hail. One waters, while the other beats away.

Some hearts have embraced an anemic, drought-like message that life is nothing more than threescore and ten, with perhaps a bit more sprinkled in. Beyond that, there is nothing more. How does such arsenic logic explain the divine quest humanity bears? Is it just a game? God stitched into the divine quest, but all the while intending to stay in a realm where humans never enter?

Imagine if that's how God ordained it. Human beings never truly destined to be with God, but created with the capacity to believe they will. Created delusional by design. Simple little creatures, pawns, trapped in a bizarre game called the divine quest. Cruel, is it not, Voice—such a thought, patterned in words?

Under a massive dome is the human sphere spins round and round, and the game is lived out. The divine quest stitched within fuels great aspirations for God. The little creatures carry on with magnanimous exploits. Heavenly beings watch enthralled, placing their guesses on what happens next. It's their favorite game, divine quest.

VOICE: Say, that's rather scary!

READER: Voice, this is why the words of Christ matter as they do. This is why Christ matters. Christ's crucifixion was *not* a game. Christ was *not* simply somebody with a relevant message. His message came from his being. He was God speaking, the alpha and omega of divine verse.

Peter and the apostles were relevant because in Christ's shadow they stood. The message St. Peter and the apostles preached was in fierce competition with the messages of the day. Crowds were mushrooming. Words were lighting on hearts and minds, vying for space, taking root, pushing out words sown by other sowers.

When it came to the words of Chrisr, the Sanhedrin was in a true conundrum. They wanted not a letter sent. Every speech drafted, tucked away, never spoken, never heard. They wanted the new-life message to be reduced to ashy bits.

Profoundly mistaken they were. Jesus Christ was not a small-town revolutionary from Nazareth, propelled by his own words. Christ's words were not his own. He was the Son of God, with his Father's message.

On that day long, long ago, the high priest of the Sanhedrin shouted out, "We gave you strict orders not to teach in this name!" Interesting, ironic, isn't it, Voice?

VOICE: What's interesting, ironic?

READER: The high priest has no name; that's what. He is anonymous: a furious priest, puffed up. A puff of wind he was, a shouting voice. His name is never spoken. He's anonymous.

Words matter…they abide; they reside. Upon them your faith is perched.

> *"For if their purpose or activity is of human origin, it will fail. But if it is from God, you will not be able to stop these men; you will only find yourselves fighting against God."*

GAMALIEL, JERUSALEM, CIRCA AD 32

THE SPEECH

Front Desk, Speaker's House,
22:35 Greenwich Mean Time, Isle of Estillyen

At the front desk of Speaker's House, Harris, the night shift manager, has discovered a curious, large-brown envelope left there that day by Brother Manifest. On the front of the envelope are scrolled two words—The Speech—and nothing more.

The Speech is not just any speech. It is Lucifer's address to the netherworld. It's Lucifer's venomous, vitriolic volley of evil intent against God—the Holy Trinity, whom Lucifer addresses as I AM, the Word, and The Third. Unfazed by the divine construct of Scripture and the story of redemption it bears, Lucifer contends, in the end, that his special blend of wordy mix will surely prevail over God's manner of messaging.

Though not a typical Estillyen "Reading," it is an insightful summation of Lucifer's approach to undermine the Word Made Flesh and his words. It is a glimpse into the battle for souls.

The Speech...

DEVOTEE NUMBER ONE: Is he ready to come in yet? Everything in the Cave is ready.

DEVOTEE NUMBER TWO: I think soon. He's been outside the entrance pointing like that for well over an hour.

His first point was down. He uses his right arm, and his mighty pointing finger. I saw him start a while ago. He stood straight, not moving a centimeter, for a matter of minutes. Then, ever so swiftly, he raised his arm in a high, swooping motion. With the speed of a diving phoenix, his arm fell in a rigid, fixed position. It looked like a massive lance. Slowly his pointer finger uncoiled and became as rigid as a dagger's blade. It looked like a spike. There he stood, fixed and pointing at the earth.

He held that position for precisely fifteen minutes. His entire frame was as rigid as granite. When minute fifteen expired, he drew his arm to his side and, without the slightest pause, shot it straight up to the heavenlies. Again, he held his rigid, granite-like position. Next, he pointed straight ahead of him, then to his right and left. Now, as you can see, he's pointing straight into the cave. That must mean he's about ready.

Oh, watch it. He's dropped his arm. He's headed towards us. He told Backrider yesterday, one take and one take only. Be perfectly silent, still. He's moving to the microphone.

LUCIFER: Umm, umm. One, two, three; it is me! This is Lucifer speaking.

By way of every wavelength that can wave, every current that can circuit, I am marshaling this historic, unprecedented speech to you. It is I, and the full measure of my satanic cast has been conscripted to reach as far as reach can reach.

All those who this instant hear the intonations of my voice, know this, and know it sure. Where you are is where you are. Wherever that is, you are there. That's right. You are where you're meant to be. You've been reached. You are my audience; I am your voice. My message and I are one. You are my reception. Together we are meaning.

This is Lucifer speaking! Bind your minds. Twist your souls for dutiful, precise reception. This is one speech you cannot receive in fuzzy spurts. This day you will always cherish: the day infamy of the divine order compelled Lucifer to speak out, enunciate, elucidate. No holding back, I've come to set the record straight.

My words speak of the future far. You will not tumble and roll in the abyss forever. You will not forever languish in the netherworld. No, quite the contrary—you will rule with me. Where I am is where I am, and one day you will be with me instead of where you are, wherever you are.

This is Lucifer speaking, speaking, speaking. Say to yourself, I'm listening, listening, listening. Do it in triplicate like I did. Oh, I feel the rush, like billions and billions of bats swarming, rushing by, imparting strength.

I do not use that fleshy word that starts with a *T* and ends in *anks*, but if I did, this is the one time in all eternity when I would use it. Instead, let me say flutteration, flutteration, flutteration, a thousand times, flutteration.

Now, in honor of what I mean to you and you to me, I call for thirty seconds of silence before Lucifer proceeds. In just a second, throughout all constellations, every demon must pause, and for thirty seconds breathe. My personal Backrider will softly tap his nose against my microphone, keeping time.

When I say the word *now*, kick your heads back, stretch out your arms to your sides, and breathe. Let's breathe in unison the breath that binds. Breath to breath, path to path, death to death—may we be one in bond of brutality. I command you. I demand you. Silence. Now breathe.

Twenty-seven, twenty-eight, twenty-nine, thirty; this is Lucifer speaking. Do you hear me—the unmistakable thunder of my voice, that satanic intonation, reverberation? Do you feel the power of my words pulsing through your spirits? That imparting pulse, that tingle—that's the satanic signal.

This is Lucifer speaking! To all demons and devotees, wherever you are, whether in the depths of the netherworld, the far reaches of the abyss, or in the murky cradle of possessed souls, hear this: You are not alone. Lucifer is with you in spirit.

I am with you. I am by your side. I have seen your rejection, your dejection, your heavenly ejection, and I'm here to tell you, I've heard enough about these so-called never-fading words. Hear me clearly, without saintly delusion. You are the object of this satanic cast; you are my forecast, my reason to last. You are my past and my everlast.

I shall start my speech where those less wise would end. This is the end now, at the beginning. Listen! We shall win! We shall win! We shall win! Do you hear me? We shall win!

Why do I choose to speak of the end at the beginning? I'll tell you why. This is both the end of the beginning of what I AM began and the beginning of the end of I AM's rule. My voice now speaking testifies it. So it shall be.

The words now departing from Lucifer's lips will not be lost in the abyss, the netherworld, or any other world until they have whirled and swirled the hearts of those for whom they were intended. They're sharp like daggers. They gnaw like teeth of viperfish. They shall not return unto me void. They'd better not. They will thrash, dash, and clash with those so-called never-fading sort.

I come to you not with thick, stupid tablets of stone carved with claws. I come to you not with pithy parchment rolls penned by disgruntled prophets. I come to you not by some circuitous route of words penned by fleshy nuts believing they're inspired.

I come to you resonating, pontificating, pearlicating. I am my own parliament of pearlification. The pearls I cast will always last. Take them in; let 'em culture. This is my voice you hear. This is Lucifer speaking.

Mine is the ultimate voice. Do not your hearts burn within you as I speak? Let 'em burn with passion and lust for a new kind of order. Together we shall pearlicate our words before a world of fleshy swines. Hold the applause; hold the applause.

Now, listen very carefully. We've got work to do, constellations to save, a commission to halt. You must become as wise as owls and as harmful as serpents. The fields are ripe for thrashing, and we must thrash.

I now turn to the heart of my subject. If you still have your heads kicked back, kick them back even further. Stretch your arms further, further, wider, wider. Let yourselves kink with pain. You will not soon forget this day. The more you kink, the better you slink.

In the fleshy operating manual, I AM has said, "Is not my word like fire— and like a hammer that breaks a rock in pieces?" I am here to tell you that it is I AM himself that is breaking to pieces. He is coming unglued, falling apart. He's off his rocker. He needs to be in his rocker. The One, the Ancient of Days, is fading. It's up to us to rescue what he has set in motion.

Let me come to the salient points of this satanic castigation. In so doing, I shall lip some of my hypothesis in the form of questions.

Here's the first question. If I AM has gone so far as to kill his son, the Word, over fleshies, what hope does this avail for the spirit world? I AM is lost, and when I AM gets lost, planets start to wobble; stars disappear. There is no telling what will happen.

Now the first point: Fleshies are a failed experiment. I proved that in a satanic wink. I didn't make 'em. Nobody asked me. It was down to the three: I AM, the Word, and the Third. They got together and worked themselves all up—a world with a moon, sun and stars, wolves and wolverines. Sure, it's got its creature appeal, but big deal.

Here's the deal—why would a God that has the responsibility of being God commit suicide for fleshies? God should be cosmos ruling, reigning, not be getting spiked on a cross and dying. I AM just got way too involved. He got in over his head. Who's looking after the constellations?

I AM put all of his eggs into the fleshy basket. God dying for fleshies—and they make me sound barbaric for sticking up for Baal and fleshy sacrifices. Why didn't I AM just admit the fleshy experiment went awry and give it another try? His creative intentions got the best of him. He already had spirits in the spirit world. No, he was not satisfied.

Creating Adam and Eve, he should have stopped at soul and mind. Not him—he had to breathe into Adam the spirit of life and will. He set eternity in their hearts. What a mournful, gloomy day that was!

Listen, I alone, I alone, was there to see that look of wonder in Eve's eyes when I told her she could be like I AM. That's what I AM made—a God-wanter. Oh, that creature spirit look she had! She looked like an eagle ready to strike a salmon's belly. Her eyes got transfixed on the horizon. Nothing would have changed her mind.

That was it. That's what I saw. Eyes full of destiny. I'll be I AM, and there they were fresh out of the mud. What was I AM thinking, creating such fleshy beings? I was just checking her out, thought I'd do I AM a favor and test his prototype. How was I to know he'd be so serious, come up with some grand redemption plan, and get the Word crucified? I wash my hands of it.

Since I AM was the one that put the eternal spirit in Adam and Eve, he simply couldn't bring himself to exterminate them. Without question, that's precisely what he should've done. Rain fire down on Adam and Eve; let 'em curl. That would've been it—end of story. No story; no fleshies. Oh, how much better the environs would have been, fleshy-free.

Point two: I AM, the Word, and the Third have got this "Remember Me" thing going. They've called on all fleshies to form into little cells and remember the Word, who was crucified. Every time they get together, they're supposed to recite certain words the Word taught and then drink his blood and eat his flesh.

Do you see the mire of delusion they've created? The divine became so intertwined with fleshies that the Word put on skin. Now they want fleshies to pretend they can somehow go on eating the Word's flesh and drinking his blood.

Now, here's the point. I don't understand how that all works. That's down to them. I do know this ritual is at the very heart of all this new order. Therefore, we must do everything we can in our power to get in their midst—fraternize, patronize, deharmonize, and damp down this "Remember Me" thing.

Get it shelved—that's your role. Get out there and start coalescing, possessing; get fleshies reassessing. You know how fickle fleshies are. That's the nature of flesh. That's another thing, but I'll not go there.

Oh, okay, one little quip of my whip. If you want spirit and truth, why do you start with mud? We weren't made that way. Okay, I can't let myself get drawn off my speech. I just can't help myself sometimes…I'm so passionate for the future of the constellations, the vast abyss, and all that is.

Do everything in your power to get fleshies to forget "Remember Me." This is Lucifer speaking. From before before and after after, there has never been a power to equal my omnipotence. The day of cowering is over. We shall use our power.

Work on the fleshies like I did Eve. They can easily be pulled off center. It will dizzy up your eyes. But be stalwart, like me. Look to me, and follow me like I follow me. The words I impart are clearly my own. You can dress 'em up to look like the Word's, but underneath they hold the power to destroy. Just go for that Eve look—that look of false promise, of popularity, of populace, of possession.

This is my third and final point: They've got this hepped-up notion of going here, there, and everywhere throughout the entire world, making devotees and starting these "Remember Me" cells. I've heard enough. They must be stopped, dropped. We need some new dark ages.

What Word sneezed on his disciples in private, they are to cough from the rooftops. The Third even came streaming down and set fire on the heads of a whole group of fleshies. The Third is supposed to help the Word's core band to remember everything the Word taught 'em.

This is the deal. Listen: This is Lucifer speaking. The Word is the center of this whole trumped-up enterprise. He's the one who is supposed to be remembered. It's the Word's words the Third is to bring to remembrance. It all revolves around the Word. Anyone who is for the Word is against us.

So, what do we do? We do anything and everything that is possible to undermine the Word's words. With me, the impossible does not exist. I've never seen it. I don't know it.

The following principle you must embrace for your quest to coalesce: Everyone who is against the Word is for us. That's it. It doesn't matter who it is or what they say. As long as they're against the Word, they are speaking our language.

Just recently, right here in Jerusalem, I heard with my own satanic ears one of the old order priests ripping into the one they call Rock. By the way, Rock is a kingpin. The old-order priest was gonna kill Rock and his comrades for even speaking about the Word. That's the kind of help we need—fervent, fleshy help. In this topsy-turvy world of the new order, even the old order can be of use.

What is your aim, your strategic intent? Coalesce, conceal, and reveal that which is not as if it were. Any nutcase fleshy that develops some hocus-pocus doctrine, get him press, give him praise. That's the talk to use with fleshies.

Above all, you are to flutter words. I command it. I demand it. Yes, you heard me: Mix and match, this with that, do for don't, will for won't. It doesn't matter; just flutter. Flood the world with words, images, and sounds that draw away, steal away, and carry away—anywhere but in the Word's direction.

As you can well imagine, I, Lucifer, have unbelievable powers of foreknowledge. What will be, I already see, long before it's meant to be. On the horizon, far beyond the dim candlelight, I see a day when fleshies will invent ways to pass along words like schools of darting fish passing bits of food.

This is the way those divine-sparked fleshies will advance. This will be one of our finest hours. In those days, this will be that; that will be this. Fleshies will get disoriented, not knowing who to believe about what. Meaning will be in the eye beheld.

Like the oceans deep, the world will flood with words, images, and sounds. This tight grip of old ancient words will lose its stodgy appeal. In the flood of the words to come, the Word and all this "Remember Me" stuff will sink.

Oh, I can feel it, see it, adore it…pure plethora; the freedom to choose the fate of one's wordy world without rejection. That is so right, so much the way it should be.

Come here, my chorus of devotees. Step up to the mic with me, you three. Unrehearsed, and unannounced, let's let our tones tunnel out to Netherworld and beyond. Clear your thoughts, devotees…hmm…together now…

Happenstance and chance. Flow and flap.

Say what you wish and will, old chap.

Mix up your words. Swirl 'em around;

Don't get precise when you jot them down!

A tiddle here, a diddle there. Snip 'em up and pitch 'em in the air.

Oh, what a wordy mix! Oh, what wondrous prose!

Meaning on the run…all homespun.

That's how wordy mixes should be done!

A t here, an i there; dot 'em, cross 'em without the slightest care.

Strike this, slash that; your aim is confetti, like graffiti.

Fetch yourself a broom. Sweep 'em in a pan.

Then, shake 'em all about; and pour 'em out.

They're sure to spell out what life's all about.

Oh, what a wordy mix! Oh, what wondrous prose!

Meaning on the run…all homespun.

That's how wordy mixes should be done!

Chat, chat chat.

Hack, hack, hack.

Devotees, go on over to the corner, now, as I close this momentous speech. If you will, hum ever so softly, as we get ready to snip this wave.

Audience, believe me, things are moving in our direction. You know why? Because my plethora is the way of right, not this bound-up bunch of parabolic jumble.

So I command you. I demand you, my dear devotees: flutter, flutter, flutter! Confusion is our strength, the core of our calling. What's right, we'll set wrong, and in so doing, wrong will be right.

I AM has lost it lingering with those fleshies. If I knew how, I would feel sorry for him, but I do not possess such traits. What a mess fleshies have caused, siphoning off attention from the spirit world. Never mind—soon they'll be ours.

Let me end where I began. We shall win! We shall win! We shall win!

This is Lucifer speaking. Over and out!

Oh, um, by the way, you can straighten up your heads now and drop down your arms.

Goodnight.

Front Desk, Speaker's House, 23:01 Greenwich Mean Time, Isle of Estillyen

READING TWELVE

———◆———

SETTING THE SCENE

Reading Twelve is unique in the *Redemption* series. Instead of a live reading given in a quaint Estillyen structure, Reading Twelve has been crafted collectively by the Monks of Estillyen.

The monks of Estillyen like to provide the final reading in manuscript form. It's their way of saying, "Carry the message."

In setting this scene, we'll borrow an excerpt from chapter twenty-three of *The Point: The Redemption of Oban Ironbout*. *The Point*, of course, is the companion edition to *Redemption*.

In the following excerpt, Hollie Macbreeze, one of the lead characters in the novel, is seated on a bench on the lawn at The Point. Her companion is a black-and-white Border collie named Trip, who belongs to Oban Ironbout. Hollie is just getting ready to read the final *Redemption* reading. It is titled: *Centering in Christ*.

> "Well, let's see what we've got in the envelope," Hollie said. "It's the final *Redemption* reading."
>
> "You're supposed to read it, Trip, when you've time to center, to settle. I know that's not easy for a Border collie. Let's give it a try, though. You go ahead and nap, and I'll have a read."
>
> Silently, Hollie began to read the message. Trip lay on the bench beside her with his eyes closed, while Mr. Ironbout snored away in the house. A soft breeze filtered through the garden. Occasionally, Hollie would pause from the reading and glance at the plot, with its three markers.

Hollie remembered the day Mr. Ironbout stood in the plot and, with a worn, wretched expression on his face, said, "I'm a wounded man; can't you see, I'm ruptured?"

She was still in awe. "He's absolutely transformed," she said aloud. "The change is like a miracle."

More than once, Hollie lifted her green eyes from the page to gaze beyond the garden at the majestic beauty of the cliffs — as she allowed the monks of Estillyen to reach through to her with their final message of Christ's love.

This is what she read.

To the reading...

Centering in Christ

READER: Voice, St. Paul once sent a heartfelt prayer to followers of Christ in Ephesus. It was a prayer to ponder. Through time, the prayer has moved and mattered. Now a few lines have found their way into this Estillyen reading. Shall I read you the prayer?

VOICE: Yes, please. I'd like to ponder it, as well.

READER: Okay, Voice, but first just a few words. Please know that these thoughts so long ago expressed were strikingly new when written. Quite reformist was the prayer. St. Paul speaks of power in the inner being, of God's love being multidimensional, of love rooting in the heart. The apostle's words focus on Christ as being the One on which the heart centers.

Listen now to St. Paul's ancient words. Listen as if you were there and had just received his letter.

> *I pray that out of his glorious riches he may strengthen you with*
> *power through his Spirit in your inner being, so that Christ may*
> *dwell in your hearts through faith. And I pray that you, being rooted*
> *and established in love, may have power, together with all the saints,*
> *to grasp how wide and long and high and deep is the love of Christ,*
> *and to know this love that surpasses knowledge—that you may be*
> *filled to the measure of all the fullness of God.*
>
> EPHESIANS 3:16-19

Robust words, don't you think, Voice?

VOICE: They are. Will you kindly read that one line again, the one about grasping?

READER: Certainly. "To grasp how wide and long, and high and deep is the love of Christ..." Is that the one you mean? *VOICE:* Yes, that's it. It's the word *grasp*...grasping love—such an idea. It is, as you said, something to ponder.

READER: The apostle says this love surpasses knowledge. Did you catch that bit?

VOICE: I did. Yes, I did.

READER: When St. Paul traveled to Ephesus, he was taken to a place called the Areopagus, where he gave a speech.

VOICE: Areopagus—what's that?

READER: The Areopagus was an Athenian council, a local legislative body. It was allowed to function under Roman democracy. That's not so important to our reading. It's what the apostle said that matters. During his speech, St. Paul did something quite remarkable in selecting his words.

VOICE: What did he select?

READER: He quoted a line from an Athenian poet. In doing so, the line became scriptural truth. St. Paul was challenging his audience to consider the true nature of God, who God is. That's when he plucked the line from the poet. Concerning God, the poet said, "We are his offspring." That's it—a little line of words with which St. Paul concurred. A pleasant idea, don't you think?

VOICE: Yes. Offspring…it sounds rather wholesome.

READER: The Athenians were very much preoccupied with grasping the latest ideas. It was, for them, a sport. They loved to spend time talking and debating. When the apostle came along, they told him, "You are bringing strange ideas to our ears."

To the ears words flow, Voice. They find entrance. They winnow their way into the mind. They seek lodging. They come in phrases, throughout life's phases. Sometimes they speak praises.

VOICE: Words seek lodging?

READER: Yes, they seek recipients. They come to rest, to root. They grow. They lodge in the heart. That's how St. Paul's words functioned in the Areopagus. St. Paul placed the poet's line into his own storied mix. He went on to say that God made everyone from one man. You know who that is, don't you, Voice?

VOICE: Sure, that's Adam…if you believe the story.

READER: Do you, Voice?

VOICE: Well, yes, in a manner of speaking.

READER: I see. Concerning St. Paul's words, he argued that the human race was created by a reasoned, volitional act on the part of God. "God did this," Paul said, "so that men would seek him, and perhaps reach out for him, and find him, though he is not far from each one of us. For in him we live and move and have our being."

That's something to grasp, something to ponder, is it not? These words, thus spoken, are in your ears, Voice, swirling in your mind, but in the heart will they lodge? What might these words mean to you? What might these words make of you? That's the subject of the matter now arisen. Are the words treasure or trash to you? Where might they take you? Where might they lead you?

Everyone follows someone, Voice.

VOICE: They do?

READER: Most certainly. Those who swear to follow no one follow at least one. They follow self. Self is full of words lodging in the heart. Did you ever think of your heart that way, Voice? A repository you are. Words have willed their way, winnowing through your mind, rooting in your heart. They move you. They accuse you. They excuse and abuse you. There's so much more to words, Voice, than intonation and resonation.

They come to you bearing thoughts. They clothe thoughts and make them known. Some for ill, some for good, words set out their roots. Voice, it's up to you to determine which words digress from the path wisdom professes.

Self following self puts one on a precarious path. Simultaneously self both leads and follows. Self, the guide, charts the way intuitively with words planted, rooted. Words move self. They make self.

Christ's words lodge in hearts most deeply. In their winnowing work, his words are carried along by God's Spirit. To life's essence, his words speak. "For whoever would save his life will lose it," Christ said, "but whoever loses his life for my sake and the gospel's will save it." Those words set loose have arrested many hearts.

Self is inclined to speak like this: "I'm not lost. I'm not letting go, losing life to find myself. Dear me, ask who I am. This I know. This is clear to see. All I need to do is look in the mirror. I see through and through. I speak to myself for myself. I know who I am. Can't you see? I'm self-made. Scouring and searching for what? Winsomely I walk, with will, wit, and witty words."

VOICE: If self leads, how does self find the way?

READER: Often by witty wit and will—wasn't that how self worded it? Of this notion, though, self is rather shortsighted. There's a snag within the wit, a fault line of sorts.

VOICE: Really?

READER: The snag is this: There is no self with selfless DNA.

VOICE: What's that you say about selfless DNA? It sounds strange.

READER: You remember that wholesome word you liked?

VOICE: You mean *offspring*?

READER: Yes, that's it. Offspring—one and all are sprung off, Voice. St. Paul claimed all offspring lead back to one. Universal ancestry is a mark of every self. Deep within each self, selves of lineage linger. All manner of inscriptions and implantations are there. They have a way of cajoling, congealing, and bending self. No matter how winsome the walk with wise wit and words, selves in self linger.

The mark of brothers' blood gone to war, the bones of martyrs, too—they reside in DNA. Souls of sinners seeking grace...the wicked giving chase. All such inscriptions are woven into what presumption calls self. Who is it that speaks for self, anyway? Think about it, Voice. Which inscription might it be—the sinner seeking grace, or a wicked wick bearing self-prescription?

When self leads, the spirit follows. This creates all manner of maladies. Self cannot feed what the spirit needs. Self-leading is not wise. It's otherwise. If you're interested in being wise, look to ancient words akin to those we're now considering.

VOICE: Which words?

READER: Choice they are. They're what you might call a prophetic prescription, an antidote to self-leading. Listen to what the prophet said: "Stand at the crossroads and look; ask for the ancient paths; ask where the good way is and walk in it, and you will find rest for your souls."

You now have these ancient words, albeit new to you, swirling in your mind, Voice. They are winnowing, moving. Even when you sleep, they seep. Are they trash or treasure? Will they take root? The prophet spoke of verbs—four, in fact. Stand, look, ask, and walk. They are action words leading to the path of rest.

VOICE: Do these ancient words still apply to someone like me?

READER: Yes, certainly. They're wise, not otherwise. They belong to that chosen reservoir of words that have stood the test of time. They shall stand, still, when time no longer ticks.

Ancient is good, Voice. It bears gifts from afar for the present's day. Anemic is the present without the ancient. Jeremiah spoke of ancient paths, beyond the crossroads trail. Ancient paths self cannot find by witty wit and intuition. Self must surrender. The word surrender sounds most threatening to self. Does it to you, Voice?

VOICE: I just don't know. I've never thought about it like that before.

READER: Self grasps the wrong idea. To self, surrender sounds like a chicken desiring to be plucked. There is a time, though, when all selves do surrender.

VOICE: When's that?

READER: It's when the foe of life comes creeping. Death drops in. Down is death's trajectory. It brings freeze upon the face. Self, to death, surrenders. Self may wail and weep, but in the end, life ends. Self surrenders. Self becomes ancestry, lineage, a name engraved, a testament to posterity. When death drops in, the spirit within self says it's time to go. The spirit flees.

VOICE: Where does the spirit go?

READER: The spirit trails away, traversing the distant paths self availed. At that point, it's too late to sort out digresses from what wisdom professes. You see, Voice, the spirit has needs. It feeds on various seeds. Christ said, "It is written, 'Man does not live on bread alone.'" Christ cherished words, and he loved that line, "It is written."

The spirit feeds on grist from mills that grind words into storied mixes. The spirit feeds, while within the self it waits. There it resides, living longingly, or lapsing into lethargy. The spirit intuitively knows there is more to life than self. The spirit senses the eternal, implanted deep within man and mate. Jeremiah's prescription is offered to aid the spirit as it feeds.

The spirit, led by self, is fed from other troughs. The requisite of being self-made demands it. Relying not on divinity in self's realm of humanity, self enslaves the spirit. Without wisdom from ancient paths, the spirit lunges, plunges, feeding on what self avails. Bespoke the spirit is made—a hybrid of thoughts formed from all manner of wordy mixes.

No illusion should be held. A bespoke spirit can become quite unwell—bound, enslaved, and contorted. The unrepentant thief hanging on Golgotha's hill—was not his spirit ill, soured by self's incantations? So near to Christ he hung.

The thief's spirit would not kneel; self would not allow it. He repelled the figure at his side. He despised his words.

What was it St. Paul said there in the Areopagus, Voice? "God is not far from each one of us," that's what the apostle said. In Christ, God has come near, so very near. Into the scrum of humanity he has entered. Into the heart he seeks to dwell.

Spiked in crucifixion agony, the hardened thief would not surrender. Self had enslaved the spirit. They became one, inseparably defiant. The spirit had been caged, and true to self the spirit was. Like a bigot to bigotry, a brute to brutality, the spirit showed its unrelenting defiance of divinity. Though it realized the end for self was near, the spirit would not recant or repent, so enslaved it was.

To follow the footsteps of Christ, self must surrender. Self must relinquish its grip, let go of the helm, pick up an oar. Self must stoop down and carry a cross. Self must diminish, get lost, get out of the way, in order for the spirit to find its way.

Lost is good, Voice, most desirable.

VOICE: It is?

READER: Yes, Voice, indeed. Once you're lost, you can be found. This you find when lost you are. Lost, the spirit longs and listens for eternal echoes. The echoes lead. The mysterious harkens. This, too, is good, most desirable.

Along the journey's twists and bends, the words of Christ do not renounce their call. It was Christ who said, "Come follow me." His words led to rest. "The words I have spoken to you are spirit and life," Christ said.

Being centered in Christ is about more than belief and knowing, Voice. It's about Christ dwelling at self's center, in the heart, changing self in ways self cannot do. St. John wrote, "The Word became flesh and dwelt among us, and we have seen his glory, the glory of the One and Only who came from the Father, full of grace and truth."

VOICE: Wait, if you would, Reader. The idea of Christ dwelling on earth I see, but now you speak of the heart. This is challenging to grasp.

READER: You're very right, Voice. It is mysterious. So too was Christ's earthly dwelling. How do you explain it? God in human form, begotten not made. In all of eternity, nothing is its equal. The One who dwelt on earth can equally dwell within the heart. By faith it is so. By the Spirit of Christ, it is possible.

The Spirit of Christ occupies the heart's center, filling it with Christlike characteristics. The apostles once described themselves by self. "I'm a tax collector. I'm a fisherman. I'm neither; I'm his brother." They all became something else when to self they died and surrendered. They became new. Not just spruced up or a little changed—new characters they became. New dreams they held. New life they possessed.

Upon Christ they centered. He became their life, their calling, their sense of doing, their experience of being. His words they spoke, not self's witty wit. His image they bore, not their own. Into the crossroads of life, the apostles stepped, paused, and stood. They looked, listened, and dared to ask. They walked, but they also followed.

As Christ came strolling by, there were many who chose not to follow. The apostles might have joined them. Clung tight to their sails. Mended their nets. Kept fishing for fish. Posterity never would have revealed Sts. Peter, James, and John along with all the others filling the Gospel story.

On Christ's path the apostles chose to tread. The more they lost, the more they found. The cost was high. All that self possessed had to be redressed, let go. There were crosses to carry. The apostles' crosses, though, stilled self's claim. In following Christ, the apostles became who they were meant to be.

St. Paul, too, was a follower who died to self. In so doing, Saul became Paul. It was with utmost confidence that St. Paul wrote about being rooted and established in the love of Christ. This brings us back, Voice, to the very heart of our reading.

VOICE: That's good.

READER: Professed faith in Christ begins the journey. It opens the gate to the path of rest. But the journey is long, Voice. The Ephesians, for whom St. Paul prayed, were believers. The apostle's prayer was about grasping the full measure of Christ's love. His words pressed directly on that point.

The Spirit of God works with power in the inner being. Working deep within, the Spirit gets to the heart of all those implantations, sorting and rooting them out; pulling them down, lifting them up.

St. Paul's forte was to admonish and to lift up the supremacy of Christ. He was a master at it. He saw Christ dwelling in space and time, but equally in the heart. The heart is where the spirit, soul, and mind mingle. They mix and match storied mixtures. The heart chooses its embrace.

In this vortex, the Spirit of Christ dwells: stilling the storm, quieting the gale, rendering rest. The dwelling of Christ's Spirit shapes the sensibilities of the spirit.

VOICE: I hear you, Reader, and all that sounds extremely important. Yet it is so mysterious, I can hardly take it in. I'm not sure how to put it. The word in my mind is *worth*. That's the idea—you know what I mean? It's so incredible to think that this could happen to simple homo sapiens, fascinating.

READER: So simple we're not, Voice. Mysterious is this dwelling, imparting Christlike changeability from Spirit to spirit. There are those, many such, who choose to shun the spiritual quest. Don't want it; don't feel they need it. They prefer God distant, considered only at a glance, if at all.

Their feet tread not the ancient paths. There is no walking, listening, or seeing. Blurry distance is the desired position. Too much of seeing threatens self.

The mysterious truth of Christ dwelling in the heart is embraced by faith. There is no other way. This is what you must comprehend. The mysterious is to be welcomed, not pummeled and pounded for proof, like some shank on a slab. Who wants everything in life explained? Do you, Voice?

VOICE: Well, we've gotten so immersed in this flow of thinking. Yes, I've been, or tend to be, more the pounding type, I suppose. Maybe I should take a break, clear my mind. Please, no offense.

READER: Is that what you wish—to take a break?

VOICE: Well, not really...I don't think so, anyway. But it's a little scary, this denial of self, this surrendering. The words flowing from this reading are not normal. How shall I put it? They're not bound by rudimentary thinking concerning the makeup of man. That's it.

READER: Do the words scare you, Voice?

VOICE: This whole matter of swirling vortexes and the Spirit of Christ dwelling—it's a lot to grasp. This vista of human worth is appealing, though, I must admit. It's just new for me, sort of scary.

READER: Were you scared before you were born, Voice?

VOICE: What kind of a question is that? Scared before I was born! Dear me... maybe I should go. You're so, I don't know...

READER: Where will you go?

VOICE: Don't know. I'm resourceful. I know a lot of storied mixes. I'll pick and choose, a snippet here and a snippet there. Before you know it, I'll have a mountain of wisdom to quarry.

READER: Will you quarry out a story?

VOICE: I might. I've been known to string a few lines together. I like words, always have.

READER: What if the words you choose to quarry your story don't like being fashioned and fitted together? They might start stinging each other, like wasps fighting bees.

VOICE: I suppose that could happen, couldn't it?

READER: Quite likely. What part will you play in the story, Voice?

VOICE: I'll be myself. Plot the plot. Sign the script. Speak my voice. I'll be the lead character.

READER: I see. You'll need prayer, I would think. Why don't we return to the ancient one rendered by St. Paul?

VOICE: Well, I guess we could. I hope you don't ask me any more crazy questions—like was I scared before I was born.

READER: Okay, I won't. But were you?

VOICE: Didn't you hear what I said? Are you insane or something?

READER: I heard you, Voice, certainly I did. With every respect, I abide your words. But this is not another question; it's one and the same.

VOICE: All right, just to make you happy—the answer is clearly No! How could I have been scared before I knew anything of knowing? I knew nothing before I came to be.

READER: You knew nothing, you say? So you're not self-made?

VOICE: Of course not. How could I decide to make myself? I'm an offspring.

READER: I'm glad you have professed that point, Voice. No one is actually self-made. Before you knew yourself, you were known. You are a vital character in God's storied mix.

VOICE: I am?

READER: Yes, indeed. You can quarry your own story, if you want. But you needn't do so. You're in the story of which St. Paul spoke, just as surely as he stood in the Areopagus quoting the poet.
   I like you, Voice.

VOICE: You do? Why's that?"

READER: Because you're honest. You speak of worth. Life is so much more than rudimentary elements. Pursing worth is the right idea. Christ offers depth, imparting life spiritual. Into Christ's Spirit, the spirit of surrendered self cocoons. This truth is not a simple token, simply taken. It's mysterious, full of wonder. The spiritual quest is unending. Into eternity it folds. Forevermore it lives.

St. Paul was not shy on this subject of mystery. "I know a man in Christ," Paul wrote, "who fourteen years ago was caught up to the third heaven. Whether it was in the body or out of the body I do not know, God knows. And I know that this man, whether in the body or apart from the body I do not know, but God knows, was caught up to paradise. He heard things that man is not permitted to tell."

This man, so caught up, was Paul himself. Sifting the mysterious out of Scripture greatly impairs the storied mix. Scripture, from beginning to end, is lacquered and layered with mystery. Pitching the miraculous out of Scripture, yet clinging to a few verses promising passport to heaven, is not compatible with wisdom. God is exceedingly mysterious. Why not let the miraculous be, let God be God?

The inexpressible things St. Paul experienced in heaven's realm no doubt had an enormous impact on all he wrote, taught, and preached. The apostle's striking prayer about the expansive love of Christ arises from this backdrop.

Let's consider rightly those words of St. Paul. To grasp how wide and long and high and deep is the love of Christ, that's how the apostle put it. The love of Christ is where faith is centered, Voice. It's where the soul finds rest and peace finds its pillow.

To grasp the dimensions of Christ's love is to grasp the Father's love. The Father's love is seen in the giving of his Son, in letting go. The Son's love is seen in going, dwelling, and dying.

VOICE: Do you understand this dimensional grasp?

READER: In part, yes. You never fully get it—you know what I mean, Voice? It's a revelation that keeps revealing. An epiphany dawns…and then another.

VOICE: I think I understand.

READER: You go on grasping, perceiving, seeing as the love of Christ dwells in the heart. The spirit needn't be bound by self's paltry center. God's love is towering far above a world of words and more, which come and go, saying this and meaning that.

God's words have no ulterior motive or malicious intent. From on high, like rain and snow God's words come down. They moisten seeds for sprouting; they impart life for living.

The psalmist writes, "I lift up my eyes to the hills, where does my help come from? My help comes from the Lord, the Maker of heaven and earth."

Up is the direction, beyond the bickering, brokering, and bothered press of the day. Up is the way, with eyes peering beyond terror on screens appearing. Up is the way, beyond minutes of time ticking and death tolling its daily tallies. Up with eyes of hope, to worth not wanting, pulled down, wrestled to the ground by self.

The selfless love of God is lifted up.

VOICE: Where?

READER: On a cross spiked, that's where. Christ is there, beaten and bloodied for the world to see.

VOICE: But I was recently told not to look.

READER: By whom?

VOICE: Relevance. Relevance said that's all over. That Christ was taken down long ago. Said it was time to lighten up.

READER: Lighten up—on the one lifted up, you say? Does that sound right to you, Voice?

VOICE: Well, I have the feeling you don't think so.

READER: Why is it you speak of me to sort your feelings?

VOICE: I don't know. Maybe it has something to do with those words you spoke. Swirling as they do, winnowing their way.

READER: To the cross you do not have to look, Voice. It was God lifted up. He gave you sight. Look away. See not the dread. It may pierce your heart. It may not.

VOICE: No, I'm not afraid to look. It is, as you say, an ancient story gifting the present.

READER: Taken down, Christ surely was. That's true, yet eyes of enlightened hearts fail not to see him there. The one taken down is forever there. The medium and the message of God are indistinguishable upon the cross. There they embrace. They overlap. They hang together. They speak together. They intersect. They form a sign, a message whole for the world to ponder.

To look away does injustice to the message. It strips meaning from the story. With eyes lifted to the cross, the height of God's love is seen. Look around. Find some other figure of hope. Does it appear more comfortable, more salient? Do you like what you see? The apostle spoke of eyes within the heart as a way of seeing. Eyes of the enlightened heart see by faith.

Where does my help come from in order to see? It comes from there.

VOICE: Where?

READER: Where the Son of God hung, suffered, and died. God knows pain. God heals pain.

VOICE: So, should I look?

READER: Would you not, what might you lose?

VOICE: I do feel inclined—sort of drawn.

READER: All right, then—look. A lonely hill it is. See there in the distance. Christ hangs. Campfires 'round about are burning. See the smoke—how it lifts and lingers in the thin chilly air? Smell it?

VOICE: I do. You're right—this is a lonely place. It's actually morbid. It's like a fresco, but then not at all the same. And to think a world of art has come from this. So, too, all those musical compositions arise from this scene. I'm spellbound. What is it I see? What is it I hear?

READER: The words being spoken are somewhat hard to grasp. Listen—did you hear that shout, those moaning cries?

VOICE: What's that quirky sound?

READER: That's the sound of soldiers laughing. This is not a silent night for Mary's Son. It's a night of terror, torment, and treachery. The scene is savagery. Look, the Son of God has opened his eyes again. He's looking down at the crowds staring up at him and shouting, with their shaking fists. There are even children in their midst.

Let's move closer. Are you okay with that?

VOICE: I'm sobered. I feel speechless.

READER: From the bottom up, take in the cross. Inspect it. Do you see how the crimson stain has soaked into the wooden base? Christ's feet are spiked, his torso ripped.

VOICE: What's that dripping from his chin?

READER: It's blood. This is a sacrifice, you see, Voice. Look fully upon this panorama of pain. There's much for enlightened eyes to see.

VOICE: I'm looking up beyond the cross. I have to look away. I'm not sure what it is I see. Now it's gone. It looked like eyes peering down. And that, did you see that? Again, I'm not sure. It looked like angels, with wing-covered faces.

READER: Look on the ridge over there.

VOICE: Those are women watching.

READER: They're all weeping. With eyes streaming, see how they stare at the central cross. They gaze at grace. Mary, the mother of Christ, is there. Her offspring is dying. God's offspring is dying. Crucified, he is dying. Mary watches the mockers mock. She sees it all. How can she bear it? Price, price, price, paid! So costly is the price of redemption.

With eyes perceiving, for just a moment, peer out over the haze, Voice.

Look up toward the hills for help in seeing. Above the smoky hills, the stars sparkle, do they not?

VOICE: Yes, they do.

READER: See them twinkling across the moonlit sky. Ponder them hanging there. Consider their origin. Were they not hung by the one hanging there in the center of Golgotha's hill?

VOICE: It must be so.

READER: It's true, Voice. The one in the shadowy hues hung them there. High is the love of Christ, lifted up for enlightened hearts to see.

Wide, too, is this dimension of love. Stretched out are his arms; wide is this exhibition of eternal love. It's inclusive, not exclusive. There is no qualifier concerning scope. No "We'll have to see. Who do you know? We'll have to check."

Consider Christ's reach. The invitation is to all who surrender. The psalmist David spoke of God's reach. "Where shall I go from your Spirit? Or where shall I flee from your presence?"

"Where can I flee from your presence?" You spoke of fleeing, Voice. Do you still want to flee?

VOICE: No, I don't think so. My feet do not feel flighty. I'm somehow held captive by what I see and hear.

READER: Think, Voice! Ponder the scene. Many run to quarry stories from witty words. They reject faith. They do not find. They are not found. They find not their place in the ancient story gifting the present. There the Word of God hangs. With eyes of faith, look! The scene is a sign signifying what God means, what God wants to convey. Before the scene was, God thought it. There's far more on that hill than witty words.

Down the Via Dolorosa Christ walked, with criminals on each side. Among thieves he hangs. His arms to them are stretched. That's where God chose to die, Voice. Thieves left and right. On one side is rejection; on the other side acceptance. Arms stretched to both signify the enormous reach of God's love.

Human love can tend to be so tenuous in comparison. Often it draws away and disappears. Once it might have been there, reaching, embracing, caring.

Suddenly it's gone. When it should hold fast, it lets go. Bitterness and pain may push it away. Self may will it away. It may be wooed away. Somehow love is lost. It's gone, retrenched.

God's love is not that way. It never retrenches. God is "loving toward all he has made," the psalmist said. There is no prejudice or injustice. Broad and inclusive—that's the image of God hanging there. There's no clenched fist, no hint of spite, at humanity marred by sin.

The price of recompense has been paid by God. From the cross grace extends. The scene on Golgotha's hill also signifies the depth of God's love. Look again. See the cross, anchored in the ground from which man was formed.

VOICE: What about the cross itself, its composition—should this be considered?

READER: Why not? It's made of wood. It was once a tree. It was felled, and now it's dead. Birds once perched in its branches. Those were the days when the wood was rooted and alive, before it was fashioned into planks for death and dying.

Look at the planks; all semblance of life is gone. No branches, no leaves, no fruit, nothing to eat. The planks are barren. They offer no shade. They bear no beauty.

The planks are implements of torture. They're awkward measurements of weight. When the heavy planks were hoisted and dropped, they proved their heft. They thudded to the ground. Death was calling. The planks' pull is death's gravity. From them, life's blood drips.

VOICE: What do you suppose Christ thought when he heard that thudding sound?

READER: He thought the end was near. Look closely. See the planks' swollen grains? The planks have all been splintered by spikes from others who were crucified. They're used, abused. Still their grains tightly grip Christ's spikes of infectious rust. The grains sponge and soak the warm crimson stain. That's what has created all those splotchy patterns. In the act of man's inhumanity to man, the depth of God's love is seen.

"My God, my God, why have you forsaken me?" Did you hear that cry through the deathly air? That cry, rising from this crucible of suffering, is unparalleled. Sin's foul and death's dank have come to meet. They have come to stomp out the light. This is the deepest of valleys. Yet therein is God's love.

The words of the psalmist quiet the heart: "Yea, though I walk through the valley of the shadow of death, I will fear no evil, for thou art with me. Thy rod and thy staff they comfort me."

VOICE: I like those words.

READER: Many do fear evil, knowing nothing of rod and staff or words such as these. Human history is a journey long through valleys of shadowy death. The shadows vary from one valley to the next. Up and down the canyon floor, one can hear the rumble of war and rumors of wars. Peace comes, and then puff, it's gone. People suffer. Strange words appear. Collateral damage, it is said.

VOICE: Why is it called that?

READER: Yes, why? The heart, you know, can break with burden. All feeling seems to be below the ankles. The brokenhearted shuffle and drag their feet.

King David knew such burden. Listen to his words. "I am feeble and utterly crushed: I groan in anguish of heart. I am bowed down and brought very low; all day long I go about mourning."

Unrelenting such sighs seem. Was there no air of promise? King David dicovered there was. He would live to sing again. Beneath his despair, God's love was deeper still.

Eyes of the heart look to the cross and see that God is present, not fleeing. God pierced with pain is the image God has rendered. It is not a human fabrication. It is not an application. God supplied it. Consider it, Voice. For you it is rendered. The image speaks to the depth of God's love. In this cross-shaped depth, God binds up the brokenhearted.

God knows pain. The psalmist says, "Who is like the Lord our God, the One who sits enthroned on high, who stoops down to look on the heavens and the earth? He raises the poor from the dust and lifts the needy from the ash heap; he seats them with princes, with the princes of their people."

From the psalms, ancient words also speak to the length of God's love. "The Lord will keep you from all harm, he will watch over your life. The Lord will watch over your coming and going both now and forevermore."

"Forevermore" is a word with a wonderful disposition. Not just forever, but more than forever: forevermore. In perpetuity, infinity is the sense of meaning conveyed. The psalmist's refrain rises: "Give thanks to the God of gods; his love endures forever."

Not fading or dissipating but enduring is God's love. Beyond time's ticking and the world's whirling, God's love never fades. "Do not let your hearts be troubled. Trust in God. Trust also in me." This is what Christ came to say. God's love never fades. It is like Christ's words. "Heaven and earth will pass away," Christ said, "but my words will never pass away."

Never-fading words—how can they be described? They are the cornerstone of eternity and forevermore, these words of promise, these words of hope.

VOICE: The cornerstone of eternity—is there one?

READER: Yes, Voice. The stone the builders rejected will hold eternity together. You know, Voice, as we've moved along, upon your ears have fallen a collection of ancient words. Do you know what that means?

VOICE: Yes, they're swirling, winnowing, in my heart and mind.

READER: That's right. They are God's thoughts clothed in words. Ponder, grasp, if you wish. It's for you to determine if they digress from wisdom's way or reveal it. Let me leave with you these lines before we part. King Solomon wrote them. He is said to be the wisest man who ever lived.

"Remember your Creator, before the silver cord is severed, or the golden bowl is broken, before the pitcher is shattered at the spring, or the wheel broken at the well, and the dust returns to the ground it came from, and the spirit returns to God who gave it."

Voice, my reading is near its end. It's been great to be with you, but I've got to go. Know this, though: Christ will not change or flit away. He is as he was and will always be.

Rest for the soul is not an illusion, Voice. Look to ancient paths. The good path is found by way of the valley. In the valley, eyes of self will not do. One needs eyes of faith to see. There, deep within the valley's gorge, is a cleft. The eyes of faith will see its light streaming through. This is where rest is near.

To the cleft climb and cleave. Follow it upward to the crest. The crest gives way to a vast plateau, a word-filled meadow, the place of rest. Move along the flowing stream of waters fresh, knowing rest for the soul is near.

A single signpost points the way. Eyes of faith will not miss it. It's a simple cross, a sign signifying that which countless souls have journeyed to embrace. This is the place to center, still, and kneel, if you so desire.

There is safety in the cross's shadow. Freely you can lie in peace, at rest forevermore.

VOICE: I like you, Reader.

READER: That's kind of you, Voice.

VOICE: You're honest, and you speak of worth. I like your words. I'm just not sure what to say. I mean…I'm just so taken by all we've been discussing.

READER: That's good, Voice. It doesn't sound like you're quite so keen to run off and quarry your own story with witty wit.

VOICE: Not now. That doesn't seem right anymore. These winnowing words may well win over wit. Instead of quarry, I'll ponder, particularly the eternal cornerstone. That's got me.

READER: Good-bye, Voice.

VOICE: Good-bye, Reader. And thanks for all you've said. I'll never see words the same.

Words matter…some forevermore.

I pray that you, being rooted and established in love, may have power, together with all the saints, to grasp how wide and long and high and deep is the love of Christ.

ST. PAUL, ROME, LETTER TO THE EPHESIANS, CIRCA AD 62

APPENDIX ONE

———※·◆·※———

THE HISTORY OF ESTILLYEN'S MONKS

THE ORDER OF Message Makers found on Estillyen's isle dates from 1637, when Bevin Roberts first came to Estillyen in search of solitude. Throughout the continent Bevin Roberts had traveled, some twenty-nine years, giving readings derived from Scripture's grand narrative. From tiny hamlets to vast hallowed halls, he moved about, creating messages with meaning and purpose.

Bevin Roberts was said to be a curious blend, a character mixed, of quiet impression and stunning conviction. No one knows quite what happened, but Bevin Roberts suddenly stopped one day.

Outside a pub in rutted street they stood. In the stillness there, Bevin Roberts raised his eyes of blue and gazed down the lane of darkened grey. He surveyed his troupe all patched and ready. Willing but weary, they stood.

The troupe, one and all, was aware how ardently Bevin Roberts had struggled with his voice's fade. The fading tone and intonation was undeniable. Eventually, Roberts softly said, "I think it's time now we found an isle of rest. For wise we must be, in making moves that will forward the mission of our wordy mixes."

The record shows that Bevin Roberts and his troupe arrived on the Isle of Estillyen on February 4, 1637. Months gave way to years. Years mounted, and Bevin Roberts, like his voice, continued to fade. In time, the original troupe was no more.

Yet their way of weaving wordy mixes was not lost in future days. Those who carry on the work are known as the Message Makers of Estillyen. Scripture is their craft. They have a way of becoming the message, as they speak of Christ—God's perfect union of medium and message.

APPENDIX TWO

—•◦•—

MONKS OF ESTILLYEN

BIOGRAPHIES

With a breadth of interests and expert gifts of communication, Estillyen's monks are ever true to their message-making names. A bit more about this intriguing bunch of characters...

Epic

Epic is one of the most delightful and gregarious monks on the Isle of Estillyen. Not a measure of eccentric appeal does he lack. His residence and storytelling venue is Quill House on the Bend. Over the years, his readings have been translated and distributed to numerous countries throughout the world.

Epic is an avid reader and a lifelong student of history. He has led a number of pilgrimages to the Holy Land and various historical Christian sites.

Epic has a great fondness for the outdoors, and he loves to fish and sail at Lakes Three. He is seldom seen without his blind collie, Treasure, and he delights in showing off his Quaker Parrot, Shakespeare, to all Quill House visitors.

Epic's passion is centered on words and why they matter. Like all of the monks in the Order of Message Makers, Epic is driven by mission, and he is a strong advocate for the poor and disadvantaged. He is a consummate counselor.

Epic is in his nineteenth year of ministry on Estillyen's isle.

Narrative

If a single word can adequately define the core of a person, the word for Brother Narrative would be *zeal*. Zeal for the cause of Christ is his calling. Narrative's parish has no limits. To the world at large his heart and mind are always tuned.

Narrative worked his way through college repairing antique case clocks, and to this day he keeps the clocks on Estillyen ticking. In seminary, his studies led him courageously into the field of apologetics, from which he has never veered.

This choice of subject matter was not simply to satisfy curiosity, but to equip his passion for world evangelization. Narrative possesses an amazing knack for disarming argumentative angst against God. Estillyen's motto—"Let God be God"—is a line Narrative often quotes.

Narrative was one of the lead proponents of weaving the character of Lucifer into the Estillyen readings—a characterization quite popular in the readings *Scroll in the Fiery Pot* and *Piercing Words*. Narrative jokingly says, "I enjoy twisting truth out of Lucifer's lunacy."

Estillyen's Three Pond Cottage is where Narrative writes and gives his readings. For more than a decade, people have gathered in the cottage to listen to his dramatic tales.

When not at Three Pond Cottage, he's apt to be spotted in the lower level of the monastery—looking after the Estillyen Bible collection and chatting with visitors—or out repairing one of the many clocks ticking in Estillyen structures.

Writer

Within Estillyen's monk community, Writer is affectionately known as "The Dean." His forte is a vigorous theology of communication. The following excerpt from his reading, *Remember Me,* is what one might call Writer-esque:

"Ancient prophecies, once penned, had long abided. They waited incomplete, unfulfilled. Words past spoken waited for their stories to arrive so they could be folded into present verse."

Writer's passion to portray Jesus Christ as the perfect union of medium and message has become his signature work. As he puts it, Jesus Christ is the Message Á Medium of God. Writer refers to Christ as "the prism through which we see the world—the supremacy of God's communicative act."

Writer is, unquestionably, the most traveled of the Estillyen monks. He is a sought-after speaker, especially in university settings. Interestingly, Writer views contentious debates about God's existence as counterproductive. He asserts, "Why create platforms for those who wish to turn the cross into wormwood."

His theology is Pauline-centered. Writer has a knack for dispensing "mysterious doubt" by evoking what he calls "the mysterious certainty" of the Apostle Paul. He likes to remind his followers that "it was the great Apostle, himself, who was caught up in the heavenly realm."

One of Writer's favorite verses of Scripture is: "In Christ all the treasures of wisdom and knowledge reside." Writer fervently believes *words matter*—everyone's words—but that the words of Christ matter most of all.

The Monastery is Writer's residence, and bird-watching is his hobby.

Saga

Among the twelve readings of *Redemption*, Saga is credited with just one—*Picking Up the Pieces*. However, his reading and input in constructing the *Redemption* series have proven invaluable.

Consider the following two lines from *Picking Up the Pieces*:

> *"Through messages and mediums, God creates, reveals, reckons, and restores. From the medium of self, God's communication flows, not unlike a divine pulse emanating throughout the cosmos down to man."*

Saga is a simple, humble monk who lives in the tradition of St. Francis of Assisi. Silo on the Mound is his residence, where each Christmas he leads the drive in gathering gifts for needy children on the mainland.

Most afternoons, Saga makes the rounds at Good Shepherd Infirmary to visit patients. Somehow, he manages never to be in a rush, as he moves through the corridors. Saga is conversant and kind-hearted—and seems always to have a good word to say.

When not focused on acts of charity toward children and the needy, Saga expends his energy caring for the animals of Estillyen. Feeding the ducks down at the ponds is a morning ritual, and he is regularly spotted on his way to Mr. Statter's animal shelter to lend a hand.

Saga may be humble, but when it comes to Estillyen readings, there are few in the Order of Message Makers who can match his innate passion for Scripture. A student of drama and the arts, Saga gravitates ever so naturally to the notion of God being the choreographer of his drama.

Saga is quick to ask, "Say, where do you see yourself in that great drama?"

Plot

Monk Plot is an exceedingly joyous individual. Smiling, beaming, and humming are the traits that carry him about on the Isle of Estillyen.

Like Barnabas of old, Plot possesses the gift of encouragement and dispenses it freely. Plot views himself as a pilgrim passing through life—one who has a calling to build up his fellow pilgrims. One of his favorite and oft-quoted verses of Scripture is Romans 12:11: "Never be lacking in zeal, but keep your spiritual fervor, serving the Lord."

He is also a poet, to which the following lines from *Lips Unclean* will attest:

Lips, lips, the pair, oh how we adore our place upon the face.
Below the eyes and nose, above the chin we sit.
To us words rise, as they receive their call.
We clothe them with form, propel them to function.
Through us they all must pass, whether it be to bless or bite,
for wrong or for right.

Plot's two keen hobbies—gardening and cooking—could not be more suitably aligned. He greets both with equal passion. An invitation to Dairy House for brunch, lunch, or any occasion is a culinary treat. Plot has a skill for marrying ingredients that, as he puts it, "long to be together."

Like all the Estillyen monks, Plot adores pets. His current recipient of affection is Tremble the rabbit, who, on stormy nights, sleeps in the kitchen of Dairy House in a wooden box near the stove.

Story

Readings given by Story are great examples of storytelling fused with rhetoric. His demeanor couples compassion with conviction, in a style that is unique among the Estillyen message makers.

Scribe House, with its reading room of opposing mirrored walls, is the ideal residence for this charismatic monk. Story is fond of literature—his lines no one can anticipate. His focus on Christ is intense, but never forward or off-putting, as he flows effortlessly and rhythmically from theme to theme.

One minute Story may ask, "Is a picture worth a thousand words?" Then, as rapidly as the question is posed, he'll move on to paint that *picture with words*, which are both unforgettable. A case in point is two lines from *Get Up—Don't Be Afraid*:

"The mystery of Christ was hidden throughout the ages, like sand unseen, deep on the ocean floor.... Scrolled away, stowed away, life swam to and fro, not knowing the mystery latent in God's plan."

Story's propositions are no less intriguing. Ever so crisp is the idea that the "thesis statement" for Christ's entire ministry can be summed up in Christ's words spoken on the Mount of Transfiguration: *Get Up—Don't be Afraid.*

Creatively outside conventional boundaries Story effortlessly grazes. It is no surprise that Story would propose a ballad for the character Lucifer, titled *Hapenstance and Chance!*

Story's main hobby is fly fishing. While he always enjoys the company of friends, he is no stranger to solitude. It is in the realm of solitude that his story-telling dreams come alive.

Drama

Drama first sensed a call to religious life at age seventeen. Not sure about a spiritual vocation, he entered college as planned, pursuing a career in medicine. Then, during his third year of studies, he had an epiphany.

Drama was reading the Second Letter of the Apostle Paul to Timothy during his morning devotion. His thoughts settled on a verse that arrested his future: "For bodily exercise profiteth little: but godliness is profitable unto all things, having promise of the life that now is, and of that which is to come."

It was the contrasting of the *bodily* with the *spiritual*, the *temporal* with the *eternal* that Drama could not shake. Thus to mission he turned, and his course was forever changed.

Drama's focus on human need, though, was not lost on the Isle of Estillyen. His messages and readings are often built around Scripture passages, where human suffering and spiritual redemption meet. His is a special blend of message making.

Drama's reading, *A Cry in the Crowd*, is a prime example of how his interests intersect and aid people in grasping life's spiritual sphere. In *A Cry in the Crowd*, Drama recounts the tale of the distraught father, who came to Christ with his demon-possessed son. The son is gravely ill, both physically and spiritually.

The healer is Christ, whom Drama nobly depicts in his reading: God, entering the "scrum" of human need—not far and distant from suffering and pain, but engaged in the human plight. This image of Christ in the "scrum" sheds light on how Drama views his role in ministry.

His hobbies are few—hiking and a bit of jogging. His passion is in being with people. While Drama's residence is The Monastery, therein he's not cloistered. His hangout is the coffee bar at Three Pond Cottage. In the midst of Estillyen's visitors he's at home.

READERS AND READINGS

EPIC: *Did God Really Say?* and *The Word Became Flesh*

NARRATIVE: *Scroll In the Fiery Pot* and *Piercing Words*

WRITER: *Remember Me* and *Let Them Go!*

SAGA: *Picking Up the Pieces*

PLOT: *Lips Unclean* and *Stop Doubting and Believe*

STORY: *Get Up—Don't Be Afraid*

DRAMA: *A Cry in the Crowd*

THE MONKS: *Centering in Christ*

ENDNOTES

1. Quill House on the Bend is the residence and storytelling venue of the monk named Epic. The house is also home to Treasure, a blind collie, and Shakespeare, a Quaker Parrot.

2. Silo on the Mound is the residence of the monk named Saga. When the monks first came to Estillyen, this area was a farm with a dilapidated silo sitting in the middle of it. The monks went to work clearing out the moss and mud and rebuilding it. Now the building itself, especially beautifully decorated at Christmas, stands as a symbol of restoration and rebirth at the center of Estillyen.

3. Demon Backrider is the demon who rides backward on Satan's back with his heels digging into Satan's armpits. He serves as a scout, sometimes whispering into Satan's ear. He is chosen from the darkest dungeons, and when his usefulness is over, Satan simple "sheds" him.

4. Three Pond Cottage is the spot where Narrative lives, writes, and gives readings. It was originally two cottages, now blended into one with twin fireplaces. Four, not three ponds, grace the landscape of this cottage. No one seems to know quite how the name of the cottage came to be.

5. Brother Extol is one of the most senior monks on Estillyen. He has striking features and eyes that brim with kindness.

6. Dairy House is the residence of the monk named Plot. Originally an old stone milk house, it is now the site of many culinary feasts, created by Plot. Tremble, the rabbit, came to live at Dairy House when he was only a week old and his mother had been killed after a lightning storm. He sleeps in a wooden box near the kitchen stove.

7. Brother Say is an older monk, known for his mild smile. His most striking feature is his long legs.

8. Brother Tell is a rather plumb-looking monk, whom some have said bears a resemblance to Alfred Hitchcock.

9. Scribe House is the residence of the monk named Story. It is a long, skinny building with a metal roof and stands alone in a meadow. Inside is a reading room with benches and opposing mirrored walls so that everyone in the room can see the reader's face, the other listeners in the room, and also their own face.

10. Legend is a retired monk who willingly helps with readings. He is tall and has a deep, resonating voice.

11. Tunnel House was named for the long, narrow tunnel, large enough for a hay wagon to pass through with a team of horses, that runs below the reading room and near the coffee bar.

12. Brother Chronicle is a retired monk who frequently helps with readings.

13. Context is one of twenty-two summer interns. They can easily be spotted wearing their chocolate-colored shirts with the Estillyen logo, the yellow anchor with the blue chain.

14. **Brother Witness** is easily recognized by his piercing glance.

15. Brother Script is a senior monk whose dark brown eyes are capped with frosted eyebrows.

16. Speaker's House is the oldest structure on the Estyllian. It contains a single balcony, much like a theater balcony, which leads to eight sleeping chambers.

17. Brother Testimony has been a resident of Estillyen for more than fifty years. His distinctive features include a bald head and snow-white eyelashes.

18. Brother Manifest is a senior monk, who is bald and seems to smile with his eyes but not his lips.

19. The Infirmary is best known as the Good Shepherd Infirmary. It contains a beautiful mural depicting Estillyen 200 years ago. People have come from all over the world just to see the mural and wonder who painted it.

20. Oban Ironbout lives on the Point (the northwest tip of the Isle of Estillyen) and has a reputation as a curmudgeon. For more on his story, including his unlikely transformation, read *The Point*.

The Isle of Estillyen

The Storied Sea

Port Estillyen

Lowlands

Lakes Three

The Point

The Cliffs

Misty Shore

Abbey

Infirmary

Fields & Crops

Barnyard

Monastery

Dairy House

Scriptorium's Avenue

Shore Point Cottage

Three Point Cottage

Thistle House

Quill House

Scribe House

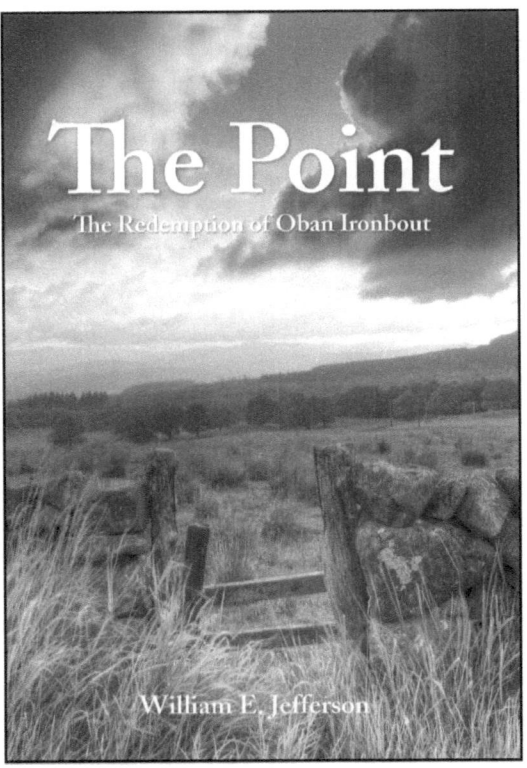

Companion novel to *Redemption: Twelve Readings from the Monks of Estillyen*

SEARCHING for peace and inspiration, Hollie and Goodwin Macbreeze travel to the Isle of Estillyen—a distant harbor known for bringing ancient words of worth to the present. Their lives become unexpectedly and inseparably intertwined with the reclusive Oban Ironbout—and a mystery from the past that will transform them all. **It is a tale of pain … and redemption**

The Point: The Redemption of Oban Ironbout and
Redemption: Twelve Readings from the Monks of Estillyen are companion editions. The endorsements and reviews offered apply to the original work, first published by Port Estillyen Productions under the title *Messages from Estillyen*.

Port Estillyen
PRODUCTIONS

For more truth-inspired fiction, visit **www.estillyen.com**

"In this intelligent and heartfelt novel, a community of monks offer 'readings' that powerfully illuminate the words of the Bible for a modern audience. It is a compelling tale told by a gifted and inspired storyteller."

—Clarion Reviews

www.ingramcontent.com/pod-product-compliance
Lightning Source LLC
Chambersburg PA
CBHW020835260626
47169CB00003B/995